Spud Publishing Inc. Presents:

Debut

SPUDPUB

Editing by Diane Fickeria

Coverart by Irish Williams

Book design by Daniel (@global_desing) on Fiverr

Published by Spud Publishing Inc.

Visit us online at www.spudpub.com or reach us at info@spudpub.com

ISBN: 978-1-7380255-0-3

Printed in Canada

CONTENTS

INTRODUCTION

Debut was conceived on a quiet Canadian prairie evening, riding on the hopes and ambitions of a handful of creative, talented, and at times masochistic friends. In the early stages, it was a small and informal project. Debut was meant to get our names out into the world, to build and collaborate on something we were proud of. It was to prove that, in spite of every reason not to, we could do it.

As with any ambitious undertaking when a group of creative people come together, what we began with is far from what we ended with. From the humble beginnings of a small anthology, born in the dredges of our Discord server, we put our best foot forward. We grew, and surprised ourselves by establishing Spud Publishing Inc.

There is a lot of love, sweat, care, and personal growth that went into the stories, art, and the project itself. As founders of Spud Publishing Inc., we are both humbled and honoured to work with such a great team who have blessed us with their patience, understanding, and excitement.

We'd like to thank our authors, our artists, and our editor. Without any of them, this would remain an unrealized idea. Last of all, we'd like to thank you, our readers. The very people which leave us inspired to create and share it with the world.

Welcome to our Debut.

Gnomey Birthday

Amy Gerein
Art by
Irish Williams

Azzie popped the top on her energy drink as she walked out the door of her rented duplex, pausing to lock the door before bopping down to the driveway. The street was silent, wrapped in the relative darkness of the very early morning.

Old school AC/DC played in her earbuds as she danced towards the car sitting in the driveway. She took a sip from the bright pink can in her hand. Not bad for some random energy drink that Price Point, the warehouse store where she worked, had started carrying. It fit her price range too—cheap.

She set the drink on the roof of her ancient car and worked to unlock the door. The 1976 Camaro was older than her oldest brother Ben, and like Ben, it had its own handful of problems. The door needed two hands to unlock, one to turn the key and one to jiggle the handle just right—a little bit up and a little bit to the left.

Maybe she should look at getting the handle fixed if she couldn't figure it out herself. It was her birthday today; she could spoil herself with a little car repair. She chuckled. Yep, she was going to spoil herself alright, but it was going to be with a breakfast burger on the way to work, not fixing idiosyncrasies on her car.

Tip of her tongue sticking out the side of her mouth, Azzie wiggled the handle until the door popped open. She reached up to grab her energy drink and started to slide in without glancing into the vehicle. Which meant that the hard pointy object she sat down on came as a surprise.

Jumping back up, Azzie looked down at her seat from safely outside the car.

A garden gnome looked up at her from the driver's seat. *What the heck?* Where had this thing come from?

Azzie cast her eyes around her yard, looking at her silent residential neighbourhood. Whoever had left the gnome was hiding really well or, as Azzie expected, long gone. Most people weren't insane enough to be up and leaving for work around three o'clock in the morning.

Since she couldn't drive to work with a gnome sitting in the driver's seat, Azzie reached down and plucked it up with one hand. It looked vaguely familiar with its long white beard and pointy bright red hat. Shrugging because those were common enough gnome features, and who was she to pass up something free, Azzie tossed her new passenger into the seat beside her where it bounced before settling. Azzie slid into her seat; attempt number two: successful.

Switching her music from her headphones to her car, Azzie silently thanked the vehicle's previous owner for upgrading the sound system and headed towards the nearest Burger King for the promised birthday breakfast burger.

* * *

"That's why you look familiar!" Alone on the freeway, Azzie shouted, pointing at the passenger seat with her burger in excitement. "From that random photography class Ben had to take! I knew I would figure it out eventually." Azzie nodded her head in satisfaction, head bobbing along with the music. "I'm a smart cookie."

She glanced towards the gnome. "Didn't Curtis name you Timmy?" He didn't reply, as yard decorations are wont to do, lying on the seat where he had been tossed. Azzie nodded again, convinced that Curtis, her second oldest brother, had named the gnome. "Yep. Pretty sure. Curtis figured you looked like a 'Timmy' and Ben hated you even more. Apparently, gnomes don't need names. Or their picture taken."

She chuckled, remembering how sour Ben had been. *'You don't need to name the stupid thing. It's not alive,'* Ben had mumbled, *'It's just a stupid assignment.'* Ben had never really *got* art. Or why he had to take a photography class to become more 'well rounded.'

None of that mattered now because all Azzie knew was that she was driving with a gnome named Timmy riding shotgun. She was also fairly sure that Ben had shoved his unloved model into the back of the shed. Their eclectic Uncle Steve, who had given Ben the gnome, hadn't wanted it back but had left strict instructions for the family not to dispose of it.

Azzie squinted at the road. Curtis must have pulled it out of the shed and left it in the car. He was the only one with a spare set of keys to her vehicle and enough knowledge of her schedule to know when she was sleeping. He also knew how to open the car door… This was what happened when he lived on the other side of the duplex. It was probably payback for the gnome covered boxers she had given him for Christmas.

Cackling as she crumpled her burger wrapper and tossed it in the back seat, Azzie crowed, "Curtis! Expect to find this gnome on your bed tomorrow!" She settled back against the seat, happy to finally have a reason to use those emergency spare keys he had given her. Returning a garden gnome was *obviously* an emergency.

Azzie turned the music up as the freeway headed out of town, dancing in her seat, prairie landscape spreading out before her. So far, this birthday was awesome. Since it wasn't every day that a person turned twenty-six, Azzie decided it was a sign. The rest of the day was going to be great.

"Pretty nice wheels you've got here."

The voice came out of nowhere and Azzie startled, swerving the car to the left, across the lane beside her, and into the far shoulder before swinging back to the right in her surprise.

"Holy shit!!" She tried not to hyperventilate, focusing on the road. She had never been more grateful for the empty, early morning roads.

Back in her lane, Azzie slowed until the car was barely moving as she looked around the interior. Somebody in the back seat? Nope, clear. Or at least nothing in the rear-view mirror. She twisted to get a better look. Who the heck was in her car and why were they just speaking up now? Surely, if someone had stowed away, they would have said something at Burger King and demanded free food.

As she had guessed, there was no one in the back seat. On the way back to the front windshield, Azzie's gaze caught on the gnome in her passenger seat. Or rather, the gnome that was now pulling himself onto the passenger seat from the sea of garbage on the floor.

"Holy. Fucking. Shit."

This time Azzie slammed on the brakes, sending the gnome back into the mess of old wrappers and empty bottles. This wasn't happening.

What was in that burger? It couldn't have been laced with hallucinogens. No one gave away expensive drugs. Not in burgers. And especially when they knew they wouldn't be there to see the results.

"Better get off the road." The gnome was once again trying to regain his spot on the passenger seat, his stubby fingers searching for purchase on the fake leather.

Azzie didn't want to imagine what her face looked like. She was sure that her eyes were popping out of her head. There was a freaking garden gnome talking to her. In the middle of the night. A gnome that was supposed to be inanimate in a shed across town.

"The car. Off the road." He sighed, finally getting up onto the seat. "Why do I always get this reaction?"

Azzie snapped her mouth shut and stared out the windshield. Right. So much for an awesome birthday.

* * *

Safely on the shoulder of the road, hazard lights blinking, Azzie gripped her steering wheel until her knuckles turned white.

This wasn't happening.

She was too young to have lost it like this.

Maybe Curtis had rigged up a microphone to the thing. But it wasn't Curtis's voice. She glanced at the gnome.

Even if he had managed to attach a microphone, there was no way that Curtis had turned an inanimate object animate. And the gnome was definitely moving, apparently of his own free will.

He had started off petting her seat with his chubby hands and having abandoned that, stood to peer into the attachment of her door handle where it created a little cup that held spare change, the top of his hat not tall enough to reach the bottom of the window. He picked up a coin, inspected it, and put it down.

Azzie watched as he tentatively walked over to the edge of the seat, getting on his hands and knees when his feet kept slipping, and peered at the floor and the tower of garbage that almost reached the top of the seat. Hadn't he seen enough of that particular area of the car already?

He poked an empty bottle that used to have orange juice in it. Azzie cringed. She didn't want to think about what was in that bottle now; she was going to throw the whole thing away. Some day.

The gnome stood up and walked towards her so he could take in the back seat.

"You should really clean up in here." He wiped a stubby finger under his nose. "It's starting to smell."

Azzie's control snapped. Her fingers scrambled to unbuckle her seatbelt and open the car door at the same time. Eventually successful at both, she threw herself out of the car, barely catching her balance in time to save her knees from the pavement. Slamming the door, Azzie ran out in front of her car.

Air moved rapidly in and out of her lungs, her stomach tying itself in notes, Azzie stared at the empty road in front of her. She looked back at the car. She couldn't see the gnome. Had he really been moving? Maybe she had been dreaming the whole thing. Pinching yourself in a dream woke you up, right? She pinched her arm.

"Ahh." Apparently *not* dreaming.

She had to go back to the car. She didn't want to go back to the car. But she needed to go back to the car. The rational part of her brain was coming back online as she started to pace, her breath returning to something resembling normal. If she didn't make her shift, she might have to ask Curtis for rent money. Even if she didn't, it would make fixing her car harder. Treating herself to anything more than a birthday burger definitely wouldn't happen.

"I got this. I can do this." Azzie ran in place a few strides, knees pumping, body hunched over. She stopped, ran her hands through her long brown hair, fingers getting caught in the hint of curl. Impatient, she spun her hair up onto her head, and wrapped it with the hair elastic she kept on her wrist. One more deep breath out and Azzie slunk back to the car.

She crouched and peered through the window. The gnome was lying on the seat. Actually lying on the seat as if it hadn't moved at all.

Azzie stood up and whipped open the car door. "Ah ha!"

No response.

The gnome didn't move, inanimate, in the same spot she had tossed it earlier, completely oblivious to her outburst.

"This day is not going to go as planned." Azzie took one last look at her silent passenger and slid into her seat. Intent on blocking out the gnome she felt obligated not to leave on the side of the road, she pulled back onto the freeway, and focused on getting to work on time.

* * *

"Azalea! Finally!" Azzie's supervisor Darren threw up his hands, clipboard almost flying out of his right one. "What took you so long?"

Azzie pulled out her phone and looked at it.

"I'm not late. It's not even 3:45."

"And we're already behind! Two forklifts down, don't know what's wrong with them, but the service guys won't be awake for hours. You're on double duty." Darren pointed at her emphatically. "I want you taking down pallets like a madman. Or madwoman. Whatever. Produce and housewares. You've got an extra stocker since George's lift is down. Hopefully somebody else can tell him what to do." Darren stalked off, gesturing with his clipboard, rubbing over his almost bare scalp with his free hand.

Azzie sighed. Today had started off so promising. Darren didn't normally get stressed, but two broken forklifts four days before a corporate walkthrough would put them behind and leave no one in a great mood. Especially since she was driving while the more senior George was stocking. She hoped she didn't have to be the someone else who had to show him what to do.

"Well, well, well, if it isn't the birthday girl. Welcome back, Azalea."

"I was here yesterday," Azzie snapped at George, who had come up beside her, good mood completely evaporating. "And don't call me that." She turned away from the older man who was slow clapping in her direction.

After two boys, Azzie's mother had decided that her first daughter needed a fanciful name, sparing Azzie's younger sister, April, the horror. So Azzie had been named after a random flower. Oh, she had gotten the 'it was your great grandmother's favourite!' spiel but she wasn't sure she believed it. She had looked up the flower once—those things could not overwinter in Saskatchewan. She doubted if her great grandmother had ever even seen an azalea. Either way, she didn't appreciate anyone using her full name. Especially not George.

"I see you get to forklift today instead of those of us more senior. Ain't right." George shook his bald head. "Ain't right."

"Beauty before age, old man." Azzie turned and stomped off towards the lockers.

"That's not how it goes!" George grumped.

Azzie refrained from flipping him the bird over her shoulder, but it was a near thing.

Struggling with the lock, it took her several attempts to get her locker open. "Freaking locks. Freaking old men. Freaking broken forklifts. Freaking gnomes. Freaking—"

"Birthdays!"

Azzie turned around, still crouched in front of her now open metal cubby.

"Happy birthday!" Neil and Cara, her favourite coworkers, stood behind her, a cupcake with a burning candle and an enormous amount of frosting stood on a plastic plate held between them.

"Blow it out." Cara gestured towards the candle.

Azzie fell out of her crouch, butt hitting the floor, back against the wall of lockers. These two. They almost made working here worth it.

Neil shook his head, black hair falling over his eyes, and put the plate under Azzie's nose. She dutifully blew out the flame. Then, removing the candle and putting it onto the plate, she took off the wrapper and attempted to shove the whole top of the cupcake in her mouth, icing smearing all over her face.

"I told you." Neil turned towards Cara. "I knew she would get icing everywhere."

"I didn't want to believe you," Cara said, producing a stack of napkins from her pocket, "but I came prepared just the same." She shoved the paper napkins towards Azzie, her eyes bright with laughter over her round cheeks.

Azzie took a couple of napkins from the stack. "Thank you," she mumbled through the sugary blue icing.

"That might stain your face." Neil tilted his head while he looked at her. "You might end up with a blue beard. Or goatee. Or something. A Smurf beard!"

"Better than getting a gnome," Azzie grumbled under her breath.

"Excuse me?"

Azzie waved away Neil's question. She pulled her safety vest out of her locker, shoved her keys in, and shut the door before getting up.

"Fancy breakfast burger this morning?" Neil seemed fine changing the subject while Azzie ate the rest of her cupcake.

"Obviously," Azzie spoke around her mouthful.

"There are more of those in the break room." Cara tried to give Azzie a disapproving look, watching Azzie try to save some crumbs that fell out of her mouth. "In case you actually wanted to taste it."

"I tasted it."

"Uh huh. Whatever." Cara was smiling now. She hadn't been Azzie's best friend for this long without being able to kind of appreciate her antics. "But seriously. I think we're all going to need those cupcakes before this shift is over."

Neil grimaced. Azzie made a face then headed to the break room and the next cupcake that awaited her.

* * *

"These cupcakes were the only thing that helped me make it through." Azzie balanced another one in her hand as she dug her keys out of her locker. She had lost count of how many she had eaten but had saved a few more for herself by glaring at George whenever he went to take one. The sugary rush had Azzie moving pallets like a madman despite George's inability to stock properly or stop complaining.

"Same." Cara peeled a wrapper off a cupcake. Only her second. Azzie didn't know how she did it. She suspected that Cara had several more at home. The woman didn't know how to bake in small batches.

"At least it's over. And neither of us has to stay to help actual customers."

"Amen." Cara hoisted her cupcake in the air before swiping at the icing with a finger and popping it in her mouth. "What are you up to now?"

"You mean besides lying in my bed and trying not to remember how much I hate forklifts?"

The two broken forklifts hadn't been the only problems that day. Azzie's forklift started the shift working fine, but it didn't continue that way. The forks dropped to hit the shelf before they were free of the shelving unit, the lift slid into racks going around corners where the floor wasn't wet, and the forks had randomly tilted down, dropping a pallet on the floor. Thankfully, no one had been hurt and it was just a skid of Kleenex, but the wooden pallet had slid off after the tissue and flattened the whole lot. Azzie, and Darren, declared it a minor loss, especially since she now had fifteen squished Kleenex boxes to take home free of charge.

When Azzie had tried to show Darren the problems she was having with the forklift, the stupid thing worked perfectly, and he sent her back to work. Without an extra forklift to switch to, he barked at her to be careful and work away from everyone else, so he didn't have to write up more complicated accident reports. He had already grumbled about the Kleenex incident.

"Yea. Besides that." Cara finished licking the icing off her cupcake before speaking.

"I'm just going to go enjoy this cupcake. Then I'm going to lie in wait for Curtis and confront him about shitty birthday gnomes." Azzie went to make a fist with her hand but stopped when she realized she was inadvertently squishing the cupcake between her fingers.

Cara, who didn't know the whole story because Azzie still couldn't believe it, nodded sagely. "Solid plan."

* * *

Azzie's alarm went off. 4:30 pm. Curtis should be getting home any time now. She hit the snooze button and stuck her head back under the blanket. Realistically, she had time before he actually got home, travel time and all that.

Eyes closed, Azzie buried her face farther into the extra blanket she was using for a pillow. Since she had left work, the day had thankfully been uneventful. She sat in her car, waited for everyone from her shift to leave the parking lot, and delivered a stern lecture to the inanimate garden ornament laying on her passenger seat. When she got home, she brought the gnome inside Curtis's side of the duplex, helped herself to one of *his* frozen pizzas, watched *his* Netflix, and fell asleep on *his* couch. The gnome spent the day shoved deep in the chest freezer in Curtis's kitchen.

The alarm went off again.

"Ugh." Azzie rolled to a sitting position. She had to get up this time if she wanted to be conscious when Curtis got home. The gnome could stay in the freezer though. Maybe it would ensure that he remained inanimate. Exactly when had she started referring to the thing as a 'he?' Surely garden gnomes were its, long white beards aside, since they weren't alive.

A key turned in the lock and Curtis walked in. Azzie scowled when he didn't appear surprised to find her on his couch. His face split into a wide grin when he registered her huddled under the blanket.

"Did you like your birthday present?"

Oh, how Azzie wanted to wipe the grin off his face.

"Hmmm?" Azzie stroked her chin. "The present where you left a talking garden gnome on the front seat of my car, or the one where you're going to buy my groceries and clean my toilet for the next month?"

The grin slowly fell from Curtis's face, and he looked at her in confusion.

"I didn't leave a garden gnome in your car."

"Yea right, you didn't!" Azzie jumped up from the couch, fumbling in the blankets. She almost fell back into the seat but kicked out a leg and flailed her arms until the blankets fell off and she could step out of them. "There was a freaking *garden gnome* in my car this morning. I figured, fine, whatever, funny payback for the gnome boxers at Christmas. But that wasn't it. Somehow, this gnome *comes alive*, which I still don't know how you managed, and when it decides to speak up, it scares me half to death and I almost wound up in the ditch. The in-between-the-lanes ditch!" At this point, Azzie was almost yelling, arms swinging as her agitation grew.

"Oh."

"Yea, 'oh.'" Azzie threw her hands up in the air. "So, after a shit day at work, that started off just fine I want you to know, I get to come home and sit in your living room so I can confront you about the stupid gnome that I shoved in your freezer and—"

"You put him in the freezer?" Curtis perked up, something like alarm crossing his face.

"Uh, yea, I didn't need some *decoration coming to life* on me again."

Curtis spun around and headed to the kitchen. "You can't put him in the freezer! He'll die if he's in the freezer too long." He pushed open the freezer lid, letting it rest on his head, then his back, as he dug to the bottom to pull out the gnome. "What were you thinking?"

"That it's an *inanimate garden gnome!*" Azzie stomped to the kitchen.

Curtis emerged from the freezer with the offending gnome in his hand, let the lid slam closed and tucked the gnome under one of his arms, rubbing his hands together to warm his fingers.

"Oh, sure, I can't put the gnome in the freezer, but you can put him under your arm by your smelly armpit."

"You don't understand," Curtis blew on his cold hands, "and besides, armpits are one of the warmer parts of the body." He offered her a small grin over his clenched hands, unable to resist verbally poking her.

Azzie glared back at him, tempted to smile, but held it in, resisting his attempt to lighten the mood. This was why they couldn't sit together at serious functions.

Curtis's grin dropped and he huffed out a breath. Giving up on warming his hands, he moved to the counter. Taking the gnome out from under his arm, he placed it in the sink and turned on the water, running it until it was warm. He sighed in relief as the heated water ran over his fingers. Grabbing a towel, he dried his hands and placed the towel beside the sink, meticulously smoothing it. Azzie was sure she had never seen him lay anything out that nice.

"Let's leave Timmy in the sink to thaw out. I don't think he was in there long enough to be in real danger. We'll talk in the living room where the hardest thing you can throw at me is a pillow."

"You have forgotten about the remote."

"You can't throw the remote at me if I have it," Curtis said, voice serious before he ran out of the kitchen cackling.

* * *

"There are some things that you don't understand, and I wasn't allowed to tell you until we knew for sure." Curtis turned the remote over in his hands, apparently unwilling to put it down within Azzie's reach.

Azzie adjusted her legs on the couch, pushing at the blanket beside her with one hand for something to do. She had let Curtis get the remote, though she shouldn't have. She still wanted to toss something at him. Even an eraser would do. Her gaze moved around the room.

"There is nothing here for you to throw at me. The room is planned that way." One side of Curtis's mouth tilted up at the corner.

Azzie raised what she hoped was one eyebrow. "You specifically left nothing in this room that could be grabbed and thrown at you?"

Curtis shrugged. "You're not the only one who has considered throwing something at me while I'm trying to hold a conversation. And unlike you," Curtis smirked at her, "some of those others may have intended harm."

"Curt—is there something else we need to talk about?" Azzie sat up, feet on the floor, worry for her brother momentarily erasing her frustration.

Curtis gave her a small grin. "It's not what you think. Or rather, it's not *who* you think. There are no people who come in this room and try to throw things at me. Gnomes on the other hand…" Curtis trailed off, a mischievous spark in his eyes as he cocked his head towards the kitchen.

Azzie's irritation returned. She huffed and pulled her legs back onto the couch, crossing them under her.

Curtis watched her rearrange herself and then sighed.

"Quit sighing and get on with it already."

"I was contemplating offering you food first, to butter you up, but I have a feeling that's not going to work." He gestured at the paper plate on his coffee table.

"Why don't you have normal plates anyway?" Azzie started. "No, wait. Don't answer that. It's off topic. Get back to the freaking garden gnome."

"This *freaking garden gnome* has a name," the irritated voice spoke from the kitchen followed by a thump. Then the gnome in question walked out to the living room. Or maybe he waddled. Azzie couldn't decide but either way, she wasn't happy about it, eyes bugging out as she watched him get closer.

She scowled and crossed her arms over her chest, giving the gnome a pointed look before directing her gaze back to her brother.

"Hey, Timmy." Curtis offered a small smile and a wave which was half-heartedly returned.

Curtis turned back to Azzie. "Have you ever heard of cryptozoology?" He sounded like he was launching into a well-worn lecture, then waved his own hands to erase the statement. "Never mind. Of course you have. That's what I study."

Right. That was the name for what Curtis did. Cryptozoology. The study of things that didn't exist. If she ever remembered what it was called, it might be a miracle.

"Ah, yes, where you stick your nose in dusty old books and make shit up for a living."

Curtis opened his mouth to respond before closing it and scowling. "There is some speculation as to what, exactly, cryptozoology entails," the irritation left his voice as he continued, "but, for myself, it's the study of creatures that are thought to exist only in myths and legends. Like Bigfoot and Ogopogo. And living garden gnomes." Curtis picked up Timmy, who was standing by Curtis's feet, and sat him on the arm of the chair before leaning back. "They're all real, but most are capable of hiding themselves, one way or another, from the majority of humanity." A grin cracked Curtis's face. "I don't *make shit up* for a living."

Azzie stuck her tongue out at him. "And how come I can see them? And you, I suppose, you weirdo." She watched as Timmy rubbed his hands across the material of the couch. *Tactile little thing.*

"That part I don't know." Curtis pressed his fingers into his eyes. "The trait seems to run in families, but I know some other CZs that are geneticists. They've looked into it and haven't been able to find a link. Especially because it doesn't appear to be dominant or recessive, just something that skips the first child." Curtis looked at the ceiling quizzically, the words speeding up as he got into the topic. "And the last. Which points to it appearing at some point in development when—"

Azzie cut him off before he could ramble too far into the 'things Azzie doesn't need to know' category. "See zees?"

"Oh, right. It's short for cryptozoologist: a C and a Z. Less of a mouthful. It's a generic, globally accepted name. Anyone who is involved in the field can claim the title. Really, anyone involved and anyone who can see them." Curtis's eyes danced. "Congratulations, little sister. For your birthday, you have become a cryptozoologist."

"Ugh." Azzie flung her arms out to her sides and tilted her head back on the couch. "You couldn't have gotten me a pair of socks or an embarrassing shirt or something? This is not what I wanted for my birthday."

"You clearly haven't raided your *own* fridge today. I did give you 'a pair of socks or an embarrassing shirt or something,'" Curtis said dryly while Timmy giggled into his beard. "And just because you can see the things doesn't mean you need to fully embrace cryptozoology as I have." Curtis shrugged.

"Because driving a forklift at Price Point is such a glamorous job that I shouldn't get rid of it."

"That's not what I meant, and you know it." Curtis pointed at Azzie. "You don't have to get involved at all. Or you can keep your job and only worry about this stuff every once in a while. It's not like there are cryptid crises very often."

Timmy nodded his head in agreement.

"Cryptid?"

Curtis relaxed into the chair a bit. "It's a good generic term for the creatures, humanoid and otherwise, that CZs study and work with. It's less of a mouthful than 'creatures that are only thought to have existed in myth and legend, but nobody has definitively proven they don't exist.'"

"I'm surprised nobody has come up with an acronym for that."

Curtis glared at her. "It's been tried, but thankfully none of them have caught on. You know better than to get me started on acronyms. It's bad enough that I've incorporated CZs into my vocabulary."

Azzie grinned. He was right. She knew how much he hated them and how it was not a good idea to prompt his rant. He would go off on a tangent on how AI could mean anything from artificial intelligence to artificial insemination to Adobe Illustrator.

"And the deal with the gnome?" Azzie prompted when it looked like Curtis wasn't going to rant about the world's excessive use of acronyms.

"Right. Timmy." Curtis gestured to the gnome. "Did you want to chime in?"

"Nope." Timmy shook his head, legs bumping back and forth on the arm of the chair.

Curtis rolled his eyes and muttered something that sounded like "classic" under his breath.

"I already mentioned that this trait only shows up in middle children and there isn't necessarily a direct family lineage." Azzie nodded at

Curtis's words. "Well, Mom is the first child, and knows nothing about it, though at least one of her siblings does, and Dad—he's not a first or last child—but I have never had any indication from him that he knows about this stuff."

"So, how did you find out? Or was it like one of those superhero movies where you were suddenly like *'I see dead people'* and had to figure it out for yourself?"

Curtis's lips curved at Azzie's sad attempt at a movie reference. "I don't see dead people." He stopped as he reconsidered. "Well, I suppose that might not entirely be true, but I don't see normal dead people. Zombies, vampires, and probably some other things could be considered dead people, though I haven't interacted—" Curtis cut himself off when he noticed that Azzie's jaw had fallen on the floor.

"Right. That's irrelevant to this part of the conversation." Curtis resettled himself in the chair. "I don't remember when I saw my first cryptid, but I didn't figure it out by myself. I was approached by someone who was waiting to see if I carried the trait."

Azzie didn't say anything, hoping that Curtis would get on with the story without too much extra prompting, since she was too busy reeling over the fact that vampires existed.

"Do you remember Mom's brother Steve? The weird one? He gave Timmy to Ben for that photography class?"

Azzie bobbed her head.

"Well, the gnome wasn't really for Ben." Curtis tilted his head towards Timmy, who nodded sagely. "He was for me."

"I guess Steve had kind of estranged himself from the family for almost a decade at that point, always off on some trip or another," Curtis continued. "But he happened to be back in town around the time Ben was taking that class. I don't know how it happened that Mom was talking to him about me—,"

"About you?" Azzie was surprised. Ben and Curtis were both good kids. She was more the wild child of the family, with the much younger April being just as studious as her older brothers.

"Yea, me. I don't remember talking about it, but, apparently, I had mentioned switching out of engineering into biology, to study the unusual creatures that lived on campus. Ben had repeatedly told Mom that there was nothing weird about the gophers at the university, so Mom called Uncle Steve. All we knew about his job at the time was that he studied the histories of mythical creatures. And," Curtis tilted his head when Timmy held up a finger, "that's still all Mom knows about his job. And mine for that matter. Anyway. I didn't switch degrees then, but it was when Serrano came into my life. He showed up with a plastic garden gnome, claiming Mom had told him Ben needed an interesting object for his photo class.

"Timmy served two purposes that semester: Ben's inanimate model, because he really did need something to take pictures of, and my official introduction to the world of cryptids." Curtis gestured grandly at the gnome who was trying his best to sit regally while still being a plastic figurine.

"So, you did leave him in my car?"

Curtis shook his head. So did Timmy.

"I didn't," Curtis answered. "But I had brought him over from Mom and Dad's. I tried to make the shed cozy for him, after Ben put him in there, but I couldn't visit often and with nowhere else to go…" Curtis shrugged. "Sometimes it's lonely here, and I figured April had been around long enough that if you were going to join the CZs it would probably be soon. But this isn't how I had imagined introducing you to him."

"Back up." Azzie held up a finger before Curtis could move on. "You said Timmy and Serrano came into your life at the same time. A pepper came into your life? Had you just discovered what a grocery store was?"

Curtis barked out a laugh. "Ha, no. Uncle Steve goes by Serrano in the CZ world. I have no idea why, and I've tried to ask." He coughed and mumbled into his hand, "Probably thinks he's hot shit or something." In his normal voice, he continued, "It's weird trying to refer to him as different things, depending on who I'm talking to. Since he mostly dropped out of the family again, it's not as big of a deal anymore. But he's still around. I don't think he's *here* here, at the moment, but I phone him when I need to."

Curtis looked at the gnome sitting beside him. Timmy met his eyes and nodded solemnly. "You should start taking Timmy with you when you go out. No one has taken the time to put together any standard information, so there is no pocket cryptid ID book. Timmy will be the next best thing."

Azzie snuggled deeper into the couch, pulling the blanket tight around herself. She chewed on one of her cuticles while she tried to process.

Curtis finally stopped playing with the remote and slapped his hands on his thighs before standing.

"There any frozen pizzas left? You destroyed that one, and I'm starving."

Not waiting for an answer, which was good because Azzie didn't know if she was capable of giving him one, Curtis strode out of the room and into the kitchen. Azzie glared at the gnome across the room, giving him shifty eyes, and Timmy glared right back.

* * *

Azzie stared at the ceiling while she lay in bed, dressed in the gnome pajamas she had found in her refrigerator, head propped on a brand-new poop emoji pillow—her real birthday presents from Curtis. Her head was still reeling from what he told her that afternoon. Or maybe it was the half an ice cream cake she ate after Curtis pulled one out of the freezer. Or maybe it was the energy drink she drank twenty minutes ago because there was nothing better in the house. Maybe it was a combination. Whatever it was, Azzie wasn't sleeping, and she didn't have many hours left to sleep in.

The numbers on her alarm clock rolled over. Midnight. It wasn't worth sleeping now, was it? Good thing she had napped on Curtis's couch for most of the day.

A soft scraping sound floated in from the living room. Azzie turned her head to the side. Button, her small tortoiseshell cat, was curled up on the pillow next to her, not yet at the point of the night where she moved and basically sat on Azzie's head. The noise wasn't the cat. Which meant someone had broken in. Or it was that damn *gnome*.

Curtis had insisted the gnome come home with her. And he had insisted that she call him Timmy, not any of the other, more creative, names Azzie had suggested. She sighed. She wasn't sleeping. She might as well go talk to the gnome, who also wasn't sleeping. Did garden gnomes even need to sleep?

Azzie crawled out of bed, careful not to disturb the snoozing Button and pulled on a giant sweater before tiptoeing out of the room.

In the living room, she couldn't see anything moving despite the little nightlight she had begrudgingly left on for the garden ornament. Yawning, she turned to go back to bed.

"Can't sleep?" Timmy popped his head out from behind the wall separating the kitchen from the rest of the house, at around the height of her waist.

Azzie jumped straight in the air, striking what she hoped was a praying mantis ninja pose when she landed, one foot in the air, arms bent at the elbows in front of her. She wobbled as she stared, trying to hold the position.

The stupid thing chuckled at her. The nerve.

"It's a lot to take in," Timmy said as he jumped down from the counter that he was obviously standing on, given where his head had appeared. "I already made hot chocolate."

Hot chocolate sounded good. Azzie supposed he probably hadn't poisoned it. He was a gnome after all. She didn't think he had pockets in his molded plastic pants to keep anything in. But were those even pants? Maybe those were just his legs… It didn't matter. Hot chocolate would be nice, and poison wasn't something normal people kept in their houses, right?

Not that Azzie could probably consider herself a normal person anymore, but still.

Flicking on the light and sitting down at the table, Azzie watched Timmy push back a chair and use the rungs on the legs to climb up to the seat. Then he put his hands on the table and walked his legs up the back of the chair until he could crawl onto the tabletop.

I guess I could have lifted him up. Azzie stirred her hot chocolate with the spoon Timmy had thoughtfully provided. She didn't even want to consider how he had gotten the two mugs down from her cupboard, let alone made hot chocolate and placed said mugs, and the spoons, on the table. The gnome was barely taller than her cat and seemed far less agile, despite having opposable thumbs.

Timmy stood to stir his own hot chocolate then lifted a portion out with the spoon, slurping it up. Some of it ran down his beard to drip on the table. Azzie watched in fascination as the liquid didn't absorb into the hair. She didn't think there even *were* individual hairs in his beard. But it didn't look plastic anymore…

"Ah. That's good," Timmy drank another spoonful and sighed before sitting down on the table, his back against the mug. His red pointed hat stood above the mug's lip, tip happily falling forward instead of back into the hot liquid.

"So, you're a gnome."

"Yes. I'm a gnome." Timmy had his fingers threaded together, hands resting on his little belly, eyes closed. "Any more intelligent questions?" He squinted one eye at her.

"I don't think anybody has ever accused me of asking intelligent questions." Azzie picked up her own mug, took a sip and contemplated whether she could poke him to see if he felt like plastic when he was alive. "This is delicious. And not made out of the powder that I have in my cupboard."

"That stuff is garbage." Timmy didn't open his eyes. "Gnome secret recipe."

Azzie glanced down at the mug, then at the closet full of cleaning supplies just out of the kitchen. Maybe she did have to worry about poison…

"It's safe. Perfectly acceptable for human consumption." By the time Azzie looked back up at the gnome his eyes were shut, but she figured he had to have opened them to gauge her reaction.

"So," Azzie paused, drawing out the word, not sure if there was a polite way to ask a sometimes-inanimate garden gnome if he was really made of plastic. "Umm, are you, I mean, do your—" Azzie's phone rang, cutting her off.

She had brought it to the kitchen on reflex and stared at the number calling her now. She didn't know it, but the area code was local. Maybe she got to go into work early tonight. She wasn't sleeping, might as well make some money.

"'Sup?" Azzie drawled into the phone. She might be awake, but she didn't need to come across as cheery, answering her phone at this time of night.

"Azalea?"

Azzie straightened. She didn't know that voice either.

"This is she."

"Oh, good. I was hoping I had written the number down right." Who the heck had given this stranger her number? "I don't know if you've heard of me, but my name is Serrano—"

"Uncle Steve?"

"Ah, um, yes, you might know me by that name." The man on the other end of the line swallowed. "But I'm calling you to welcome you to the cryptozoology family, so I would prefer you call me Serrano, at least in this context. Best not to mention it to your mother, though. She doesn't know me by this name."

Azzie nodded then remembered he couldn't see her. "Right," she said instead.

"I'll keep it brief," Uncle Steve, er Serrano, went on, "I know it's early, but I can't imagine you've gotten a lot of sleep tonight."

"I work in a couple of hours."

"Oh, yes, he mentioned that, too."

"He?"

"Curtis."

"Oh."

A pause stretched between them.

"Yes, well." Serrano cleared his throat. "I'll let you get ready for work then. You have my number now. Call me if you need me, if you have questions Curtis and Timmy can't answer. Take care of Timmy. Don't get addicted to the hot chocolate." The phone disconnected, but not before Azzie heard him mutter something about abandonment issues and hot chocolate withdrawal.

"Remind me to talk to Curtis about who he can give my number to," Azzie grumbled, still looking at her phone.

Glancing up, her gaze locked on Timmy, who had opened his eyes sometime during the conversation.

"Hot chocolate addictions and abandonment issues?"

Timmy shrugged. "Gnome hot chocolate is incomparable. And it's not my problem if it was time to move on. I'm not the one who kept being left behind for *more interesting* things."

* * *

No one should be allowed to go back to work after having a conversation with a garden gnome and one's crazy uncle, all on barely an hour of sleep. Azzie refused to count the extended nap on Curtis's couch as rest. But she didn't know how she could phone in sick and tell them that she had been up "talking to a gnome." Or maybe she could? Would somebody try and put her in the psych ward? Maybe she needed a trip there anyway. You *probably* got to sleep there since you *probably* couldn't bring garden gnomes.

Azzie's next yawn cracked her jaw, but she took a gulp from yet another energy drink, this one in a bright blue can, before placing it on the top of the car and unlocking the door. She tossed the bag containing her lunch into the passenger seat and slid halfway in. Then she did a double take. Her lunch bag had landed right beside the dratted plastic gnome.

"Again?" Azzie dropped onto the seat, fingers of one hand rubbing at her eyes.

Timmy nodded. "Did you miss the part where Curtis said I get to come along?"

Azzie managed to keep her groan to herself but just barely. "Apparently."

"No standard information?"

"Yes, yes, the bird watchers guide to cryptids." Azzie waved her hand at him and sighed. It was going to be another long day. She pulled her left leg into the car and shut the door. The old car door required more effort to close than should be allowed and the resulting shudder of the vehicle caused the can she had forgotten on the roof to tumble down, spraying bright blue liquid everywhere.

"Ugh. Not again." Azzie tried to run her fingers through her hair in frustration, but got stuck part way through, running into the elastic that held her hair on top of her head.

"Just leave it."

"I can't leave it. You get money back for those cans!"

Timmy shook his head. "Leave it. Curtis has been tending to some sort of weird rabbit who lives around here. It will happily eat your aluminum can. And that radioactive looking liquid might improve its complexion." Timmy tilted his head, stubby fingers stroking down his beard. "It's been looking a little pale."

"You don't know what this *weird rabbit* is?"

"I don't know everything."

"And here I was under the impression that you did, and that was exactly why you were supposed to be my 'guide' in the whole 'journey to become a cryptozoologist' thing." Azzie air quoted, sarcasm creeping into her voice. Not enough sleep and bothersome gnomes were not a good start to the day.

"I know more than you. That's all it takes." If garden gnomes could look smug, Timmy did.

Azzie took one last look at the can on the ground before grumbling about cocky gnomes and putting the car in reverse down the driveway.

* * *

"Can't you at least shrink yourself to the size of a keychain or something?" Azzie stared at Timmy.

Timmy shook his head adamantly. "That is not part of gnome magic. This is the size I am, always."

Azzie scowled. She didn't want to bring him into Price Point. He did not need to 'further her education,' as he put it, from the dash of her forklift. She continued to stare at him. He stared back.

Azzie looked away.

Timmy crowed in triumph and scrambled between the seats to pull himself onto her lap.

"Fine." Azzie scooped up the warm gnome, his plasticky surface feeling pliant under her fingers. "But you have to be inanimate when other people are around."

"Obviously." Timmy cooled and lightened in her hands, the smug expression remaining on his now inanimate face.

Azzie tucked him under her arm and grabbed her lunch bag. Time to go.

Walking up to the side door, Azzie nodded at a grumbling Cara, who offered only a slight wave in return.

The warehouse door opened, and Neil swung through the frame. "Look alive, suckers, because this shift is not going to be an improvement on yesterday." Neil swept an arm past himself, ushering them into the building.

"You know the two forklifts that were down? Well, they were fixed during regular people hours," Neil answered his own question as they walked toward the front of the building and kept on talking. "And they appear to still be working. But there are four more down. Darren is losing his shit."

Cara made a face. Azzie swore. She was over it. First her birthday hadn't gone anything like she had hoped and now work couldn't even play nice. *And* she had this dratted garden gnome to cart everywhere.

"Let me guess. George has to stock again and is making everyone's lives miserable, and the shift hasn't even started?"

Neil shook his head. "Thankfully, no. George called in sick this morning. Something about his joints being too sore from stocking yesterday." Neil rolled his eyes and Cara chuckled. "I mean, it could be true. Or it could be that he thinks stocking isn't *manly* enough for him."

"You don't think he sabotaged the forklifts, do you?" Cara asked Neil.

"Nah. They've looked them over, looking for obvious problems and nothing. Supposedly the mechanics couldn't find anything wrong with those two from yesterday. They just worked again while the guys were here."

Azzie mumbled under her breath. This wasn't happening. Under her arm, the plastic gnome was starting to get warm and was she imagining that he was wiggling?

"Look guys, I have to go put this ridiculous gnome somewhere. Do you know who's driving and who's stocking today?"

"We're stocking, as per usual." Neil gestured to himself and Cara, both of them glancing between Azzie and the gnome with raised eyebrows. "You, oh forklifting queen, have three sections to forklift for. We'll try to be nice." He grinned.

Azzie stuck her tongue out at him and turned away, heading to the forklift bank at the back of the building to find her mechanical steed.

* * *

Safely away from the prying eyes of her coworkers, Azzie set Timmy down on the dash of her forklift. He was no longer rigid and carrying him like was almost made Azzie feel bad. Almost. But not enough to quit doing it. Carrying around a garden gnome was weird enough.

"You need to be vigilant today."

"Can we skip the cryptic messages? It's just some broken forklifts."

"Maybe." Timmy shrugged. "Or maybe not. There are creatures that like to cause havoc on mechanical things, creatures that are good at hiding in plain sight. But they won't be invisible to you any longer. Be wary."

"What should I be looking for? Giant frogs? E.T? *Pale rabbits?*" Azzie looked up from her driving assignment, but the gnome had returned to his fake plastic state. "A lot of help you are," she muttered. Leaving him on the forklift, Azzie walked away, needing to ditch her lunch bag and grab her safety vest from her locker.

* * *

Timmy hadn't been kidding. Azzie had to spend the shift being overly careful and she didn't like it. The forklift she was driving had been one of the ones that was down the previous shift, and it had developed a mind of its own. This time, she wasn't so lucky to just be dropping pallets of Kleenex. The forks would tilt precariously with any balanced load, no matter how she maneuvered the controls, until Azzie was forced to set the edge of the pallet on the metal racking to try and rebalance.

She had tried taking a wrench to the easily accessible bolts, but none of them moved while the forks were down. She was contemplating scaling the mast to try wiggling the bolts from that vantage point but figured Darren would walk by at that exact moment. Darren was *not* having a good day and getting written up for unsafe work practices she had already tried to talk to him about wouldn't make Azzie's day any better either.

"It's got to be a cryptid." Timmy was on his hands and knees, gripping the edge of the dash and staring up at the lift.

Azzie sighed, looking between the gnome and the misbehaving forks. "I'm starting to believe you."

"As you should."

She rolled her eyes. This guy. Didn't he know that he was some ridiculous plastic gnome? She was opening her mouth to tell him to be less cocky when something jumped from the shelf in front of her to the pallet of watermelon she was lowering to the ground, tipping the load slightly down from its level position. The load stopped its downward motion, the lift control jamming under Azzie's hand.

"What the—" Azzie didn't finish her sentence before the thing was peering at her over the edge of the pallet.

The creature was vaguely frog-like in shape but much, much larger. Like if a cocker spaniel had decided to become an amphibian. It didn't appear to have any fur, just skin of a colour that Azzie couldn't nail down. Was it grey? Green? Kind of blue? Any human with skin that tone would have been pronounced dead. It stared at her over the corner of the pallet, its long finger-like digits popping the little suction cups at their tips on and off the watermelon box. Its eyes were larger than she would have expected, giving a further nod to the froggy resemblance, but they were a bright green that she would have expected to see on the glistening skin, rather than its eyes. While she watched, several more pairs of eyes joined the first, heads peeking up over the creature's shoulder to glare at her.

A movement above the pallet drew her eyes to where another of the creatures climbed headfirst down the metal racking. It crawled, stretching out its front legs while its longer back legs stayed bent, ready to spring its slender body forward. Getting within jumping distance of the pallet the thing brought its hind legs underneath itself and sprang. It landed behind the others, disappearing while the load rocked.

Azzie sucked in a breath. This couldn't be good. She really wished she had had the chance to lower the forks before the pallet had started tipping with its new passengers. Or that she hadn't decided to take down one last bin before joining everyone else on break.

The pallet rocked some more and on a swing towards the forklift cab, she could see the newest creature on the farthest edge, jumping up and down. It stood upright, large joints sticking out against rather slim limbs. A grinding croak sounded from its mouth, encouraging several of the others to stand and begin bouncing, rocking the pallet dangerously. The original creature stayed perched by the cab, watching Azzie's reaction, back legs bent as it squatted, toes and fingers over the cardboard side of the box.

"Don't you dare!" Azzie slammed her hand down on the emergency stop button, attempting to turn off the forklift but got no response. After a few more fruitless attempts to lower the forks and turn off the lift, she got out to watch from the aisle. The crouching creature followed her with its eyes while the others started to bounce more vigorously. "There are watermelons in there. I don't want to clean those up!"

The troublesome ringleader screamed and started to jump higher, its followers joining in until the whole forklift was rocking back and forth.

Azzie dove back inside the forklift, banging Timmy with her hand, in her hurry to try, yet again, to lower the load. "Got to get this thing down before they topple it. Bring it down. Hurry. *Hurry*." Azzie punched the control, desperate. When the forklift failed to respond, she risked a glance back up.

The crouching creature looked down at her and when the forks still refused to move, it grinned, revealing a wide mouth full of sharp pointed teeth. Frogs did not have sharp pointed teeth. It flicked up a couple of ears longer than its head, pointed straight out to the side, further destroying the frog illusion. Then it got up and joined the others in their destructive jumping.

As the forklift started swinging violently, Azzie decided it really was time to abandon ship. Grabbing Timmy from where he was clinging white-knuckled to the side of the forklift cab, she sprinted around the corner towards the next aisle. Deciding that wasn't far enough, she raced past two more of the wide aisles, where she threw herself and Timmy into a bin of pillows, peeking over the box and through the racking.

The forklift continued to rock with its uneven moving load. Azzie watched as more creatures crawled down the shelving to bounce on the pallet until the forklift gave up the fight, lousy piece of machinery that it was, and toppled forward.

Timmy jumped, despite the hands he had held over his ears, eyes squinched shut. Azzie almost screamed, watching the destruction as if in slow motion. She was *so* going to get fired.

The cardboard bin the watermelons were shipped in had taken too much strain from its questionable passengers, and when the watermelons rolled into the weakened front of the box as the forklift fell, the cardboard gave out, sending melons crashing to the floor in sprays of chunky red flesh and green rind. The spray coated the forklift, the aisle floor, and up the sides of the houseware products around it. Azzie startled when the juice hit her face, and something landed in her hair, despite being three aisles over. She huffed out a breath. That's what you get for wanting to be able to watch the action.

The ground shook as the forklift followed the watermelons to the floor. Azzie squeezed her eyes shut. Timmy gave a small whimper. Azzie's eyelids flew open once she realized she could hear fast, scuttling movements accompanied by staccato suction noises.

The creatures were climbing the walls, scurrying from racking to pallet, until they reached the height of the shelving. From the top of the steel, they cackled in weird, hoarse voices while a few of them leapt higher, making it to the ceiling before scuttling to the light fixtures.

By now, Azzie could also hear running footsteps. She wasn't surprised that everyone had heard the fall in the break room, clear across the overly large building. She better go back out. Maybe she could claim that she had been going to the bathroom? Nope. She had hidden in the wrong direction for the bathroom. She got distracted on the way back from the bathroom? That wouldn't fly either since she would never have left the forks up to pee. The gnome needed some air? She was close to the side door. It might work but it wasn't going to let her keep her job. And it would mean she had to admit that her garden gnome was alive and there was *no way* that was happening, no matter how much she needed the rent money.

Making up her mind that there was no way out of getting fired, Azzie crawled out of the pillow bin and took a deep breath.

"I'm leaving you here," she said, facing away from Timmy. "I'll come back and get you before we have to leave."

"I don't want to stay here by myself." Timmy's hat was pulled down over his eyes and his stubby arms were wrapped as far as they could go around his equally stubby legs. His hands didn't reach all the way around his calves and his little fingers were trembling.

Azzie cast her gaze around. "Fine. You can go over there." She pointed to the center of the store towards a display of garden gnomes.

Timmy peeked one eye open. "I suppose that will do." He stood up and put his arms out towards Azzie.

Picking up the gnome like she would a small child or a puppy, she realized that Timmy was still shaking. She absently rubbed his tiny back as she headed away from the pillows, feeling the little quivers that moved his small frame.

"Just do your 'I'm a fake gnome' trick and you'll be fine over here." Azzie set Timmy down among what she hoped were actual plastic gnomes. "Unless they start tossing around garden ornaments, you should be OK."

Timmy nodded as he looked around the display then lifted one hand in a wave, the other down by his side, before taking on his rigid plastic look.

As safe as she could make him, Azzie took a deep breath and turned around. She was slightly closer to the bathroom now. She might be able to feign ignorance. After all, it would also explain why she hadn't made it to the disaster at the same time or sooner than her coworkers. Maybe she could save her job?

She had barely taken a step when the warehouse was plunged into blackness. Screams came from where the forklift had toppled, and Azzie's breath whooshed out.

"Gremlins," Timmy's voice said behind her in the dark. "You definitely have gremlins."

* * *

Azzie thought that a shift couldn't get worse than the one the day before, but this one was determined to prove her wrong.

Once the breaker had been flipped and light restored, she had promptly gotten a lecture about loitering in the washrooms and leaving lifts unattended with the forks in the air. Which wasn't what had happened at all, but she couldn't tell Darren that the gremlins had done it. She looked unhinged enough, trying to explain how the lift had jammed and the emergency stop wouldn't work while attempting to keep herself from looking at the grey-green creatures flitting back and forth overhead. It didn't help that the wretched things kept looking at her and grinning, showing off their pointed teeth while waving their ears. It took more effort than Azzie cared to admit not to flinch every time one paused and pulled back its lips.

After the lecture, Darren had her on another forklift and pulling pallets as fast as humanly possible. She didn't understand why she was allowed to drive after the past couple of shifts. Or why she still had a job.

Now she got to scrape the watermelon disaster off the floor because 'it wasn't a custodian's forklift that fell over.' It might not have been so bad if Darren hadn't insisted she drop pallets before dealing with the mess. It had given the gremlins time to run around with a heater, somehow drying the watermelon into some sort of disgusting floor fruit leather.

"Of all the hairbrained things to go wrong the day after my birthday. Don't these stupid gremlins know that if you have a bad birthday, you get to have the next day to make up for it?" Azzie attempted to slide a putty knife under a rubbery piece of watermelon that was determined to stay on the floor. The fruit didn't budge so she reached into the bucket of water beside her and pulled out a sponge. She slapped it down on the offending piece of melon. "Suck on that."

"I suppose it could be worse." Timmy stood beside her, holding a piece of watermelon that she had already pried loose, and looking around warily for gremlins. "It could be zombie goats or leprechauns. Or badgers." Timmy shuddered. "I hate badgers."

"Put that away." Azzie took the piece of dried fruit from him and tossed it in the trash wheelbarrow beside the bucket of water. Timmy shrugged. "Badgers? Like magical badgers?"

"No, no." Timmy shuddered again. "Real, normal badgers. Have you ever met a badger? A North American badger? They are the most troublesome creatures. Apparently, English badgers are much more accommodating, but do the badgers here make any allowances for a humble garden gnome to exist in peace? No! They are intent on destroying our nicely made homes and keeping us out of the best hidey holes."

"Regular badgers." Azzie slanted Timmy a look. "I'm so glad we're not dealing with regular old badgers." Sarcasm crept into her voice, but she couldn't help it. She was scraping dried watermelon off a concrete floor because gremlins tipped over her forklift and this ridiculous garden gnome was worrying about *badgers*. She wasn't even sure they had badgers here. She had never seen one. Then again, she had never seen a talking garden gnome before either.

"Just be happy we're not dealing with badgers." Timmy seemed oblivious to her sarcasm, which was probably for the best. He nodded and moved on to toeing a piece of watermelon with his plastic boot. "Gremlins are much easier to deal with."

"And how, exactly, am I supposed to deal with gremlins? A frying pan perhaps?" Azzie didn't even think about hiding the sarcasm this time.

Timmy shrugged. "I don't know," he admitted, "but it couldn't hurt."

Azzie grinned. That answer wasn't helpful in the least, but she had always wanted to hit something with a frying pan. Besides, she needed a new one anyway.

* * *

Brand new frying pan acquired, but watermelon still somehow in her hair, Azzie once again found herself sitting on Curtis's couch, watching *Monster's Inc.* This time, she had ordered in Chinese food. All her favourites. Which weren't, she was happy to note, Curtis's favourites. Maybe the day would get better once she watched him grimace his way through a plate of deep-fried shrimp and chow mein. Curtis was more of a steamed shrimp and rice kind of guy. She may or may not have ordered him some, but only for after she watched him try to eat the other stuff.

Azzie had just finished putting more noodles on a tiny plate for Timmy and stuffing half an egg roll into her mouth when Curtis came through the door.

"Tell me everything you know about gremlins," Azzie said around her mouth full of food.

"I can't." Curtis dropped his bag beside the door and headed to the coffee table. He peeked through the selection of take-out containers and grimaced. "I've never studied them."

Azzie's mouth fell open. She had to shove the egg roll back in when it started falling out, forcing her to chew before saying, "You do this for a living. How have you not studied the thing that's bothering me the most?"

"First, I'm happy that Timmy isn't the thing that is bothering you the most anymore," Curtis said. He waved at the gnome before heading into the kitchen. "Second, I didn't know you had an issue with gremlins. I normally study things that are large, actual problems." He came back to the living room with a plate and a fork. Curtis didn't use chopsticks unless there was no other option. "Like when a small tribe of Bigfoot were kidnapping hikers out of boredom, or some knock off sea serpent calling himself the cousin of Ogopogo started capsizing all those fishing boats out in Nova Scotia. Actual problems."

"These gremlins jumped on a pallet of watermelon that I had in the air until the forklift fell over."

Curtis snorted in disbelief, adding a small amount of chow mein to his plate. When she didn't respond, he looked up.

"Oh. You were serious."

"Obviously." Azzie held up her new frying pan, while Timmy nodded solemnly from his perch on the arm of the couch. "Timmy tells me this can't hurt but didn't really have any other useful suggestions. I have to do *something*. They've been wrecking the forklifts and playing with the lights."

"Serrano would know better than I do. He's gotten more involved in smaller, local species research than I have."

Azzie groaned. She wasn't looking forward to talking to her estranged uncle again so soon. It wasn't that Uncle Steve, or *Serrano*, wasn't a nice guy, though she didn't know him well enough to be sure, he just came on a little intense about the whole thing and Azzie couldn't find the energy to interact.

Curtis raised an eyebrow at her as he picked breading off his shrimp. "Fine. Fine. If you don't think a frying pan will do, call Serrano."

Curtis nodded, tapping at his phone until it connected to the TV. Serrano appeared, blinking at them from the large screen.

"How did you do that so fast?" Azzie directed her question at Curtis, but it was Serrano who answered.

"I've been keeping this virtual meeting open in the background. Curtis has the link and I anticipated you calling at some point." There was a pause. "Timmy." Serrano nodded at the gnome. Timmy did not nod back.

"You knew I had a gremlin problem and didn't think to tell me anything this morning?"

"You have a gremlin problem?" Serrano's face suddenly filled the screen, like he was trying to look through his camera to see the offending things. His red hair stuck out wildly from his head. He might call himself Serrano because he thought he was into the hottest CZ topics, but Azzie thought it should be because he looked exactly like how someone should look after eating a serrano pepper. If he ate the hot pepper, would it get even better? Azzie shook her head. Nope, back on topic.

"At work. I have a gremlin problem at work. Not here."

"Ah. We can relax then. Gremlins are often an immediate problem if they are in the room if, for no other reason than, they demand the attention." Serrano sat back from the screen. "Now, do you have a plan?"

Azzie held up the frying pan so her uncle could see.

He nodded sagely. "That will help fight them off, but it likely won't solve the problem."

"Well, how do you kill gremlins, then?" Azzie set the pan down.

Serrano opened his mouth to speak, but Curtis cut him off.

"If at all possible, as cryptozoologists, we aim to preserve various species. It's better to find a solution to deal with the gremlins than to eliminate them completely." Curtis aimed his irritation at their uncle.

Serrano nodded, eyes thoughtful. "That's true," he said, stroking his chin as if he was some philosopher of old, deep in thought, or like he once had facial hair. "That said—if it's you or the gremlins, girl, always choose you."

Curtis coloured. "Obviously. I never meant that she shouldn't kill them if they had a knife to her throat."

"They do that?" Azzie put her hand to her neck. Timmy patted her arm in sympathy, leaving greasy handprints on her shirt sleeve. Apparently, they didn't make utensils small enough for gnomes and toothpicks as chopsticks didn't work. Fat little gnome fingers were not that nimble.

Serrano shrugged. "It's hard to say what gremlins will get up to. It's not their norm to attack people with weapons; they are much more interested in machinery and various other technology. But they also fight dirty, so if they think that's what's best for them it's been known to happen."

"OK." Azzie swallowed. "Killing gremlins is plan B. What's plan A?"

Serrano made a show of shuffling things around in front of him until he pulled out a notebook. "Ah. Here it is. I knew I had notes on gremlins somewhere."

"In a notebook. On your desk. Without knowing I had a gremlin problem." Azzie's voice was dry. "How convenient." Serrano ignored her, appearing to skim through his notes, but Curtis glanced at her and rolled his eyes, grinning.

"Gremlins tend to work in groups under one general leader. Groups are referred to as hordes, and hordes are generally made up of members of the same family unit. Horde leaders may be from within the family or be chosen by group consensus from outside. In the majority of cases, leaders are always male, though sex cannot be determined by looking at them." Serrano looked up. "The best way to hurt the unit is to take out the lead figure. However, that can lead to further complications as you have a group without order, which can potentially cause more havoc…" Serrano trailed off as he read down the page, running his thin fingers through his erratic hair.

Azzie and Curtis sat in silence while their uncle read, depleting Azzie's Chinese food. Azzie was gratified to see Curtis cringe every once in a while, as he ate the chow mein noodles. Timmy had finished with his noodles and was now diligently dunking tiny pieces of deep-fried shrimp into a giant container of sweet and sour sauce. Well, giant to him anyway.

The silence from Serrano's end of the video call dragged on long enough that Azzie pulled out the small order of steamed vegetables and plain rice that she had ordered for Curtis. He smiled gratefully and quickly abandoned his plate.

"Here it is!" Serrano slapped a hand on the notebook in front of him. Azzie and Curtis both jumped. Timmy kept dunking shrimp into sweet and sour sauce.

Serrano started to read aloud. "Should the leader of a gremlin horde be eliminated, the remaining gremlins lack direction... blah blah blah... to compensate for this oversight the CZ looking to defeat a horde must tame the leader, rather than kill him. Taming a gremlin is quite simple. While incredibly interested in machinery, gremlins are loathe to wear metal pieces on their body."

Serrano kept talking as if he was reading, but his eyes no longer tracked the words on the page. "To tame a gremlin, simply pierce its ear and insert an earring. The earring must be previously worn by the CZ and must not be cleaned between wearers. The presence of human body oils allows the metal to sit in the gremlin's ear without causing harm and forms a loose connection between the previous human wearer and the gremlin. This bond will be further strengthened when the human shows themselves to be a worthy leader of the horde. Worthy leaders ensure that hordes are provided for and stimulated with access to various machinery and other technologies..." Serrano trailed off again before looking back at the screen.

"The solution is simple really. Find the leader. Pierce its ear. Put your earring in. Then you have a brand-new gremlin horde to call your own." Serrano tugged on his right earlobe, showing a light blue stud and indicated the lack of earring on his left. "I've done it before."

"And if I only have plugs?" Azzie pulled on her own ears to show her uncle the pink piercing plugs she wore in place of earrings.

Serrano scrunched up his face, scrutinizing her stretched piercings through the screen. "I suppose one of those would work, but you would need a very large hole and that might not make the gremlin pleasant to work with afterwards. I would suggest finding an old pair that you haven't cleaned or putting something between your ear and the plug to freshen up the oil."

Azzie looked down as she thought. She probably had something, somewhere.

"You could always change the earring out," her uncle continued, "but during the period where there is nothing in the gremlin's ear, you risk it getting away and losing the horde."

"I'm starting to think that trying to find a family of kidnapping Bigfoots was a better time than trying to take over a gremlin horde," Azzie muttered to Curtis.

"Bigfoot," Curtis corrected her, "and nah. That was weeks of trying to search every part of a massive forest before giving up and pretending to be a lost hiker. This sounds like it will be over much faster."

"How, exactly, do you pierce a goblin's ear?" Azzie asked, not convinced that she was better off trying to tame a gremlin horde than pretending to be lost in the woods.

Serrano jumped in, immediately explaining that the best thing to pierce a gremlin ear was a thin sewing needle, followed by a slightly larger one, and the best way to restrain the gremlin was by straddling its back while it laid face down on the floor, one knee on the ear to be pierced.

"One final thing," Serrano cautioned, lifting a finger, "I have heard it happen on occasion that there are two leaders in a horde. This can happen when a subdued leader joins their horde to an independent one. As with everything, there are always multiple ways to handle this situation. One is to add another piercing to the pierced leader, attempting to coerce it over to your side. The other is to tame the independent leader. This will cause a rift in the horde as there is no clear head of the larger group. The horde will likely split into its original factions, and you will be left with the ones that followed your leader originally."

Azzie nodded as if this were the best advice she had ever heard, but it really wasn't. Curtis was bobbing his head along beside her. Timmy had moved on to eating more noodles after turning up his nose to Curtis's offer of rice.

An alarm went off, the noise ringing through the TV.

Serrano jumped up, moving away from his camera. "I've got to run. Let me know how the fight goes!"

Serrano ended the call, and the TV took over, popping up an image of *Monster's Inc*'s Mike Wasowski. Azzie grimaced. He looked nothing like the gremlins except for his colour. It was eerily close to the shade of their eyes.

"There you have it." Curtis set his plate on the coffee table and rubbed his hands on his knees. "Easy peasy. Just capture yourself a gremlin horde and become their almighty ruler." He reached over and pressed play on the movie. "Almost makes me wish I was the one to come across the gremlins."

* * *

Azzie slowly pushed open the side door of the warehouse. It was dark outside, as it always was when she went to work, but today was the first time she felt like she was sneaking around.

She had come over an hour early for her shift, hoping that Darren was already there, working in his office before everyone else showed up. She lucked out. His car was in the parking lot, and he had left the door unlocked so he didn't have to remember to come open it later.

Lazy, Azzie thought, rolling her eyes. What happens if someone else snuck in? A dark warehouse. The middle of the night. Only one person in the building. It had all the makings of a horror movie. Azzie grimaced. Hopefully the gremlins had left Darren alone. She didn't want to be found here if it really had become a film scene.

The space was too big to take in with one glance, but a quick look through the racking to the small second floor above the break room showed the light on in the supervisor's office. She thought she could see the silhouette of Darren's head.

Azzie let out a breath she hadn't realized she was holding and jogged back to the car, careful not to let the warehouse door slam behind her.

"OK, Timmy, we're clear." She slid back into the Camaro where Timmy was again riding shotgun. Azzie reached for the backpack she had dumped into the foot well by Timmy's seat while he attempted to drag the frying pan up from the floor. The pan was probably twice his weight and Timmy's feet slipped out from under him, sending him careening backwards. The frying pan fell back to the floor with a thunk.

Azzie scooped the pan up, shoving it under the bag in her lap. Timmy righted himself on the seat and watched her rummage through the backpack for the millionth time.

Flashlight? Check. Azzie moved it to the water bottle holder on the side of the bag, making it easy to grab in a hurry. Or if Timmy needed it since she wasn't planning on using it if she didn't have to. She shuffled through the bag, pulling out items she needed to carry inside.

The little sewing kit that her mom insisted she keep was going to prove itself useful tonight. She had used her limited stitching skills to lengthen the strap so Timmy could carry the kit across his back. Azzie handed the small pouch to the gnome then reached across the car to help him get it over his hat and onto his back when his stubby arms prevented him from doing it himself. Timmy nodded at her solemnly in thanks.

Frozen water bottle? Yep. The bottle was wrapped in a towel inside a plastic bag. She might be planning to pierce a gremlin's ear, but she didn't have to be mean about it. She remembered some old movie where they punched a needle through someone's ear and into an ice cube. Hopefully gremlins responded well to the cold.

She took the bottle full of thawing ice out of the wrapping meant to protect her backpack and set it on the floor before pulling out a winter glove. Since she didn't want to deal with a wet backpack and trying to unwrap the bottle later, carrying the bottle it was. And she wasn't risking freezing her own hand just to be nice to the gremlin who was making her life miserable.

Azzie took a deep breath, then reached out to Timmy with both hands. He let her pick him up and place him in the backpack on top of her lunch. She zipped up the sides until just his upper torso was visible.

"Don't fall out," she whispered at him.

"I won't."

Frying pan? Accounted for. Azzie opened the car door, sliding the pan through the strap of her backpack to put the bag on as she got up. She pushed her left hand into the winter glove and picked up the bottle. The frying pan she tucked under one arm before attempting to quietly shut her car door. She didn't think the gremlins would be paying attention to noises outside, but she wasn't taking that risk.

Car door closed, Azzie took a long breath and headed toward the warehouse.

Inside, the dim emergency lighting cast the steel racking in an eerie glow. Azzie swallowed and crept through the open produce section to the garden gnome set up in the middle of the building, glancing up obsessively to make sure the light in Darren's office was still on.

At the display, Azzie knelt, setting down the water bottle and frying pan before taking off her backpack. She lifted Timmy out of the bag and slipped the pack inside a nearby garden shed. She wanted to keep Timmy with her, but she didn't think he would be safe riding in the backpack. There was no way that his stubby plastic legs could keep up with hers, despite the fact that she was only five-two, and her legs could not be considered long. All legs are long to a gnome that doesn't even reach a short person's knee.

As Timmy arranged himself with the other garden ornaments, Azzie cast her gaze around the dully lit warehouse, watching for gremlins. She lifted her hand to her right ear, feeling around the plug in her ear lobe for the gold hoop earring she had stuck in the night before. It was one of those hoops that could be slept in, where the closure was even with the rest of the ring allowing it to spin freely. She hoped the gremlin wouldn't mind it too much.

Not finding her nemeses, Azzie picked up the water bottle and frying pan, taking a deep breath before standing.

"Good luck," Timmy whispered by her feet.

Azzie leaned down, tucking the frying pan back under her arm, and put her fist out, which Timmy promptly bumped with his own. "Stay safe."

Timmy nodded stoically and assumed a cheery garden gnome expression, going inanimate.

Azzie looked at him a moment longer. The little thorn in her side had grown on her at some point, and she didn't want him to get hurt. If sometimes-plastic-gnomes could get hurt, that is.

Azzie gripped the handle of the frying pan as she stood up. Its weight felt good in her hand, almost secure. Or at least, it was making her feel less freaked out. The thought of fighting off gremlins had kept her up all night, panicked and drinking too much of Timmy's hot chocolate. She hoped she didn't have to pee in the middle of this.

Taking a deep breath, Azzie shoved the handle of the pan under the back band of her bra, her Guns N' Roses T-shirt tucking up as it went along for the ride. The top curve of the pan fit securely under the waistband of the jeans she had stolen from Curtis's closet. Hers hadn't been loose enough to stick part of a frying pan into. She didn't know if it would hold there for long, but she wanted to have at least one of her hands free. She would have to come up with something better if carrying frying pans around was going to become a regular life occurrence. One more deep breath and she moved away from Timmy and the garden gnome display.

The farther she got from the gnomes, the more she panicked. She should have brought Curtis with her. She didn't know what she was doing. She didn't have any extra skills as Curtis had so *helpfully* pointed out more than a few times in the last couple of days. Who did she think she was to take down a gremlin mob boss and take over a horde?

Azalea Bates, she thought to herself as she walked into the produce section, *today you get yourself a horde. Not of gold or jewels or fancy old cars but gremlins. Creepy little beasts who are probably going to destroy the only functioning car you own. Today you protect the world, or at least this warehouse, from the giant frogs!*

She took a power stance by a bin of watermelon that hadn't smashed to the floor, feet planted, legs apart, one hand on her hip, and the other fist punching the air above her head.

She broke down giggling to herself. *This is absurd.* She abruptly slapped a hand over her mouth. *Shit.* Had she given away her position?

Azzie stood still, casting her eyes around, her right hand reaching for the frying pan at her back, the left still holding the frozen water bottle by her hip.

It probably only took a few seconds, but to Azzie it felt like hours, before bright green eyes started to blink out of the darkness. The giggling had definitely given her away. Maybe it was for the best though. If they came to her, that meant she didn't have to work as hard to find them.

Azzie hadn't thought this through enough. She wasn't familiar with fighting. At least not serious fighting. She used to playfight with Curtis as a kid, but now they only threw punches they never intended to land. What she did know from action movies was that it was better to have a wall at your back. Or a corner. Something that meant she could see what was coming at her and nothing could come up from behind. Glancing frantically around, Azzie took off for the bakery and the closest empty corner she could think of, frying pan handle poking between her shoulder blades.

Azzie's breath huffed out as she ran. The suctioning sounds of gremlins jumping from racking and running along the floors kept getting louder. How many of them were there anyway? The frying pan limited her ability to twist around and count as she tried to maintain the space between them.

Pushing through the swinging doors into the bakery, Azzie reached the corner and turned around, panting, hands on her knees. The distance between the produce section and the back of the bakery wasn't that far, but it had been a while since she had run *any* sort of distance. Might have to work on that. Reaching behind her with her free right hand, she maneuvered the frying pan out of her clothing. It had stayed in her waistband better than anticipated. One more deep breath and she straightened, pan held out to the side, bottle of ice at the ready in her other hand.

The running and jumping sounds of the gremlins had slowed, but she couldn't see them beyond the slowly swinging doors that separated the bakery from the rest of the store. As she watched, dark shapes began to creep in, setting the doors swinging faster, before they spread out, eyes blinking at her from the darkness. Some of them stayed crouched on the ground, but most found places amongst the baking equipment and supply racks, and at least one pair of eyes glowed at her from the ceiling.

Crap. The ceiling. She didn't have any idea how to keep track of that one. The gremlins could crawl down the walls at her back. Nothing she could do about it now except try to remember to look up. At least there weren't ceiling tiles for it to hide in.

"Any chance you want to take the easy way out?" Azzie tried reasoning with the gremlins. "You could just leave. Or show me your leader or something."

A lone gremlin stepped through slowly swinging doors, upright on its hind legs, coming forward until it stood in the pocket of light before her, lips pulled back and snarling.

Azzie's attention snapped from the gremlin to the warehouse barely visible through the small windows set in the bakery doors. She hadn't realized she could see the light from Darren's office glowing onto the racking until it winked out.

She sucked in a breath. How much time did she have to wrap this up? Probably not enough. If Darren was leaving his office, that meant she had maybe fifteen minutes to fight a gremlin king, pierce its ear, and make it seem like she hadn't been here very long before the rest of her coworkers showed up.

Maybe he would just go back into his office after running to the printer or something? She risked a glance at her watch. She had only been here 10 minutes; there was no way that Darren should be coming down to the main floor yet. There were not many people keen to get to work on this team.

Azzie looked back at the gremlin. She breathed in and out. The gremlin breathed in and out. The entire horde crept closer.

Azzie started to panic. No more deep breaths for her. The gremlin took a step closer.

Darren's light flicked back on.

Azzie felt her muscles relax for a split second seeing the light glowing out over the warehouse again. Thankfully, Darren wouldn't be able to see her behind the bakery doors, fighting invisible demons with a frying pan. She had already started carrying around a garden gnome; she didn't need to add swinging a frying pan around the baking area to the list of her new, quirky traits.

The gremlin made a growling sound in the back of its throat. *Probably mad that I'm not paying attention to it.* But seriously, it wasn't that tall. Even standing upright, it only came up to about her waist. It slid its lips back farther. Those teeth, though. She gulped. This was not going to be like scrapping with Curtis. This was going to be like fighting an angry dog that walked around on its hind legs part-time.

Azzie bared her unimpressive teeth back at the gremlin and took up her praying mantis ninja stance, frying pan close to her face, water bottle out in front of it. She didn't have time to wobble as the gremlin took her pose as a cue, crouching down and launching at her.

Azzie dropped her stance as she stumbled backwards, brushing the wall behind her as the gremlin's leap brought it closer. Shit. This was not going how it was supposed to go. Nanoseconds before the gremlin would have latched onto her with its teeth, she threw up her left arm, and it bit into the water bottle instead. That didn't stop its body from slamming into hers, driving her back into the wall.

"Eew, eew, eew!" Azzie squealed and squirmed away from the gremlin and the wet feeling of its hand on her neck. She could feel its fingers sticking to her as its feet scrambled for purchase. She was still trying to twist away when it pried its teeth out of the plastic.

Suddenly free of the additional weight, Azzie's arm swung back, her muscles still trying to pull away from her attacker. The ice in the water bottle had started to melt and water splashed across her face, running into her eyes as it poured from the new exit holes.

Just what I needed. I can't see what I'm doing. I'm probably going to die by gremlin.

Azzie felt the gremlin crawl up her with its weird feet, not affected by her thrashing as she tried to dislodge it, forgetting she was holding a frying pan as it hit the wall, the contact reverberating up her arm. The gremlin stopped with both feet on her shoulder, one hand yanking her hair. A weird beckoning sound emerged from its throat and more gremlins emerged from the shadows.

Shit shit shit.

Azzie swung the frying pan above her head, hoping to take out the gremlin still perched there. The stupid thing managed to duck and miss her upward swing, but she caught it on the back of its head as she swung her arm towards the floor.

The gremlin tumbled from her shoulder to land on the floor beside her where it flipped over and glowered, a louder growl slipping through gritted teeth, hatred filling its slitted eyes. The other crept towards her.

A second lone gremlin stepped into the light near the door with no apparent intention of attacking. Its ears flicked out from its head and Azzie caught a glimmer. This one had an earring. A rogue, subdued gremlin. *Fuck.* Had someone sent this horde after her? Or loosed them in the warehouse? Or something? Maybe having a gremlin horde didn't actually give you that much control…

The gremlin at her feet shifted, crouching like a frog, blood trickling from its lip. It had to be an independent leader like Serrano had talked about. Why else would the other gremlins have responded to its weird croaking.

Azzie glanced up at the gremlin near the door before returning her attention to the one at her feet. It was at least within catching distance. She didn't know if she could pass the stream of giant froggy gremlins coming towards her to get to the pierced one.

The gremlin leapt. Azzie closed her eyes and swung her frying pan, suddenly nervous with the thought of hitting it again. She didn't see the pan connect, but she felt it. And she heard the gremlin hit the ground for the second time. She peeked out of one eye. Had she killed it? What would happen if she killed the leader? Did they all answer to the other leader? Did they disband? Why did nothing Serrano told her feel useful right now? And why, *why*, couldn't she seem to remember any of the details?

The gremlin rolled over and sat up, shaking itself. *Whew, not dead.* One less thing to worry about. Which was good because several more gremlins were preparing to launch their attack. Azzie didn't bother trying to count them. As they jumped, she swung out with the frying pan, trying to keep herself between them and the wall, keeping them apart from their leader.

It was more work than she had anticipated.

Panting, and getting worse at hitting gremlins, Azzie had to resort to running into the wall to dislodge some of them. The leader hadn't joined back in, and the gremlin attack was slowing. Azzie risked a glance around. Most of the gremlins close to her were on the ground, though none of them appeared to be dead. Some of them looked to be regrouping. A handful more stayed back, hovering around the pierced gremlin, clearly waiting for their own instructions.

Azzie drove the handle of the frying pan into the bag of flour sitting on a stack beside her. Ripping the bag open, she sucked in a breath, closed her eyes, and swept the flour out in front of her. Choking sounds filled the air around her as the gremlins breathed in and started coughing.

Opening her eyes, Azzie dove and scooped up the stunned gremlin leader. She bopped it on the head with the frying pan when it bared its teeth at her and started to struggle.

"Timmy!" Forgetting about Darren and the risk of being discovered, Azzie screamed for her gnome. And just when had Timmy become *her* gnome? Whatever. Timmy had the needles. She needed to get to Timmy.

The recovering horde protested her sprint past them and through the flour cloud, hacking as the powder settled in their lungs. She crashed into a rolling cart full of supplies, toppling an open bag and sending a waterfall of sugar down her side, rushing toward the door. The gremlin in her arms didn't react to the cascade of crystals down its face, eyes unfocused and staring. Racing out of the bakery, she moved as fast as her legs could take her, thigh muscles burning, lungs screaming in protest.

Skidding to her knees beside Timmy, an aisle away from the gnome display, Azzie awkwardly juggled the gremlin, dropping the frying pan in the middle of the floor, as she fumbled to add the gnome to her armful. Legs wobbling, she stood and almost fell as she shoved through the doors of the garden shed a few steps in front of them. Crouching and letting Timmy jump to the floor in the relative safety of the dark space, she placed the gremlin on the ground.

Azzie held herself over the gremlin, a knee on one of its ears as Serrano had instructed. She placed the partially frozen water bottle on the tip of its ear. She thought she heard it hiss in pain, flinching under her.

"Sorry." She glanced down, though she couldn't see its eyes. "It's probably going to get worse."

"Azalea." Timmy had dug the flashlight out of her bag and turned it on, the light shining along the floor and sending shadows up the walls of the shed. He thrust a needle under her nose as far as his stubby arm would allow, sounding oddly serious.

She looked up at him, concern stopping her from taking the needle.

"I know this is best. But you still need to consider what you are doing. By claiming this gremlin, you will need to know that you can provide for its horde. Are you prepared for that?"

"I'll make it work. I'll figure something out. Or find some other CZ who can."

Timmy nodded solemnly and gestured with the needle.

This time Azzie took it.

She placed the towel wrapped foam that Timmy gave her next under the goblin's ear, positioned the needle, and pushed. She probably should have been more prepared for the resistance of the gremlin's flesh, but just when she started to worry the needle slid through hitting the towel beneath.

Pushing the first needle all the way through, she slid the second needle into the wound. That needle in place, she reached up and unhooked her earring. She slid the hoop into the gremlin's ear as she pulled the needle through. Earring latched, she slowly got to her feet and backed away, not that she could get far inside the shed.

The gremlin lay on the floor. She could see it breathing, but it wasn't moving. She nibbled her lip, worried. The gremlin pushed itself up on its arms until it was crouching in the frog-like position she had first seen it in. It turned to look at her over its shoulder, the newly pierced ear flicking back and forth. Azzie let out a breath.

"Yea. Sorry about that," Azzie apologized, hoping the piercing didn't hurt too bad.

The gremlin turned, still crouched. Its body tensed and it leapt into the air. Azzie didn't have time to put her hands up to try and ward off the attack.

But an attack didn't come. The gremlin just landed and perched on her shoulder.

"Oh, umm," Azzie cleared her throat, "OK."

Taking a breath, Azzie pushed the door open enough to see the rest of the gremlins crouched in a half circle around the garden shed. Why hadn't they come in?

She stepped out, taking a quick count, the water bottle rolling out and leaking everywhere. There were only about a dozen gremlins, not including the one on her shoulder. Six of them sat around the shed while the others crouched with the pierced gremlin a short distance away.

The gremlin on her shoulder stood up, placing one hand on her head as it had before. A series of throat sounds swirled above her. When the other leader didn't move, the sounds got angrier. She watched as the horde closest to her turned, baring their teeth to the others.

Were they all going to fight? Azzie couldn't take it. She was exhausted and she still had a whole eight-hour shift to get through.

The other gremlin leader regarded her and the gremlin on her shoulder. Before either Azzie or her gremlin could react, it sprang forward landing on Azzie's chest and pushing her back into the shed doors. It grinned at her before leaping off, running towards the employee door, its horde on its heels.

Azzie watched them go. As it had leapt off her, she had gotten a better look at its earring. A blue stud. Like Serrano's.

Timmy tugged on Azzie's pant leg, and she slid down the shed to collapse on the floor beside him, gremlin peering down at the gnome. Her phone rang.

Pulling the phone from her pocket, she glanced at the screen. Serrano. Of fucking course.

She answered the call and put the phone to her ear, not saying anything.

"I'm going to assume since you answered that you're still alive and everything went well," Serrano's voice came through the phone's speaker. "Especially since neither gnome nor gremlin fingers are able to activate smart phones."

There was a pause as he gave her a chance to reply.

"I see," Serrano paused again, shorter this time. "Well," his voice brightened, "Congratulations on your new gremlin horde, Azalea."

The call disconnected and Azzie let her hand fall to the floor.

She offered the destroyed water bottle to the gremlin on her shoulder. It took the offering cautiously, trying not to touch the cold ice with its weird little fingers. It looked back at her.

"What am I supposed to call you?"

The gremlin replied with a series of sounds that she would never hope to understand, much less replicate.

"Is it OK if I call you Bob?"

The gremlin didn't reply, but she thought she saw a small nod before it licked at the water bottle with a weird purple tongue, split like a lizard's.

Azzie leaned back on the shed, patting Timmy on his hat.

"Well, Bob and horde, I could use a nap."

* * *

"Couldn't manage to show up on time again, Azalea?" George sneered as Azzie walked back into the building half an hour later.

Azzie glared at him, shoving her hands in her pockets and walking to her locker.

For all that it had taken out of her, the fight with the gremlins hadn't been very long and Azzie had gone home to shower before coming back to work.

The gremlin horde was currently ensconced in her bathroom, playing in a partially full bathtub with Timmy for supervision. She had left some towels laying around in case they were inclined to curl up and have a nap. Button had been hissing at the bathroom door when she left, evidently able to see the gremlins just fine and spitting mad about it.

"Five minutes is hardly late, old man."

"Back in my day, five minutes early was late," George boasted. "And I was never late."

"It seems that times have changed with age, huh?" Neil slung an arm around George's shoulders.

George swore and shoved Neil aside before stalking off in the direction of Darren's office.

"I don't even want to know what happened in the bakery overnight, but somebody call an exterminator and somebody else get over there and clean it up. Now!" Darren barked from behind Azzie.

She groaned, realizing she was the reason for the mess in the bakery.

She had found flour in her hair when she had gotten home and had only been partially successful at brushing it off her jeans when she decided she didn't have time to find a clean pair. And there was something in her pocket that she hadn't noticed before...

"And make sure you clean it up all the way to the garden gnome display," Darren added, turning away. "This job is bullshit," he muttered. Azzie snickered.

"Come on, champ, let's go clean up the mess." Neil swung his arm around Azzie's shoulders. "We have to do something to amuse ourselves since Cara thinks she gets a day off."

Azzie turned, Neil following behind, his arm still on her shoulders. "I've got a surprise for you."

Neil looked at her quizzically.

Azzie tossed the sugar she had found in her pocket in his face then raced to the bakery, Neil yelling in mock horror and running after her.

* * *

It had been three days since the claiming of the gremlin horde and Azzie was getting a haircut. She hadn't talked to Serrano about his involvement with the gremlins, but she had talked to Curtis. Probably more than Curtis wanted to talk about it. But he was the only one she could talk to, so he suffered through.

The horde had been relocated to a junkyard full of broken-down old cars owned by another CZ. They were still Azzie's, but the junkyard owner was pleased to have some sort of security for his place. Apparently, small house cats weren't the only animals able to see the cryptids and most were eager to avoid gremlin encounters.

The gremlins had seemed happy enough when Azzie visited yesterday, as she watched them attempt to drive a car that they had started. Who knew that they could fix mechanical things as well as break them. Maybe she would have to let them tinker with her beloved Camaro. Just maybe.

"Can you tilt your head down?"

Azzie tilted her head so the hairdresser could trim the hair on the back of her neck.

"Done. What do you think?"

Azzie eyed her brand-new haircut in the mirror. Her once long brown hair was now short, somewhere between shoulder length and pixie cut but not quite a bob, and silvery white. Her mother would be appalled that she had basically dyed her hair grey, but bleached blonde was worse.

Besides, this colour matched the colour of Timmy's beard exactly. The gnome sat on the counter by the mirror. She caught him wink at her. She winked back.

"I love it."

Happy birthday to me.

SILVERBIRD:
A HALFWAY HOME STORY

IRISH WILLIAMS
ART BY
ROMY POISSON

"There's a kelpie in the koi pond."

A sigh came from the other end of the call. "A... what?"

Reeve bit the inside of his lip. Teeth found purchase on old scar tissue, like it was the well-worn "oh shit" handle of a truck that had seen too many teen drivers at the wheel.

Covered nose to tail in a carpet of algae, water weeds tangled in its black mane, a horse-like creature stared back at him as it munched away on an unfortunate koi fish. That was what gave it away: the munching. While a horse might have had its weird little mouth and freakish buck teeth all at the front like some vegan vacuum cleaner, a kelpie, by contrast, had a maw more like a dog. It chewed. It munched. The koi hung limply from its mouth in iridescent calico strips of cartilage and pale meat.

The kelpie stared vacantly back at him with eyes painted an unsettling yellow colour he was pretty sure had no business on any kind of horse.

"A kelpie, Alex..." Reeve glanced around to see if there were any other pedestrians on the manicured walkway as unsettled as he was at seeing a soggy murder horse. Unfortunately for him, he was alone when it came to human companionship. It was late enough in the afternoon that the migration of parents and kids cutting through the lush garden park into the lands of suburbia had already come and gone. The loitering ducks didn't seem too concerned, though. They were still clogging the bright red foot bridges and huddled at the shores of all the interconnected little koi ponds, enjoying their daily feast of leftover lunch breads. "Geeze, put that folklorist nerd shit to use or I'm not helping you study anymore."

That pulled a laugh from the other end. "Yeah, yeah. You sure it's not someone's—"

"Some little kid's escaped pony?" By now Reeve had started walking again, eager to get as far away as he could from a creature famous for its tendency to snatch and drown any would-be rider before feasting on their innards. A creature from *folktales,* he had to remind himself. It probably wasn't there anyways, just a product of his misfiring mind. Besides, he had to reach the bus stop. If he could catch the last of the peak service buses, he'd not be stuck alone with his uncooperative thoughts for an hour till the regularly scheduled bus showed up.

"Pft. This neighbourhood?" He looked over his shoulder half expecting the kelpie to be gone. "Could be. Could be one of those miniature horses, too." The kelpie had sloshed its way onto the shore. Weirdly, rather than hooves, it had feet like that one type of big, black bird Reeve could never remember the name of; the blue-necked ones that kind of looked like punk rock emus and zookeepers needed to carry shields into their enclosures to avoid catching the attitude that went with it. "I can't tell the difference."

"One's fat and the other looks like someone put a horse-shaped sweater in the dryer."

Reeve rolled his eyes. "Wow, very insightful. Clearly, you're an expert."

"Can you take a picture?" The question was abrupt, more so than normal for this type of check in. Alex usually settled for a description of whatever had unsettled him, cracking off-the-wall jokes about it until some kind of calm returned.

"Sure. If you're collecting pics of wet horses this week, I can promise you you'll find better ones on kinky furry sites." He slowed and stopped before putting the phone on speaker to fiddle with the camera app. Juggling his guitar case in the mix didn't help any. The item slipped suddenly off the top of his shoulder at one point into the bend of his arm and came dangerously close to hitting the ground; a "brush with death" for an instrument in a soft case.

Reeve, once he remembered he'd made a joke, was pretty sure Alex had inhaled whatever he was drinking from the sound of things. One of his friends must have been with him, too, because there was a burst of loud laughter picked up in the background.

"DUDE!"

"Hey, no judgment. Get your freak on in peace, just do it when I'm not home." Reeve, finally in control of the guitar case, centred the murder horse on screen for a decent enough picture to send. "Fair warning, this one likes fish sticks."

More sounds of fumbling and distant cursing from Alex's end pulled Reeve's attention pleasantly elsewhere as he resumed his trek to the bus stop. At least with a picture, Alex could confirm if it was an escaped horse or pony of some sort. He could call Animal Control and get it back to wherever macabre petting zoo it had wandered off from. Alex could even tell him it was some performance art weirdo in a horse costume, and that would make more sense than what his brain had started to cook up after the day he'd been having.

Alex told whoever he was with to shut up a moment, clearing his throat. "Speaking of home, I couldn't get the battery block working, but a mechanic buddy of mine needs practice. He offered to rewire the whole RV at half cost."

"Shit, I'm about to take the seven, Alex. Where the hell am I going? Are we crashing at Cindy's again?"

"Well, that's the good part; same buddy has *also* offered us a spare room for a while." There was some more murmuring, this time from the other person and a harsh "shush" from Alex. "What are the chances you can get over here to the Storm Brew in… I don't know, less than an hour?"

"Lemme guess: offered it for free?" Reeve rolled his eyes, knowing there was some kind of catch, from Alex's tone. "And I'm also gonna go out on a limb and guess your *buddy's* garage is attached to their house or something?"

"Something like that…"

Reeve massaged the bridge of his nose. "Every time someone tells me nerds don't get any…" Still, half price for that kind of an overhaul was nothing to sneeze at. Just replacing the old RV's septic tank had been an ordeal.

"It's not like that, it's more… look, I'll explain it when you get here."

Reeve caught sight of the bus cresting a treeless hill in the distance right before it disappeared into a maze of maple-covered side streets nearing the park. If the driver didn't blow through any of the stop signs along the way, then he had roughly three or four minutes until it arrived.

"Yeah, yeah. Bus is on its way, gotta go. Grab me a muffin or something before they run out; I'm starving." Whatever Alex started to say in reply was cut off as Reeve ended the call and stuffed the phone in his pocket.

"You can sing?"

Reeve froze mid-step.

Stress of the day, and the illustrations in Alex's textbooks from last night, had given Reeve's mind ample ammunition to threaten him. The kelpie on its own was an unsettling but ultimately harmless figment of imagination to chuckle over, not even the weirdest by any stretch. Harmless, but it should have been a warning sign.

"You should sing, I bet you sing like silver birds!" declared the voice.

There hadn't been anyone around when he'd checked a moment ago, but that still didn't rule out a jogger who'd caught up to him and seen his guitar case.

Please be a jogger.

Reeve turned towards the sound to find a short man dressed up like some hobo clown he'd seen once at a circus when he was little. The man had a mallard duck tucked under one arm and wore a horse-head mask, a finely detailed one as opposed to some generic latex monstrosity. Real hair covered the surface, and it seemed like animatronic "muscles" had been built beneath the skin allowing it to occasionally twitch or emote. Wet golden eyes, much too large in proportion to the rest of the face, were even outfitted with pupils that constricted in reaction to the play of dappled light filtering through the branches overhead.

The mouth moved, rudely chewing on a calico chunk of koi.

Shit.

Reeve bit the inside of his lip, the little spike of pain serving to pin him in the moment before he could focus on the rhythmic, tactile sensations of his feet slamming into the ground as he ran.

He couldn't *stop* running until he was almost at the bus stop, heaving in shallow breaths, doubled over. The soupy, floral scent of gardenias blooming somewhere was unmistakable and heavy in his straining lungs. Reeve struggled to focus on that distinctive smell for a while, then the patterns of brown and grey pebbles suspended in concrete beneath his boots, the weight of his guitar case on his back, anything to calm down.

He looked back over his shoulder and watched as the horse-headed man waddled up the path after him, waving and shouting. Reeve swallowed hard. He had, for a few moments, gone deaf to the voice on the phone and the realization he'd called Alex back on reflex.

"Reeve?" Restrained worry laced Alex's voice. "Talk to me, bud. Re-"

"Y-yeah, 'm–here." The phone came close to slipping from his sweaty grip.

"You good? You sound out of breath."

"I will be." The run had left Reeve feeling as if he'd downed too much coffee, heart fluttering, fingertips tingling. "Look, I'm about to get on the bus…" He lowered his voice, seeing other people staring back at him from the bus stop. Reeve cupped his hand around his mouth to further shield the conversation. "That kelpie just turned into a guy with a *horse head,* so my imagination is really firing on all cylinders right now. Today has—it's just been a bad day."

"Need me to come pick you up?"

Reeve winced. "No, I- I can make it to the coffee shop." He abruptly hung up again, pocketing his phone.

The last thing he needed was for Alex to feel like he needed to swoop in for a rescue, especially when it had sounded like Alex was with someone.

"Wait, wait! Your legs are too long!" yelled the horse-headed-kelpie-man behind him, throwing the now vocal duck aside in his continued efforts to catch up.

Reeve knew he shouldn't have looked back.

The blue metal awning of the bus stop didn't shade much in the late afternoon. Four others already stood waiting, pretending like they weren't staring.

"Such a delicate bird!" Reeve winced as the voice suddenly crowed from ahead of him where the little man now hung from the bus stop pole and gestured in random directions with the skeletal remnants of the koi. His proclamations were more and more like that of a circus announcer. The creature's head slowly lost the equine features in favour of human ones: a patchy black beard, cherub cheeks, and a squat nose set between pale eyes the size of golf balls.

"A dainty little clockwork bird tucked in its music box!" The newly formed face tittered with flashes of buck teeth beneath his lips. He stilled, mouth agape and eyes wide. "No! A *proper* nightingale. One of Circe's melodic neighbours wailing their *Reaper's Chorus!*" He spun around the pole, shouting. "They'll melt the wax right out their hunters' ears and drive them gloriously mad, they will! Those beautiful, beautiful *Silverbirds!* Ha ha! The deadly beauties will lead their would-be hunters to the rocks upon their harrowed shore, turning moonlit waters *crimson!*"

Reeve ignored the figure as much as he could. The shouting was loud and grating, ringing with a discordant undertone that had him tensing his jaw until the taste of copper was on his tongue.

To Reeve's left, an elementary kid craned her pigtailed head up at him, smiling innocently as she held her father's hand. The two were regulars along the route, enough that Reeve had nicknamed her "Shelly" on account of her carrying around massive seashell hauls during the summer. He had yet to find something suitable to call her father.

Shelly waved at him, and Reeve did his best to wave back, to pretend like everything was normal in order to not come across as "sketchy." It was a task he failed. Shelly's father politely shuffled them farther down the queue.

This day can't get worse.

"You can sing; you can see; you can hear! My, how you've grown!" The creature Reeve had now mentally dubbed Horseface crowed gleefully.

Don't acknowledge it. It's not there. It doesn't matter what it says. Calm. Down.

Reeve focused on the weight of his guitar case hanging from his shoulder, on the plastic of the pass in his hand as he tapped it with roughened fingers. He ran the crisp edge of it under his thumbnail as the bus rolled up with a squeal and sigh.

His phone buzzed with a text in his back pocket. Alex, no doubt concerned about the sudden silence.

Horseface kept rambling, shouting whatever it did about silver songbirds making people go mad with their singing.

Get on the bus. Sit down. Text Alex an update. Forty minutes till the stop near Storm Brew.

Get on the bus. Sit down. Text Alex. Forty minutes till the coffee shop. Everything is fine.

It had been a while since a hallucination presented so vividly, certainly since one had followed after him. Another meeting with his psychiatrist was definitely in order. This new prescription wasn't doing its job, either, worse than the last one and the one before. About the only medication that really worked was the Alprazolam he resorted to when a panic attack hit too hard.

Reeve boarded the bus and sat down near the rear door, resting his guitar case between his knees and his forehead atop that. He tangled his hand tightly in the coil of the shoulder strap for a familiar texture.

As much as he tried to ignore it, he could still hear Horseface outside.

Why such a bizarre little man had gotten his heart leaping out of his chest would forever be a mystery; panic attacks usually were, but like hell was he about to waste even half a pill on that little weirdo. Pills were damned expensive and, even split, the Alprazolam made him nauseous. He just needed to work on calming down.

Several people continued to stare because of his shaking and laboured breathing; pretending they weren't whenever he looked up to see what was keeping the bus from taking off. Reeve gripped the strap of his guitar case tighter.

"Just... a bad day," he sighed to himself, watching as a few more people made it in time to board. That had probably been what triggered the whole... kelpie thing. He'd had a tutoring session. Bass. Fourteen-year-old little twerp who thought he should be Robert Trujillo after two months but wouldn't practise slap or basic scales.

The pay had been good, then the parents had the same expectations as the kid and thought two months of private lessons should have their precious brat "skipping levels" in band class.

What the hell did that even mean?

Whatever. Now he needed to find other work.

He focused on the woven texture of the case's handles and edges, something solid, as he finally began to time his breathing. If he could calm down, he could text Alex that he was fine and mean it. Maybe he could even calm down enough that Horseface disappeared; he'd done that before. Really, he shouldn't be this worked up over any of his hallucinations by now. He knew he shouldn't.

Everything was fine.

Reeve pulled his phone and quickly typed out a text to Alex, letting him know he was on the bus and safe. He only briefly looked at the *"looks nothing like a kelpie??"* text Alex had sent a moment ago in response to the photo.

Shelly was up front, watching him from over the back of her seat the way kids did; her father was scrolling through his phone in the seat beside her. Most of the other passengers were settling down or chatting away as the bus finally rumbled along. Everything *was* fine and it always had been.

Reeve slumped deeper into his seat, trying to take things slow in the aftermath of panic and shame, hand wrapped tight in the fraying case strap. For once the soft murmurs of bus conversations and the warm, rhythmic hum of the engine was soothing. They almost drowned out an odd sound that bothered Reeve's ears like tinnitus. That particular sound was lower in pitch but just as annoying. It wasn't something mechanical from the bus either, more like audio feedback. He looked up and around, hoping someone else was hearing it too and that it wasn't yet another of his personal annoyances. If it was then at least it was better than Horseface's shouting.

Nothing immediately stood out until Reeve looked to the front of the bus where a guy in a retro 80's tracksuit stood limply with sleeves rolled up. His body was covered in occultic symbol tattoos that Alex probably would have been gawking over.

His face, though; there were reasons Reeve avoided horror movies like the plague, especially with his imagination. Maybe the guy was just the type to have eyes tattooed on his face. Maybe it was just face paint.

Reeve rested his forehead back on the guitar case, his fingers worked to open the zipper on the side where he kept the bottle of Alprazolam. Maybe half a pill in this situation was warranted.

"You, Silverbird, are as much a danger as you are *in* danger. Your mother told me."

Reeve jumped, the bottle clattered to the ground and rolled elsewhere along with several other items from the junk pocket.

"Shit!"

Beside him was Horseface, gesturing at him with the koi's tail as if he'd been there the whole time. He stunk exactly like a horse wet from sloshing about in a stagnant pond.

More of the passengers had begun to turn their attention towards him, a few moved away.

Shit. Shit. Shit.

Reeve dropped to the ground, feeling around for the bottle.

Everything kept shifting, the bottle, the guitar case, a bunch of loose picks and pens. The bus took a turn, and he nearly went tumbling were it not for bracing himself against the case.

The low ringing sound was louder, almost like the angry hiss of a fireplace log.

Someone was asking if he needed help.

Horseface was cackling, brandishing the skeletal fish tail like a wand at the tattooed jogger lumbering towards them.

Louder. *Louder.*

High-pitched squealing. A mechanical voice overhead was belting out something about seats... seeds? Reeve couldn't make it out beyond the muffled thunder of his heart, gushing like a river in his ears.

Someone tried to take the guitar case, he felt the tug through his death grip.

Someone tried to *take it from him,* and the world went mute except for his voice.

"GET THE FUCK AWAY!"

* * *

A sterile stench of industrial cleaners and old coffee hung heavy in the air; electronics buzzed in the unsettling quiet.

Reeve looked up from the metallic shine of his handcuffs to the camera mounted in the corner of the ceiling and then the cheap crust on the walls of what counted for "soundproofing."

The plastic chairs creaked with every little shift in weight.

The female detective sitting across from him shuffled papers.

"Reeve Pie...see...noi? I'm not sure how to pronounce this." She looked behind her to the second officer standing by the door, unhelpfully silent.

"Peisinoe." Reeve mumbled. "It's Greek, um... *peace-annoy.* We can stick with Reeve." He glanced briefly at the two who shared the tiny, stale room.

The detective was new. She sat in the second chair, wearing a crisp navy-blue pantsuit and white blouse; her badge was worn from a length of ball chain around her neck along with a Saint Michael medallion. Unlike most lady-cops he'd seen, this one had avoided the high ponytail look and gone with a pixie cut instead.

She'd said her name earlier, but hell if he could remember it so "Detective Pixie" it was. The guy behind her though was a constant pain in Reeve's life.

Officer Decklan wore his usual jeans and tucked T-shirt, work belt heavy at his hips. His stance was "at ease" in a way that seemed like he was trying to give the impression he'd spent time in the military. He might have fooled some people with his peppered jargon and that buzzcut, but Reeve had spent *just* enough time around the real deal that Decklan was simply a ridiculous poser. A poser with a gun, but a poser, nonetheless.

The woman nodded, gesturing with her pen to the recording controls.

"I'm making sure we have your name correct for the recording, Mr. Peisinoe." She had it right enough that time. "There's a note in your file that you prefer to use your mother's maiden name."

Reeve said nothing.

"And you live at 3724 Cypress Lane, correct?"

He nodded, adding: "An RV out back, not the house."

"And do you know the date and year, Mr. Peisinoe?"

At that point, Reeve had to sigh. "Yeah, I know that." Decklan shifted his weight more evenly.

Reeve shut up.

While the detective may have been new, Decklan was another story. Reeve was pretty sure the guy had it out for him by now. What concerned him was that Decklan was supposed to have moved over to major crimes. Why was he there with a detective anyways? Heck, why was a detective there *at all?*

"I'd still appreciate it if you would answer, Mr. Peisinoe."

Reeve wasn't in the mood for the good cop, bad cop routine. Not with Decklan in the mix. However, what he was in the mood for meant very little while he was cuffed.

"Thursday. May fourteenth. Twenty twenty-six. Now I'd appreciate it if you would let me call my brother and a lawyer."

"You only get the one ph–" Decklan was cut off with a harsh look from the interviewing officer. "What? Punk's already lawyering up. You know he knows something."

Reeve bit his lip to keep from speaking back.

There wasn't much to it: he'd had an episode. A very public one on the bus, and no doubt someone had tried to help him without knowing he had grounded himself using his guitar case. Anyone even *touching it* with all the other mess going on was a recipe for overload. Everything after that was all one big blur, half a nightmare.

It was a lot to explain; a lot for people like Decklan, who honestly didn't give two shits. The poser would call him a mental case in the *same breath* he swore he had a relative with similar issues.

It wouldn't be the first apology Reeve knew he'd have to give for blowing up at someone like that either, but it was this situation with the cops that was really setting him on edge again.

He didn't want to make things worse for himself.

There wasn't a clock in the room and the cops had taken his phone, along with everything else, but he knew it had been several hours since he'd been arrested. Most of it had been spent sitting around in processing, getting photographed and fingerprinted. The rest had been spent waiting in the empty room, cuffed to the table. Alex was probably worried sick.

"–names of your accomplices."

Reeve blinked, looking up as he realized half a conversation had occurred without him. "What?"

"Your little shopping spree," Decklan raised his voice. "Smashing up display cases. Don't you remember?"

He didn't.

Amidst the protests of the other officer, Decklan picked up a tablet from the table, scattering sheets of paper.

He hit play and a grainy video began. It wasn't from the bus like Reeve expected. The camera had a view of a back alley, somewhere uptown from the look of it, too clean and empty of rubbish. The rear exit door the video focused on eventually slammed open and Reeve watched as a young man in half a suit exited, running full tilt like he was being chased. He carried something tightly wrapped in his fancy grey jacket.

That was fairly normal on the scale of weird he'd experienced over the course of his life, what wasn't normal was that it was *himself* Reeve was watching. The figure even had the same thin white stripe of hair coming off his left temple that Reeve did, the same ponytail.

"Lemme guess, you don't remember this, either?" Decklan scoffed.

"I... what?" His heart clenched in his chest.

"A few hours before we picked you up, this camera caught you hightailing it out the back of the museum carrying at least one of the items reported stolen. Then, we understand from witnesses in the bus incident, *you* ran up to the stop like a bat outta hell, all twitchy and whispering on your phone."

Wait.

"You threw a fish carcass at a little kid for God's sake! You think that makes a good alibi?"

"Officer Decklan, if you don't want to fuck up this case–" Detective Pixie warned.

"Ain't nothing to fuck up! The moment he gets a lawyer they're gonna do that damned insanity defence!" Decklan leaned onto the table. "Just tell us where you stashed what you took and who your other buddies are. You covering for your brother? That why he's the last person on your call list?"

Reeve only heard pieces of Decklan's rant, spotting Horseface squatting in the far corner of the room, waving at him with familiarity.

Oh no.

"Dangers are on the horizon, Silverbird!" Horseface grumbled. He eyed the two cops, settling on the detective and pointing at her. "Does she know?" Horseface waved at her, then shouted. "Can you hear? Can you see?" He looked back to Reeve. "Are you able to make her yet?"

The door shut, both officers left the room in the moments Reeve had spent reeling over the reappearance of this very persistent hallucination. He could still hear their muffled argument from the other side.

Horseface stood in one unnaturally fluid motion, arms spread wide, every bit the showman. The odd creature's moves were heavily exaggerated as he sashayed his way into the detective's empty seat. The table only came up to his shoulders.

"Why so upset when you can see, and they cannot?"

Reeve kept his mouth shut, pressing his forehead against the scratched surface of the table.

This is not happening.

Alex would know something was up when he didn't show at the coffee shop. He'd have called the hospitals by now and probably the police station.

Maybe he was already in the lobby sweet talking someone into at least letting them meet. Maybe he had already called some lawyer buddy of his; Alex had a number of oddly connected "friends" these days.

He had better make use of one.

Reeve looked up, seeing Horseface tapping his muck-encrusted nails against the plastic.

"A mirror was stolen," Horseface said simply, slowly. The creature's form rippled and stretched, reshaping into something more feminine: an approximation of Detective Pixie. "A *mirror* you saw. What is there to remember for you?"

Reeve refused to speak. The figure probably wasn't even there, but the camera sure as anything was still running.

Lawyer. Keep your mouth shut and wait for a lawyer.

That video of him, of someone who at least looked like him, was damning. The bus incident was damning too, but at least he remembered enough of that to know it was real. There were cameras on the bus; the cops didn't have to take him at his word.

This is just a misunderstanding.

The guy on the video wasn't him. It couldn't be. Decklan had said the video was taken a few hours before he'd been arrested for the incident on the bus. He'd been walking to his tutoring appointment then, since the clients neglected to call to tell him they'd cancelled. He'd passed by who knew how many of those suburban homes with front porch cameras.

Where had he been before then?

Detective Horseface kept watching him, golden eyes still very much the overly large, dewy stare only a horse could level at someone... or a kelpie. Couldn't those things shapeshift in some stories?

"Breathe, Silverbird. I come only to pay my debt to your mother." Horseface cocked his head sharply to one side. "Though, I believed you much sharper of wit. Ha! No matter! Birds like you learn to fly quickly under pressure!"

The creature laughed, resting his chin in his hands.

"Speak nothing, then, young Silverbird, but listen well. A foul construct has been sent for the old vessels and to collect your beating heart. You don't need to know why just yet. You only need to *run*, Silverbird. You must run and show them why they should fear a caged bird's *song.*"

Reeve's entire body was pulled painfully taunt, inner lip chewed bloody. Having a hallucination that was actually *explaining things* to him was new.

Don't respond. It's not real. Calm down and it will go away.

Where had the cops taken his meds? Where was Alex? What the hell was going on?

"Ah, well, if *that's* your response, perhaps you do deserve to die tonight. Alas, I tried, young Silverbird; farewell!" Horseface, in the span of a blink, was gone.

Reeve dropped his head exhaustedly back on the table in the same moment Decklan returned with a smarmy grin.

"Good news! Your partner just decided to turn himself in!"

Reeve groaned. There wasn't a partner; not unless Alex had decided to do something absolutely stupid.

Decklan seemed to enjoy the process of hauling him off to the holding cells. The man had an iron grip around his arm, manoeuvring Reeve around like a kid piloting a doll. Thankfully, Decklan had cuffed him from the front this time, small favours. Detective Pixie hadn't returned with him.

Breathe.

He couldn't forget that. It was too easy to hyperventilate now, and Decklan would be the one jackass to take his going limp for "resisting arrest."

Breathe.

They passed an office window where Detective Pixie was gesturing fervently to another, higher ranked officer seated at an important looking desk. She'd caught sight of them passing by, and her gestures seemed to include them now. Something in the back of Reeve's mind finally clicked that she might have been protesting Decklan's "old school" way of dealing with him or maybe interviews in general. Either way, it wasn't as if it mattered right in that moment.

Decklan spoke, repeatedly expressing how he believed Reeve was "faking" his illness. His cousin, apparently, also had a schizophrenic disorder and it wasn't like Reeve's.

Reeve tuned him out after a while.

The tirade was one he'd heard before and as always, he found himself in a position where saying anything in his own defence would do more harm than good. What Reeve wanted to say was: if it wasn't the same then *good for that cousin.* Maybe that cousin was better managed; maybe that cousin had already found their perfect combo of meds and wasn't stuck with having to constantly switch them out. Maybe *that cousin* didn't have to worry about the cost or unreasonable insurance requirements or a consistent set of doctors who would just *listen* for once.

Muddled voices preceded their emergence into an open area populated by desks and their jockeys. Civilians sat at some, discussing lost property and tedious complaints involving yards, dogs, dogs in yards where they weren't supposed to be. Separated from the bullpen area by a low half wall topped with plexiglass was a series of metal doors to holding cells and drunk tanks. They were the kind of spaces meant for detainees not quite ready for general lockup yet and faces peeked out from windows of some. One guy was banging at the wire mesh of his, yelling that he was innocent.

Same, buddy, same.

Decklan chuckled, their course taking them past everyone towards the metal doors. Reeve had been expecting the holding cells to be their final stop until Decklan had smacked his shoulder, nodding in the direction of the bullpen.

Sitting in a spare chair, at a desk with one of the bullpen officers, was a complete stranger.

No, not a stranger exactly.

Reeve recalled the father and little girl at the bus stop. The funny pair that rode almost daily down to the beach in summer. Little Shelly and her seashells.

"Your *partner* is very chatty. Looks like we'll be wrapped up soon," Decklan snarked.

The father sat there alone, and something wasn't right about that at all.

Where was Shelly?

Last week she'd been in her seat during the bus ride putting dozens of colourful ties in her father's hair. Both of them had been infuriatingly adorable rays of sunshine. Never one without the other, and Reeve had been jealous about that kind of childhood, having missed out on it himself. Vicarious living at its finest.

Reeve stopped. He kept his feet planted and braced, refusing to move any closer.

Sitting there in the chair wasn't Shelly's father at all.

"Keep walking." Decklan shoved him forward, audibly pleased that his ploy in walking past this "partner" seemed to be having an effect.

Not real.

The person sitting in the chair looked like the nameless man Reeve knew from riding the bus, but he sat far too stiffly, facing forward. Wispy threads of smoke emanated from his body, exposed skin on his arms bruised purple. Tattoos Reeve knew the man hadn't been sporting that afternoon, were scrawled up and down his flesh.

His mouth was twisted up in a silent scream, eyes plucked out and stuffed with wads of filthy cloth. A *real* eye had been shoved into a vertical slit carved between his brows while others were simply drawn on, higher on his forehead and his cheeks and his chin. He was like the man in the tracksuit.

Each crude illustration blinked out of sync with the central eye and gazed in many directions at once.

"What the *fuck.*" Reeve tried to step back, stumbling as Decklan nearly picked him off his feet.

"Hey, move it!"

Reeve watched as the monstrosity's tongue curled up, a second eye opening from the tip in his direction.

Not real. Not real. Police station. Not real. Not real. Meds. Alex. Not real. Not real.

The man flopped forward onto the desk, surprising the officer who was taking his statement and several others. Smoke had gathered at his back as a horrid mass of gel-like "something" ripped its way out like an eldritch cicada.

Not real. Not real. Run. Not real.

There was nowhere to run, not here, not with Decklan holding him.

People were reacting to the man like he was having a seizure, calling for someone with medical training, and Decklan was yanking Reeve away from the source of his terror.

Not... real?

Whatever it was that emerged from the nameless father's body stood unnaturally still amid the chaos; six feet tall, flayed skin and bones haphazardly stitched together, painted up with those freaky occult symbols.

The new hallucination didn't garner any attention from the room other than Reeve's. Why would it? It just had way too many eyes and a tentacle-eyed tongue, smoking like a burnt hamburger. Smelled like it too, old and half rotted.

Decklan shoved Reeve into one of the temporary holding cells, "forgetting" to remove the cuffs as he slammed the door shut.

What... just...

Reeve turned on his heel to the small window in the door, peeking out through the wire mesh.

The creature loomed as it had on the bus, that shrill whine of noise gaining volume, changing pitch.

There's a foul construct coming to take the old vessels and your beating heart...

Horseface's cryptic words began a loop. They weren't real. Nothing but the fear and paranoia were real. The freak with the eyes *wasn't* real.

Reeve couldn't bring himself to step away from the window of his cage, watching as the creature set its eyes on a nearby officer, reaching out with spindly, spider-like fingers.

This isn't happening.

The creature *wasn't* stepping into the body of a cop. It *wasn't* slipping itself snugly into his skin. The creature *wasn't* walking towards Reeve's holding cell. It *wasn't* yanking on the handle with stolen hands, *wasn't* rattling the door with every attempt.

It *wasn't* drawing a firearm.

There was a slow cascade of officers yelling once they noticed the gun, but they *couldn't* notice. None of it was real. It was all in his head. They couldn't see what he did. They couldn't.

Ever since he'd been a child Reeve had seen things no one else did, worse he *knew* no one else saw them. It was like being the first person in the world to beta test next-level augmented reality. Only, there was no way to turn it off; there was nothing *to* turn off.

Reeve dove to the side as the "possessed" officer took aim at the lock of the door. Even if he knew it wasn't real, his mind still screamed: *don't get shot.*

Gunshots barked until the clip was emptied. People were yelling. Other shots echoed dully before the door was wrenched the rest of the way open. Two bullets, at least, had hit the cop. Neither seemed to bother him.

Reeve looked up to see wobbly, drawn eyes blinking down at him from a new face, that cop's face, as the visage rapidly began to turn sallow.

The body went limp at the waist, folding over against the door frame as black smoke began to rise from its back. The whining keen began anew.

SCREAM.

The world went mute around Reeve as he drew up every decibel sleeping soundly in his bones.

It was the bus all over again.

He'd screamed then, too, that much had stuck around his memory; so did the cold and the sound of everything filtered through an industrial fan. Something cracked in his throat, a long-stuck key on a sax finally giving way to a completely new octave. This sound couldn't possibly be from him. It was echoes, reverb, and feedback cranked up to the max from an amp fit to play in stadiums; a discordant bellow and harmonic shriek stuck in cosmic orbit around each other.

Everyone was trying to cover their ears. Overhead lights flickered and burst. Bits of glass cascaded through gaps in the plastic covers and from the windows and partitions around the office space. Reeve ran out of air.

His first gasp had him choking on nothing.

It didn't matter anymore that he stood a good chance of getting himself shot. Anything was better than being stuck in a nightmare moment. He struggled for breath, staring wide-eyed at the smoky body snatcher when a sudden mass of people from the bullpen jumped the barricade of the low wall. Plexiglass snapped, clattering all over the place amidst crystalline debris as the mob tackled the thing from behind.

Reeve took the chance to mad dash his way out over the dogpile spilling into his cell, landing face first on the linoleum when stumbling over moving bodies didn't work out so well. He felt the cartilage in his nose snap, on the floor or by getting hit; it didn't really matter. Cuffs complicated getting back up.

The entire station had suddenly become a mosh pit. Most were scrambling after the creature in the cell while detainees beat on their doors and shouted loudly.

Everyone was bleeding from their ears.

Reeve scrambled to the other side of the wall to take cover, arms up to shield his head.

There was no sense in trying to fight the hallucination anymore. It might not have really been a body snatcher after him, but *something* was happening in the police station, maybe just an ordinary shooting; either way, he needed to get somewhere safe. Where he was wouldn't work for long.

More shouting came from other places. More people. More havoc.

The recurrent ringing sound sent a chill up his spine. Too close.

Reeve looked up into the face of yet another cop leaning over the short wall, one with too many eyes; they had their service pistol drawn.

"Leroy! Drop your weapon!" a woman yelled.

Reeve scrambled as another part of the mob went after the snatcher's new body. Weapons discharged. He couldn't tell from where.

He made it under a desk, huddled as small as he could make himself. He could barely breathe. Everything hurt and the shaking wouldn't stop.

Not real. Real. Real. Run. Alex. Meds. Run. Eyes. Shut up. Run.

A hand landed on his back with a suddenness that nearly had him jumping out of his own skin.

Detective Pixie.

She gestured for him to keep low.

Reeve could only nod. His throat was toast. It wasn't as if he knew what to do under the circumstances either. Too many doors were blocked with electronic locks. The place was a maze. Detective Pixie had more of an idea. Reeve wordlessly stuck behind her as she led him out through a fire exit that emptied into the building's underground parkade at the end of a narrow hall.

She pushed him off to one side of the door, keeping the concrete walls between them and anyone who might have followed. Several seconds were spent cautiously looking back through the window of the parkade door.

"Alright, you're going to stay here for a little bit while I head back in to deal with all that shit. Got it?" She pulled a second set of cuffs, gesturing to a spot near an assortment of access pipes and a chain link bike cage.

There was *no way in hell* he was about to be locked up like the goat from that one dinosaur movie. Reeve shook his head, pointing insistently to a red fire bell and light flashing not too far away. There wasn't any scenario in which the body snatcher hadn't heard that alarm. Almost on cue, the ominous keening started up again, distinct from the klaxon's blaring alarm.

Reeve caught a glance of someone new through the narrow window of the door, someone trailing black smoke as they moved. He pulled Pixie towards the cars, and she nearly punched him until the snatcher opened fire on the door itself.

"Cease fire!" Detective Pixie yelled. "Friendly, I have a civilian!"

Reeve kept his hold on her jacket, pulling her into the maze of vehicles.

The parkade door slammed open, bullets screamed through a rain of dusty insulation foam and concrete. Safety glass pooled alongside glittering patches of oil stains.

"Officer Garret! Cease fire, you son of a bitch!"

That *thing* wouldn't listen.

"What the hell is wrong with you?!" Detective Pixie kept trying to reason with a person no longer there.

Reeve hesitated to pull on the hem of her jacket again, to try telling her they needed to run *now*.

Officer Garret opened fire, steadily walking towards them.

Pixie returned the barrage, hitting legs and shoulders, trying to bring the man down without killing him.

It was all too loud and too fast to follow. Reeve could do no more than crouch low and wait for someone to run out of bullets long enough that he could bolt.

There had been the distant sounds of an empty magazine being ejected and replaced. Another shot and the fire alarm died out miserably.

Officer Garret was still standing.

Pixie cursed, hauling Reeve up by his collar after her and farther into the sea of cars and broken glass.

His mutual hold on her jacket was ironclad and constant, grounding. As much as Reeve wanted to run, he couldn't force himself to let go.

She yanked him farther between two bumpers, struggling to keep pillars and cars obscuring them, as the sounds of footsteps kept moving forward. The snatcher didn't seem to care about shooting them any longer or else was out of ammunition like Pixie.

Reeve could only numbly see her goal this time. She was leading him towards the parking gate, a final fire door beside it.

Pixie yanked him hard along behind her. There was no cover in darting to the final door.

Run.

The footsteps. The sickening, keening noise.

Run. Meds.

Pixie's grip. Forward momentum.

Run.

That "not real" thing with the eyes.

Run. Alex.

Two shots. One sent concrete fragments into the air near his feet. The second coincided with a sharp pain in his side.

It's here for your heart. Maybe you do deserve to die tonight.

Reeve began to stumble, scramble. It slowed Pixie.

"Get up!" There wasn't any sugar-coating. "Hold your fire!" The very tone of her voice was shrill, broken, like it would be the last thing he ever heard.

Almost.

The next cacophony of sound came from twisting metal.

Reeve scrambled; turning around, he caught sight of first a gun being levelled at him and then an airbrushed white horse with wings being ridden by a woman in a chainmail bikini. The body snatcher had been sent flying by their unusual cavalry, crumpled up in a heap a dozen yards away along with the security gate.

It really wasn't that strange, at this point, and even less strange when a familiar voice shouted out from the window of the beat-up old vehicle bearing the mural.

"Get in!"

"Alex?" Reeve choked out, throat trashed enough from screaming that he regretted it instantly.

Pixie moved first. She practically dragged Reeve towards the rusty, vintage van, yanking the sliding door open. Detective Pixie quickly cleared the back and levelled her firearm at the lanky, scruffy-haired young man who was leaning out the driver's window lighting a bit of cloth hanging from a bottle.

"Who the fuck are you?" she demanded.

Alex's eyes darted to the weapon and its locked slider. *"Your driver and saviour,* so show a bit of respect instead of an *empty* gun," he bit back. "Now, get in the van; we don't have a lot of time!"

"Not until you tell me what the *fuck* is going on at my precinct!"

"How 'bout I show you!" Alex lobbed the Molotov cocktail before sitting back down inside. "Get in the van, Reeve!"

What?

Pixie slammed her hand across the opening, wordlessly daring Reeve to not even so much as *think* of getting in the van while she was there. "Not until you *answer me.*" Her gaze remained fixed on Alex.

Reeve honestly wasn't which one of them would throw the first punch if it came down to it. Alex, scrawny as he was, would *not* survive that fight. Reeve had the vague notion that he was going to have to tackle Pixie somehow and preferably in a way that wouldn't get him arrested for real.

The two kept their stalemate up until the moment "Officer Garret" got back on his feet.

Even Pixie paled.

Flames danced around crooked limbs and melting polyester fabric; blood sizzled in the heat. The body of the once-man jackknifed sharply as the snatcher hurriedly tried to jump from its host resulting in a sickening crack of ribs and a spine blooming out from where the macabre parasite emerged, writhing in agony.

The shrieks were deafening. Reeve tried to cover his ears.

"Go." Detective Pixie kept staring at the burning horror. When Reeve didn't immediately move, she grabbed hold of his jacket and shoved him into the van. "MOVE!"

"Took you long enough," Alex grumbled.

Reeve rolled into the back along with Detective Pixie. The floor of the van smelled like grease and old glue, completely bare of carpet. He didn't need to ask where Alex had gotten the van; there were too many areas of rust that had completely eaten through. He could clearly see the concrete flooring of the parkade through one hole. If it *hadn't* come from some junkyard he'd be surprised.

Everything lurched as Alex slammed the vehicle in reverse, tires squealing just after Pixie got the door shut on her second try.

"Reeve, just FYI, that wasn't a picture of a kelpie you sent me," Alex yelled back at him. "Kelpie is a water horse that just wants to drown and eat you; those are green n' made of weeds. You hear me? A GREEN

HORSE!" Alex was still yelling. "You sent me a picture of a pooka covered in algae! Didn't you get my text?"

Reeve and the detective both lost their footing as Alex took the turn out of the parking garage backwards, shifting gears.

"What the hell are you talking about?" Pixie had grabbed onto the back of the passenger seat to keep upright.

"A shapeshifting fae." He accelerated into the night. "Reeve! Did it say anything to you?"

Real?

"Is that what that thing was?" Pixie's voice cracked.

"No, *that flaming torch* was bad news; we're lucky to have gotten away." Alex kept glancing in the rear-view. "Reeve, buddy, you still with us? Say something will ya?"

None of this could possibly be real. It was all one horrific episode.

Reeve shuddered, curling in on himself.

Not real. Not real.

He started tuning things out, focusing only on one thing at a time; from the mechanic smells of the van to the folds of a cloth bundle shoved between the front seats.

Streetlights flashed by as they drove along empty midnight streets.

Pain from his side was beginning to catch up with the rest of his aches. A graze that had damaged his jacket more than anything.

Shot. Did I really just get shot?

"Reeve? You still with us, buddy?" Alex repeated.

"–'e… was… tryin'–… to kill… me," Reeve managed. Speaking hurt.

"Will one of you make *sense!?*" Detective Pixie yelled. "Everyone at my precinct just lost their friggin' minds and started attacking everyone else! *WHAT* was that *thing* you set on fire?"

Alex didn't get a chance to answer. The van lurched as it was hit from behind, dislodging the grey cloth bundle stuck between the seats.

A bit of rounded metal rolled free, clanging to the ground. An old and lightly tarnished silver tray with geometric designs around the edges.

The van was hit a second time and Alex scrambled to gain control of the vehicle.

"Bad News is back. Everybody hang on!"

A police cruiser lined up behind them for another go, neither blaring its siren nor flashing its lights.

Alex shifted gears again and pulled off the kind of sudden U-turn that stunt drivers earned their pay over. Reeve knew Alex could handle a stick, but this level of skill was unreal; when the hell had he learned to *drive?*

Alex gunned it down the street, taking a right angle turn fast enough to lift them on two wheels and somehow managed to keep going.

From the view out back, the cruiser remained on their tail if a bit more behind.

Reeve clung to the ridges in the floor trying not to accidentally bite off his tongue; Pixie white-knuckled the passenger seat.

"How the hell is this guy still alive!?" she growled.

"I don't know! Fire usually works! Stop shouting at me!" Alex glanced back, spotting the loose tray at the same time Pixie did.

"That's th—you're from the heist!"

"Not the time! Reeve!"

"Make time!" Pixie again aimed her empty gun at Alex.

"Reeve, get your trigger-happy friend and open the back doors! Now!"

"Like hell am I about to get tossed!" She readied the weapon like a club, this time at Reeve even though he'd yet to move an inch.

The back windows shattered, a shotgun blast from the cruiser left no question of intent.

"Then don't fall out! Open the doors! Grab that mirror and aim it behind us!"

"Why?" she insisted.

Alex yelled aimlessly, hitting the steering wheel with every word. "Because I've gotta cast a spell and crush this *creature* behind us before we all die horribly!"

What in the absolute fuck...?

"Reeve! You hear that? This multi-eyed freak is fucking *real!* Now *get off your ass!*"

Somewhere between the gun in his face and every unreal thing going on around him, Alex's voice plucked the one chord that rang blessed silence through his mind.

Real.

He and Alex had grown up together in the same group home. Both had lost their parents young and violently, something they'd bonded over. The other kids had never really understood the kind of effect that left; and while Alex had been fortunate enough to start healing, Reeve had it to fuel his strange menagerie of hallucinations.

Alex had become his voice of reason, always, *always* able to pull him out of that hell, a fortifying voice that now said *real* to the things surrounding him. He said *real* to the thing that chased them. He said *real* to the danger and had shown up out of nowhere to rescue him from it.

Goddamnit Alex.

Reeve awkwardly grabbed at the old silver disk before it slid away from him during another turn. His cuffed wrists stiffly refused to move after so much abuse and his grip wasn't much better now, after everything he'd done to remain stable in the van.

His stolid expression must have been enough to convince Pixie to play along, or maybe it was the crooked nose. Honestly, he didn't know exactly what it was he looked like after the most monumental of bad days, where the possibility of dying was still on the table.

Detective Pixie grabbed a fist full of his jacket, screaming that the two of them were delusional.

Maybe they were, who knew anymore?

With Pixie acting as a safety line, Reeve forced the rear door open. He narrowly missed being hit by a shotgun slug carving yet another hole through the van.

Alex owed him one hell of an explanation if they survived whatever was happening.

Reeve strained to brace his legs on either side of the door, glaring at the thing in the cruiser.

"He's aiming the damn mirror!" Pixie bellowed.

"Hang on!" Alex called back.

For a third time that day the world's sounds were all muffled out.

The antique mirror tingled in Reeve's hands, growing warm. Alex was chanting *something*, but Reeve couldn't understand what it was. The patterns on the back of it shifted with the tempo, a combination lock of ever-changing imagery.

What the hell have you been up to, Alex?

The thing in the cruiser reacted, for once, and slammed on the brakes.

Why is it real this time?

They barreled downtown through scant AM traffic, drunks hooting at the gallant ride of an old shag-wagon painted up in 80's vintage with its Pegasus and pinup warrior on the side—a police cruiser trailing it.

Breath was knocked from Reeve's lungs as the mirror slammed into his chest. Heat seeped through the fabric of his shirt and then searing *cold*. It felt as though, for a moment, a hand had slipped beneath his ribcage to ensnare his heart between talons of ice.

Something hit the hood of the cruiser.

A sizable dent was left by the impact, the glossy blackness interrupted by an undulating grey *something* reflected in the hood. Two more, much smaller dents pressed deeper into the metal until each tore into the recognizable shapes of claw marks. The snatcher tried to shake off the invisible attacker, swerving sharply to either side. For a second, it looked like the snatcher had fumbled in reloading the shotgun, windshield shattering in a flash of white, but there had been no discharge. The glass had collapsed inwards rather than out.

Pixie's hold on Reeve tightened. She crouched beside him with enough awe that Reeve knew, without a doubt, she could see what was happening this time, even if neither of them had any concrete idea of what was going on. Chaos was set into motion seemingly without touch: Alex's magic spell, the old metal mirror.

It wasn't just the car's hood, either. All around them the windows of the buildings reflected the same undulating grey mass that, at times, looked like ink dispersed through water.

A light pole inexplicably buckled as the cruiser moved past, nearly ripped from the sidewalk.

The vehicle jerked to a violent halt, tethered to the pole by way of a thick grey-white cable only seen in the nearby office windows. Like a living thing, the reflection-bound cable lifted the cruiser up three stories, bent it in half, and crumpled it like paper as dozens of other pale shapes pressed in on the car's reflection. Bursts of smoke from the engine flared outward before the hunk of wreckage was dunked back towards the asphalt in a blossom of fire.

Reeve and Pixie sat in silence, watching the crater of flames grow smaller behind them.

Alex definitely owed him an explanation.

* * *

A belt in the shag-wagon's engine had a tendency to squeal periodically. The exhaust puttered. Overall, the whole thing had been on its last legs before Alex had put it through its paces.

Now it demanded a sacrifice of gas for its service.

Reeve sat curled in the passenger seat breathing in the miasma permeating a backroad Gas-n-Sip, finally calm and free of his cuffs.

Pixie, Detective Celia Marsh as it turned out, had decided to call a cab and insisted that she'd not blab to anyone. Not that anyone would believe her.

Heck, Reeve didn't believe what had happened either and he'd been in the thick of it.

His throat had rested enough that he'd been able to recount, hoarsely, what had happened at the park and on the bus to the other two. It still felt as though he were truly losing his grip on his own mind.

"Got you some oatmeal n' yogurt; there's other stuff in there, too, but for a convenience store it wasn't very convenient," Alex said by way of greeting.

Detective Marsh had taken to leaning on the driver's side bumper, watching dawn on the horizon. She needed her own time to process.

Alex was already pulling some first aid things from the grocery bag.

"The *hell, man.*" Reeve winced, too exhausted to help with much as Alex took the opportunity to lift his shirt for him.

"Wimp." Alex chuckled.

"I got shot…"

"Grazed. Won't even need stitches." He shook a box of butterfly bandages. "How you doing? Still got a headache?"

"I got *shot,*" Reeve repeated. "By a *cop.*"

"A possessed cop, but… yeah, a cop."

"Why the fuck did I get *shot?*"

Alex sighed, silent as he worked a while. Reeve didn't know how to process his own mental turmoil, trusting Alex to have some kind of enlightening revelation, however slight. Detective Marsh deserved the answer, too, especially after what they'd all been through.

"My fault, probably, but… Reeve, you know all the folklore stuff I've been studying?"

Reeve slowly nodded.

"Yeah, well… some of that stuff is real."

That took several seconds to sink in.

"*Some* of it, and some of it is just stories people tell, civilization's original creepy pastas. Mr. Sato… um… he's this antiquities guy I know through the university, works at the museum uptown."

Reeve nodded, breath hitching as Alex got around to the antiseptic.

"According to him, there were a bunch of artifacts that came through for this new ancient occult exhibit, only the artifacts are *real* and very *dangerous* things that got the attention of some equally dangerous people along the way."

"Alex, you're starting to rip off every supernatural buddy cop show *ever,* now will you stop talking to me like I'm five?"

"Fine. I–"

"Robbed a museum, yeah, I picked up on that when Marsh pointed her *gun* at you, you *asshole.*"

Alex grit his teeth. "Are you telling this story, or am I?"

"I don't wanna see a *gun* pointed at you ever again!"

"It was empt– ...*Reeve.*" Alex leaned back, plucking at the air.

A momentary haze saw Alex's normal lankiness and frizzy black hair change completely. His face was squared, bearded, and he... he sort of looked like a guy they had once hung out with until he'd been arrested for boosting cars a few years back.

Alex pointed to himself, even his voice had changed. "Magic, Reeve, it's weird and I've learned a little."

He waited, letting Reeve again process what he was seeing at his own pace, even going so far as to take Reeve's hand and pass it through his new beard. It looked real, but there was nothing there to feel.

Detective Marsh snorted incredulously, having glanced back at them at some point during their conversation.

"Think of it like a hologram. It's not real but you *are* seeing this, buddy." Alex snapped his fingers, breaking the illusion. "Kinda the biggest spell I know right now apart from... well, unlocking that mirror."

"You..." Reeve shook his head, the grainy footage from an alley played across his memory. "You d-did that with–"

"You're the one we've got on camera," Marsh finished.

"Yeah, I panicked." Alex still had hold of Reeve's hand, squeezing it. "I was getting chased by that thing wearing the skin suits, and Reeve's face was the first I thought of because–" He let go. "It's a lot, Reeve. I know it's a lot."

Reeve slumped farther down into the seat. "Just tell me what the hell is going on, I can't... and that... that thing with the eyes, *and the mirror.* Holy *shit,* man, what the hell is up with that mirror?"

"Yes." Detective Marsh nodded sharply, her gaze flicking briefly towards the back of the van. "Please explain the mirror and–" she stared at Reeve. "What was the thing with the eyes?"

"The snatch," Reeve grumbled. "Body snatcher...thing. It was taking over your buddies down at the precinct... I think..." He rubbed his face tiredly. "It just had a lot of eyes. I don't care if it was real or not, just... I don't want to think about that thing anymore."

Alex snorted, trying to contain his amusement at the creature's new name, as he went back to taking care of Reeve's injuries. "It wasn't supposed to happen like it did. I swear. Mr. Sato knows about magic; he helped me learn, then he called me and said he needed someone to collect the artifacts before these... I don't know... they're like a wizard mafia or something."

Reeve didn't know how to take that. Detective Marsh laughed until the silence made it clear Alex wasn't joking.

"They're looking for artifacts like these only before Mr. Sato could give them to me, a... well, a snatch showed up." He hid his chuckle with a faux cough. "That eye-monster Reeve said was jumping bodies. It's a creature the... the wizard mafia can summon up. Normal people can't see them unless they're on fire or there's smoke around to see their outlines. They possess people in positions the wizard mafia can't physically put one of their own. Radio controlled pawn, kinda."

Reeve nodded. It really couldn't get any weirder.

"They had that snatch squatting in a staff member and gave it orders to haul out the artifacts *then* to h-hunt down..." Alex slowed.

Reeve took a guess. "Me."

"They had your picture... I have no idea why other than they were calling you a *Silverbird*." Finished with first aid, Alex leaned the edge of the van.

"That... pooka thing called me Silverbird, too," Reeve admitted. "I still don't know what he meant."

"Ok, that's what you focus on?" Detective Marsh asked, overly weary.

Reeve shrugged. "Been seeing things no one else does and freaked out about it for most of my life." He nodded. "A wizard hit squad... last night... weirdly, I don't feel paranoid knowing there's *actually* people after me this time. I could care less about the reason, vindicated, actually."

She sighed, too exhausted to push any further.

"Your ride's here, anyway," Alex interjected as the taxi started to pull into the parking lot. "And taking care of my brother is my business now, Detective Marsh. You've just got to focus on what story you're going to stick to about what happened in your precinct."

"Not the truth," she scoffed. "I'm not looking forward to meeting families, either."

Both Alex and Reeve fell silent at her darker tone.

"Whatever's going on, keep me in the loop." Detective Marsh pulled one of her business cards from her jacket, sticking it under the windshield wiper as she headed to the cab. "Your wizards robbed a museum, and if you're telling the truth, they're organized crime dealing in stolen antiquities. *That's* my actual job. Make it easier for me, boys."

They watched her leave, sitting a while in the quiet buzz of the electric lights and chirping crickets.

"Well, that could have gone better." Alex sighed. "Guess we... have to call her back to pick up your stuff from the precinct?"

"How long have you been keeping all this magic stuff from me?"

"Reeve... I..." Alex took his time in answering, cleaning up the first aid rubbish all over the floorboard. "I... four months? Maybe?" He held up his hands. "I wanted to make sure before I told you anything!"

"Alex!"

"What, you wanted me to just waltz up to you and go: Hey buddy! You know how you've got this whole traumatic experience dealing with treatment resistant schizophrenia? Well, guess what? You might actually just have anxiety and be seeing critters from the unseen world! Ain't that *funny?*"

Reeve stared.

"That! That look! That's why I wanted to know my shit first 'n break it to you slow!" He stepped back, drawing his fingers through his hair. "I wanted... to give you some *peace,* Reeve. I don't... I don't have many answers for you right now, an'– hell, man, you could *still* have schizophrenia AND be seein–"

"You're an idiot." Reeve debated throwing the empty antiseptic box at Alex's head.

"... Yeah... I know."

"You're an *idiot* for dealing with this on your own. Isn't that what you're always telling me not to do? Alex, I got *shot* at, *arrested* for museum robbery, and had *one of my biggest panic attacks* because a horse-faced, koi-eating *fairy* decided to pay me a visit! ALL OF IT real, by the way!" Reeve couldn't help but cackle hoarsely at just how absurd it all was. "How the fuck did you even *learn* magic? How did you stay alive *for four months* with a WIZARD MAFIA creeping around out there?"

"It's–"

"*A lot to explain,* I get it! Now, get back in the van and drive. You can fill me in as we go. Apparently, we've got a bunch of mobster wizards after us for... fuck if I know why. That mirror thing, for sure." He hooked his thumb towards the back of the van. A glance in the rear-view only confirmed the hazy outline of a pale figure huddled in the back.

Hours later and the entity they'd let out of the mirror still hadn't returned to it, which probably wasn't good.

Alex stood outside the door for a moment longer before shoving the disposable cup of oatmeal into Reeve's hands and moving to the driver's side. He pocketed Marsh's business card.

"How did you know about the pooka? What even *is* it, anyways? It kept saying it owed my mother."

Alex shrugged, turning the ignition. "Pooka are shapeshifting fae. They're known to favour certain forms, like the picture of the dark horse with golden eyes you sent me. I don't know what the deal is with your mom, but... maybe she befriended it when she was little? It's more common than you think; some old Welsh families apparently have fae that followed their family lines for ages. Might be why you can see things, but there's a lot of other reasons, too."

"My mother was Greek, though."

"And you live half the world away from Greece. She doesn't have to be Welsh. It was just an example. As for how I knew, well... I enchanted your phone a while back while you were in the shower. That seemed like the best option; it paid off." He picked up a pair of fashion glasses off the dash, twirling them pointedly. "Unlike you, I need something to see the Unseen with."

Alex put the glasses on.

"You look even more like a nerd, and… this hunk of junk?"

"A buddy of mine who's… well, you'll see. You were supposed to meet him at the coffee shop yesterday."

"More magic. The RV is with this buddy, isn't it?"

"Yuuup. Had it moved when the thing at the museum went sideways… serious about the rewiring though. Guy's a great mechanic; this ride is his." Alex patted the dash.

"He better be. The Space Hut is priceless."

"Because you snagged it out of a junkyard."

"Says the guy driving an old shag-wagon."

"That just saved our lives!"

Reeve sighed, taking his time in getting the oatmeal down as Alex drove them away from the tiny gas station. Occasionally, he looked up into the rear-view, keeping tabs on their newest problem.

Whatever creature they had released from the mirror was much more humanoid now than when Pixie had first noticed and pointed it out. Prior to that it had been a confusing jumble of everything, shifting forms at a whim. None of them had gotten a good look at what had wrecked the police cruiser earlier because the entity had been moving through the windows of all the nearby storefronts and office buildings, interacting with the world through the glass.

The whole car chase had him rattled if he thought about it too much. Without all the reflective surfaces of the city, "Mirror" seemed much smaller and relegated to the few available in the van. Its body had a more stable form, one that was semi-transparent; a delicate crystal figure wrapped in pearlescent silk so thin the material floated in the air.

"You still haven't answered me about what this mirror is."

Alex looked into the rear-view, just as he did, and with equal worry.

"Trouble… they're supposed to stay inside."

"Yeah, but what is i– what are *they?* How much trouble are we talking about if our mob wizards were after the mirror and other artifacts like that?"

Mirror turned to regard the two humans. Reeve wasn't quite sure the exact direction they were looking; the entity's eyes were completely silver without pupil or iris.

"I think they can understand us, too…" Reeve gave a nervous wave that wasn't returned.

"Um… a… daemon? I think?"

"Ok, so wizards, fairies, and now demons, gotcha."

"Not a demon, a *daemon*. They're um… well, actually, I don't… know much about what a daemon is other than it isn't a demon."

Reeve could only shake his head. *"Alex…."*

"You asked!" He grabbed a cereal bar from their stash of snacks. "Anyways, we'll be at Grey Roads Temple this afternoon; we can worry then."

"A temple… like… Buddhist monks? Hindu?" He kept looking for some kind of reaction but received none. "You're serious? Alex, how many more surprises have you got for me?"

"Plenty, I really have no idea where to start except… ok, so Grey Roads is more of a communal house for weirdos like us than an actual temple. It's also a bit more Shinto than Buddhist and calling it *Grey Roads* is just a bit of fun with translations, considering the proper name and er– well, you'll see what I mean when we get there." Alex cleared his throat. "Still functions like a temple, though, so the deal is: as long as we stay there, we'll have to help with groundskeeping and odd jobs. Other than that, we're golden. They don't like the wizard mafia either, so it's safe there."

"Weirdos like us?"

"Yeah. Me with my magic and you with whatever voice thing you've got going on that can make an instant mosh pit… the mirror daemon too."

"Weirdos like *us?"*

"Yeah… other people can see the Unseen, too. Use magic… some that aren't… um… aren't human…"

"Alex…"

"Oh, come on, you had to have seen that coming!"

"Alex…you are the weirdest of them all."

"That's just because you haven't really got to know anyone else yet. Now, finish your oatmeal and take a nap."

Silver Consequences

Rachel Sikorski
Art by
Jenny Kong

Year 4620
Town of Vazot, Xeorene Empire
Temple District

The heavy yellow-linen curtain hanging in the entrance to Thoen, the God of Justice's temple was crooked. Despite the loud, fearful voices of the villagers outside, pulling his attention elsewhere, Aubron couldn't take his eyes off it. He almost heard his uncle's sneering voice reverberating through his head, commenting on how he couldn't even keep the small temple acceptable. He'd gotten that one a lot.

The pole over the doorway, from which the fabric hung, had been damaged in the early morning when he'd stumbled, drunk, into the temple. Despite his proclamations to his friend, Rictor, that he was fine, his uncle's death had thrown him. His last living relative he'd burned on a pyre less than twenty-four hours ago.

Eton, his uncle's closest, and probably only, friend had tried to fix it, all the while sending disapproving looks at Aubron—which he pretended not to notice. The elf hadn't done a particularly good job, but he appreciated the gesture, nonetheless.

Eton had been there when his uncle had fallen in battle, and he knew the man was struggling with the sudden loss of his friend. The creatures that had killed him, the uibixa, used to appear so rarely that some people had previously believed them to be a myth. Then, about a month ago, they'd started appearing every few nights, prowling the sand dunes outside the village. Volunteers from the town had taken to patrolling outside the walls to keep them from getting close to the townsfolk.

Aubron's uncle had joined one such patrol and, according to Eton, the creatures had been more powerful than expected, felling his uncle in a brutal fight and leaving the others to retreat. They'd barely managed to haul his dying body back into the safety of the village walls.

He had passed away minutes later, bleeding out before Eton's husband, Pel—a healer and the Head Priest of the Goddess of Medicine—could even begin to heal him.

In an uncharacteristic show of emotion, his uncle had looked at Aubron and, with his final breath, told him to "make your parents proud."

He, admittedly, didn't remember much after that. The Priest of Death had taken the body away and two days later, his uncle was cremated as per tradition. The rest of the night was a blur of Rictor plying him with mead.

A light touch on his arm made Aubron jump, and he turned to look into the narrowed eyes of Eton. As the High Priest of Hemi, Goddess of War, he was also the head of the town guard, a job which now almost entirely consisted of leading the patrols outside the walls against any uibixa that may appear. His lithe stature and soft tones often led to people underestimating him. Still, the massive God-Mark—a tattoo of deep red swirled with depictions of ancient battles that covered his entire chest—belied a man heavily favoured by the Goddess for his prowess on the battlefield.

The elf's cerulean eyes swept over him with a critical assessment before his shoulders dropped imperceptibly and he spoke, "Good to see you've sobered up. I rang the town bell. Everyone is waiting for you to address them."

Aubron sneered at the man as pain like a hot poker lit up his gut. "Considering he was your friend, I'd have thought you'd be a little more upset." He knew it was a low blow, yet the words left his mouth wrapped in bitterness anyway.

Eton's eyes flashed with anger before exhaustion overtook his features and he stepped away, fists clenched. "Of course I'm upset by Jax's death. But I still know what my duty is, as should you." His voice held the reprimanding tone the younger man had heard often in his twenty-three years.

Aubron turned away, unable to bear the crushing weight of Eton's displeasure, when the man's voice came again, stopping him, "You're weak-willed. Yet, somehow, you're now in charge. So, try not to make an even bigger mess of this." The scorn in his voice was palpable. "And you should wash your face. It instills no confidence if the new Keyholder of Vazot looks dishevelled."

The rustle of cloth punctuated Eton's exit from the temple, and Aubron forced himself to walk farther into the domed building, bile rising in his throat. *It's not my fault the old man was unwilling to let go of what my parents wanted for me.*

He stepped into the room hidden in the back of a small hallway. Once his uncle's private chamber, it was now his as Thoen's new Keyholder and Head Priest. *Only Priest*, his mind supplied, and his stomach clenched uncomfortably.

Rictor, the High Priest for the Goddess of Knowledge, had already stripped the bed and refilled the water basin. The meagre possessions his uncle owned were also gone, likely put in the small storage building out back. Aubron didn't have the heart to confirm.

He ran a hand down his face and recoiled at the dirt and soot that came away. It coated his hands in a recreation of his uncle's blood which had stained him. He shuddered at the memory.

Death was a constant, looming possibility out here. The town of Vazot was often overlooked as they were far from Xeorene's capital. A three-day ride from the nearest major center—with barely-functional sleep-stops in between for resting—made the journey gruelling. It was worsened by the raging storms, which meant it was almost impossible for ships to get in or out of the bay. In addition, bandits prowled the dunes at night, so few ever left the relative safety of the village or its immediate surroundings.

The only reason the whole place hadn't been abandoned years ago was a decree, allegedly from the God of Justice himself, that the temples and the sacred statues they housed needed to be maintained for the people of Vazot to continue to receive God-Marks, boons, and blessings of prosperity from the gods.

Aubron finished washing his face and patted his skin dry with a threadbare cloth. Dirt clung to it, and he sighed before dropping it beside the basin.

He left the room, headed out of the temple, past the crooked curtain, and stepped onto the wooden dais that his uncle often used to address the townsfolk. Stairs to the street ran down either side, with a small wooden barrier at the front. His uncle had often stood at the railing, long fingers gripping it while he spoke reassurance and prayers out to the villagers.

Below Aubron, people were murmuring amongst themselves but quieted as they caught sight of him. He looked over them, noting the faces that were missing. They'd lost a few hunters and fishermen within the last three weeks to the uibixa.

The crowd looked beaten down and Aubron couldn't blame them. Just because he'd had issues with his uncle didn't mean that was how everyone else had seen him. No, Jax had been beloved by everyone in the town. As their Keyholder and the High Priest of Thoen, he was often the mediator for problems and carried a reputation for being fair, just like his god.

The crowd's silence threatened to overwhelm him, and Aubron blinked hard, trying to recentre his thoughts. He had to speak, had to address them the way his uncle used to. Until now, he'd been content to stay back, cleaning the temple, helping Rictor with his research, or spending time with Soril.

Just thinking her name sent a wave of longing through him. *Don't go there*, he told himself.

Aubron gripped the small railing tentatively and took a deep breath. He'd been mentally preparing a speech about how Thoen and other gods had been with them as Eton and his uncle had driven the creatures away from the town. Instead, however, all he could think of was the light in the eyes of the man who'd raised him slowly fading as the life left his body.

"Friends," his voice carried over the grave crowd. "I stand before you today with a heavy heart and solemn countenance. Last night we lost Jax Sebart. He was the beloved High Priest of Thoen, Keyholder to the village of Vazot, my uncle, and a friend to many." He wasn't sure about that last statement considering his uncle had never expressed genuine interest in anyone's life but Eton's. The man, however, had possessed a gift for making people feel welcome and cared for.

"He was never one to do anything but lead from the front, even when it posed an unimaginable danger. In the end, the uibixa took his life, and he made the ultimate sacrifice for us.

"My duty to you has always been from inside this temple. Now, with my uncle passing into the afterlife by the grace of Nillioth, and on the wings of Helo, I must step up and assure you of my commitment to filling my uncle's role as High Priest of Thoen and Keyholder. The Empress will choose a new Keyholder, but, until she sends her decree, I will dutifully fill the role with honour and dedication to you all."

He tried to make eye contact with at least someone in the crowd, but very few people were even looking at him; most were looking at each other or the ground.

"I know it has been tough, these last few weeks. As uibixa attacks increase in frequency and severity, I swear, upon my uncle's eternal soul, to do everything possible to beat these creatures back and keep you all safe. You that still stand here, missing your loved ones, to you, I swear I will do everything in my power to ensure we get through this."

He stepped back and the townspeople emitted a few half-hearted claps before dispersing.

A flash of ethereal blond hair at the back of the crowd caught his eye, and all thoughts but one fled his mind: Soril was back.

Soril was a caeles, a celestial being, sent down by a specific god to watch over their assigned temple. She'd taken over as the caeles in charge of the God of Justice's temple last year–and she'd disappeared without a word three weeks ago.

Her bright gold eyes met his brown ones from where she stood at the back of the crowd, watching him with an impassive expression etched on her gray face. It was the expression he had seen her constantly make when they first met. Like most caeles, she'd often been unwilling to show much emotion around anyone.

It hurt him now that she'd be giving him such a look, even though he knew, realistically, she was supposed to maintain a certain aloofness in public.

She and the rest of the temple celestials, one for each god, had disappeared. Aubron figured most of the people of Vazot probably didn't even notice. The caeles rarely interacted with them, preferring to keep out of sight. Disdain for the mortals was a constant for them. Soril though, she was different, and he could admit he was hurt that she'd left weeks ago without so much as a goodbye.

The crowd was almost gone, so Aubron headed into the temple. He needed space. He sat on one of the stone stools in the main worship chamber. A towering statue of Thoen faced him, all shining metal and a sharp contrast to the cloth-covered wooden walls. At the base sat incense holders and the thick smell of smoke choked the air.

"It was a good speech," a voice called out from the doorway.

Aubron's head snapped up and he looked into the bright green eyes of Rictor. He couldn't help but notice the worn clothes, threadbare and aged, holes dotted throughout, indicative his friend had been researching before this moment. Ever since the death of his wife, the man had thrown himself into his research with little regard for taking proper care of himself.

"Thanks," Aubron replied half-heartedly. He turned back to stare up at the statue.

"I saw Soril," Rictor hedged, shuffling closer.

His back stiffened. "So?" He tried to keep his voice nonchalant.

Rictor let out a slight laugh. "You told me everything last night."

Aubron's gaze shot to his friend in horror.

The Knowledge Priest swept his flimsy hat off his head, tussling his shoulder-length, dark orange hair, and held it against his chest in jest. "It took quite a lot to get you to stop waxing poetic about her golden hair and how much you missed her." A pause. "You teased Genae and I relentlessly when we got married. Turnabout is fair play."

Aubron slumped, head falling into his hands. "You can't tell anyone." A relationship, such as it was, between a mortal and a caeles was forbidden. His uncle was no longer around to care, but her peers and god would have an issue if they knew.

Rictor dropped his hat on the ground, clapped a hand on Aubron's back, and sat down heavily beside him. "Of course, I won't tell anyone." He paused momentarily and then continued, "Also, there's really no one for me to tell in this awful place."

The words he left unsaid hung heavy in the air.

The heavy curtain rustled, and the two men glanced up to see Soril slipping into the temple.

She stopped short as she caught sight of Rictor. It was subtle, but he knew her well enough to see how her spine straightened as if a cord had been pulled tight toward the ceiling. Her chin raised as her eyes cooled.

"Priest Rictor," she said, her voice flat, "I need to speak with Priest Aubron immediately."

Rictor burst out laughing and waved his hand dismissively before standing and scooping his hat from the floor. "You don't have to pretend for me, Soril." She scowled at the familiar way he spoke to her, which was ignored, as he continued, "Aubron drunkenly spilled his guts to me." He left the temple with another chortle, a grin to Aubron, and a wink at Soril.

Soril's expression immediately morphed into one of annoyance. The blue veins that cracked across her face became more pronounced, as they always did when she was upset. "What exactly did you tell him?"

"Nothing you have to worry about." He stood and faced her. "What are you doing here?" He wished there was more venom in his voice, but all he could muster was exhaustion.

Her posture relaxed slightly, even though the angry look didn't leave her face. "I did not want to leave. I came back as soon as I could."

He scoffed, stood, and moved toward the statue; he needed to put some distance between them. "It's been three weeks," he snapped. There was the venom he'd been looking for. Thick and poisonous, like acid eating away at his very being.

He'd not slept more than a few minutes at a time in days, and every time he closed his eyes, he'd seen her so very vividly. She'd never appeared when his eyes were open, and it stung.

"It is true," her voice was laced with annoyance. "The gods called us back. There are consequences for disobeying."

She touched a finger to her forehead where her Mark of the Maker sat. A swirling golden pattern that dipped between her brows, signifying her as a being created to assist the gods. As if the pure golden eyes, gray skin with stark blue veins, and towering height didn't already give it away.

"Then why are you back while the others are not?"

"The others do not care," she said in a hollow tone. She had resented mortals when he'd first met her, uninterested in anything to do with the people of the town and unimpressed with her latest job posting. This fact changed as they'd grown closer although, it was still true of the others.

"It must be nice not to care about mortals being killed." He managed to keep his voice firm.

Soril flinched. "I saw the burnt pyre when I arrived. I am sorry about your uncle."

Aubron gave a half-hearted shrug, suddenly unable to breathe, pain wrapping like a band around his chest. "I don't want to talk about him." He reached down to the incense holders and started cleaning the ash from the pots.

"Aubron," she whispered, her hand brushing his shoulder.

He immediately stiffened at the comfort she offered. "Don't touch me, please." A dry sob clawed its way up his throat and threatened to choke him.

She pulled back as if burned, a muttered apology slipping out. Immediately Aubron felt the absence of her warm hand and missed it.

"Why did Thoen call you back?" he asked, desperate to change the topic.

The fabric of her airy, white dress rustled as she moved beside him and knelt to help clean up the statue's base.

Her voice was steady but quiet as she responded, "Exactly what I said. Thoen and the other gods commanded us to all return at once."

"Return so we could be slaughtered unimpeded?"

"No!" her voice raised slightly before dropping to a whisper. "He told us something about the uibixa."

"What?"

Soril was silent for a moment. "You cannot repeat this to anyone."

He bit back a scoff. "Who would I tell?"

She shot him a judgmental look. "Rictor, the next time you two drink?"

Aubron looked away as he felt his cheeks redden slightly. "I won't say anything, I promise."

His declaration hung heavy in the air before Soril seemed to come to a decision. "Thoen would not say much, only that he cannot risk any of the caeles being killed."

Aubron's hand slapped the stone tile, tipping a candle holder. "But we can die?" he spat, the words tasting foul in his mouth.

"The seal on the uibixa is weakening."

Aubron felt his jaw go slack. "The what?"

"The seal. The Maker sealed the uibixa away thousands of years ago. Thoen told us that as the seal weakens more of them escape and go hunting for mortals."

Fire raced through his veins. "How do we strengthen the seal?"

Her shoulders slumped and her hands stilled. "From what he said, we do not. The uibixa steal the magic boons of those they kill, and with each life taken, they grow in power and weaken the seal more."

"So, he called you all back instead of sending more caeles to help?" Aubron couldn't keep the incredulity from his voice.

"Aubron, they consume boons when they kill. It is one thing to get a mortal's power; it is just a small gift given by their gods. Caeles magic is a whole different story. Ours comes from the Maker himself and is much more complex and formidable. We were instructed not to interfere and given new temple assignments."

Aubron grit his teeth. "Fine. You can leave now." He waved a hand in the direction of the entrance to the temple.

Soril sighed and stood up. "Aubron, I am here to help. I cannot bring your uncle back, but I refuse to sit back and let you or anyone else get hurt if there is a way I can help."

"What do you mean?"

"I am here against Thoen's wishes. I am sure he will soon realize I am not doing my duty at the new temple, but I do not care. When you are safe, I will go where he wants." She shot him a grimace as she patted down her dress. "I am going to go get some sleep. You should as well."

She stood still for a moment before taking a step forward. The air shimmered around her, and she disappeared, leaving Aubron alone.

Fury raced through him, though he wasn't sure at who or what it was directed. He was angry with Thoen for making the caeles leave in the first place, angry at the creatures who'd attacked his home, and angry with his uncle for dying. He wasn't even sure if it was all rational.

A rush of blood roared in his ears and the overwhelming urge to hit something possessed his limbs. He struck out with his arm, knocking the pots and holders over, scattering them in a cacophony of metal slamming against the floor. Still, he couldn't quiet his mind.

* * *

The sun was setting when Aubron awoke to a skittering sound from outside his bedroom.

He stood from the bed, cautiously pushed past the interior linen curtain, and followed the sound down the temple hallway until he was in the nave.

He was startled when a small rodent with a deep blue and bright yellow coat scurried past him, heading toward the temple entrance.

He made to follow the strange-coloured creature when he heard Soril's voice from just outside.

"Get out of here, Harlequin." Her voice was biting, with an edge he'd never experienced from her before. The name lit up a memory of her grumbling about one of the leaders of the caeles, an eccentric being who meddled everywhere they went, all the while draped in a garish patchwork of clashing textiles.

The sound of dozens of voices, all different pitches and inflections, responded, "That is no way to speak to us. We are just wondering what you think you will get from coming back here?"

Aubron snuck toward the entrance. He didn't dare go outside but peering through the gap between the curtain and the floor he could make out shadows of two people on the other side.

"I do not need commentary from you," she snapped.

"Thoen is enraged by your disobedience. Very curious, then, that he would approach us to pass a message along. A warning, if you will."

"How does he know I disobeyed him?" Soril's voice had lost some of its bluster.

"He knows many things, and knowledge is a powerful tool when leveraged correctly." There was a chuckle that made the hairs on Aubron's arms stand up as a chill rolled through him. "But it is as if we know things of all times and places. Thoen knows less than he wants to be made known."

She made an annoyed noise in the back of her throat that Aubron had heard many times just before she lost all patience. "So, then, what message did he want to be passed along?"

A rustle of fabric accompanied by clicks of tongues sounded. "Ah yes. Thoen sacrificed his progeny to seal the uibixa. You think he cares about a village of mortals? Odd how that often works. How history repeats. How history breaks."

Soril gave a dark chuckle. "You cryptic asshole. Are you trying to tell me all the people of Vazot are to die?"

"That is not what we are saying. Just as Thoen did not commit the crime, inaction still belies a weak heart. You need to listen better." A pause set Aubron on edge. "You could take pointers from that mortal you seem so attached to. He seems to know how to listen."

Aubron cursed under his breath as the shadows shifted and Soril pulled the curtain back. Suddenly, they were face-to-face as she loomed in the doorframe. He tried to peer behind her to whomever she'd been speaking to but couldn't see over her shoulder.

The voices laughed before speaking a final sentence, "Coincidences and consequences, our duty-bound, Soril."

"What are you doing?" she snapped, backing Aubron into the temple. He caught a glimpse of a figure wrapped head-to-toe in draping blue and yellow cloth just as she let the curtain fall closed behind her.

He ignored her question for a few of his own. "Is it true? About us dying? Who was that?"

Soril shook her head. "The Harlequin is notorious among caeles for constantly stirring up trouble the way wind stirs up dust. That is to say, never-ending and without regard for propriety. Very rarely do they say anything worth listening to."

She moved farther into the room and frowned at him. "Why were you listening to my conversation?"

"Why were you having a conversation right outside the temple door?"

Her face flushed blue. "I was on my way to see you. They snuck up on me."

He opened his mouth to respond when Rictor's voice from outside interrupted him, "Aubron!"

They turned to see the Priest of Knowledge appear in the entranceway. He was out of breath. His leather cuirass—an ill-fitting and little-used piece of equipment—had been haphazardly thrown over his head, the buckles still loose.

"What's going on?" Aubron asked.

"I was charting the stars from the walls and ran into Eton outside of town. He sent me to get you. There's an uibixa heading this way, from the dunes, according to Dakar. He figures we can cut it off long before it gets to the walls if we go now."

Aubron nodded before turning around and racing to his room. He grabbed his leather armour and the sword his uncle had given him when he'd turned fifteen and headed back to the nave.

"We should talk later," Soril said with a frown, her lips pursed.

Aubron grunted in agreement as he threw his armour over his head and then went to Rictor to help the other man with his buckles.

Cuirass' secure, the two men left the temple at a run, Rictor leading the way.

Aubron looked beside him to see Soril running beside him, her gait so even it looked like she was gliding across the sandy ground.

"I thought you weren't supposed to get involved?" Aubron called to her.

"I am not going to sit by while you put yourself in danger."

"What about the consequences?" He let out a huff as his legs started to burn.

"They are already in motion."

Aubron stopped himself from responding as they reached the first large dune a few minutes out of the village.

As they crested the hill, he caught sight of Eton. The man cut an imposing figure as moonlight glinted off his metal armour, painted with colourful, magical symbols for protection and combat prowess. Beside him stood Pel, clad in a long leather overcoat with almost bursting pockets. One other man stood there; another member of the town guard named Dakar. He was the only dwarf in the area, having completed the perilous journey to the village years ago by himself.

"Where is it?" Aubron asked.

Eton's eyes flicked between Aubron and Soril, a frown on his face. "Dakar caught sight of it just over the next dune. Get ready."

Beside him, Soril plunged her hand into the ground. Cold air spread out from her as a pole of pure ice started to form along the sand. Next came a long, wicked-looking blade that sparked with light blue magic. Aubron had only seen Soril use her glaive once before, and he shook his head to combat the awe of such power. The weapon settled into her hand, and she lightly balanced it, slotting her hands right where they needed to go.

Dakar gave her a long look. "Glad one of ya came back," he said, voice gruff.

She looked unsure of how to respond, finally saying, "I came back to help."

Pel muttered something under his breath, and Eton shot him a glare as Dakar laughed loudly.

The dwarf unhooked a long club with sharp metal spikes from his belt and turned his focus to the dune in front of them.

Aubron thought of what Soril had told him earlier. "Do we know where the uibixa are originating from?"

Dakar responded, eyes never straying. "The boy across the street from me claims he saw them coming from a hole in the ground once, about an hour's walk northeast from here."

"A hole in the ground?" Rictor questioned.

"Why was he out there anyway?" Eton sounded unimpressed and Aubron almost smiled at the predictable response, the man's ire, for once, not directed at him.

Dakar shrugged and took a practice swing with his club. "Really couldn't tell ya. Personally, I think he's trying to scare that mother of his to death. Then again, he could be lying. He once tried to tell me about a caeles covered head-to-toe in multicolored cloth that kept speaking to him in the middle of the night." The dwarf let out a gruff laugh.

Aubron glanced at Soril whose forehead was creased in concern. She caught his gaze and shook her head for him to keep silent.

Eton hefted his great sword onto his shoulder. He and Pel had started speaking in hushed tones. The healer's hand rested on the strap of his leather satchel that, Aubron knew from experience, held a multitude of healing salves and bandages.

"There the bastard is," Pel said, voice hard as he readjusted the bag on his shoulder.

A large black mass oozed over the top of the dune, looking for all the world like darkness streaked with silver lines that glinted in the moonlight. The rippling, roiling mass seemed to shift as shadows moved within it. It slid down the hill, leaving deep lines in the red sand.

As the uibixa reached the valley of the dune, it seemed to notice them and turned to start heading directly at the group.

Aubron unsheathed his sword, Rictor following suit a moment later.

A flash of blue ice flew toward the creature from Soril's glaive. It struck with a wet smack and the uibixa folded in on itself, becoming smaller as it absorbed the blow.

Suddenly, it started to quiver and pulse before letting out a blood-curdling shriek. Wings like those of a massive bird, dipped in ink, burst out from either side of the ooze. A large, fanned tail emerged next, and as the body started to take shape, a wicked-looking beak and glinting silver eyes faced the group. The beast shook itself out for a moment, darkness dripping from its wings before launching into the sky.

It flew higher and higher, blending in with the deep blue sky—only a ripple in the night indicating its position. It flitted across the moon for a brief moment. From the corner of his eye, Aubron saw Rictor clutch his sword tighter.

Suddenly, it dove, its body angling straight for Dakar.

The dwarf repositioned himself, club held loosely in his hand, ready to be swung. Beside him, Eton's sword lit up with bright orange fire and he aimed at the creature, flames jumping from the blade to shoot toward it.

With speed Aubron didn't know these things were capable of, it banked hard to the left. The rush of magic from Eton missed and fizzled out.

The uibixa's change in direction sent it careening toward Rictor. The Knowledge Priest flung himself to the side, landing hard on the sand with a swear. Pel was immediately by his side, checking on him. Dakar ran over while swinging his club, striking the bird's side. The dwarf grunted with the impact and Aubron saw it jar his arm. Small dots of black blood dripped from the metal spikes.

The monster let out a vicious shriek and hit the ground with a shudder. Immediately, it launched itself back into the air, seemingly unbothered by the hit for longer than a moment.

Soril thrust her glaive outwards—blade pointed toward the uibixa. Ice shot out and stabbed right through the creature, sending a spray of black blood raining down on them.

"Magic is more effective against them," she called to Dakar. "If you have any, now is the time to use it."

"Helo must've forgotten that when he Marked me," Dakar snarked in response.

From behind him, Aubron heard Rictor cry with pain. He almost turned to check on his friend, but then the uibixa started another descent, streaking toward Dakar.

Aubron closed his eyes briefly to pull at the small boon he possessed. He pointed his finger at the creature and let a gust of wind push it slightly off course toward Eton.

His gift wasn't very powerful, and never had been, but his uncle had always tried to instill in him that fighting smarter was the only way to ensure victory. Never before did he better understand that idea so well. He pushed the split second of uncomfortable tightness in his chest down at the thought of his uncle.

Eton swung at it immediately, his burning sword slicing into the face of the creature that let out a high-pitched cry. It fell to the ground with one last scream before the uibixa collapsed in on itself and started to deflate, sinking into the ground. In seconds, it disappeared before their eyes, leaving nothing but a patch of black sand in its wake.

Soril let her weapon crumble into small chunks of ice and loosed a sigh of relief.

Aubron immediately turned to see Rictor lying on the ground, his face drawn and pale. "Are you injured?"

Pel spoke for him from where he was hunched over Rictor's leg, smearing something from a small jar across his God-Mark. "The uibixa blood seems to have burned him."

"A burn?" Dakar asked skeptically. "Some sprayed me as well and I'm not burned."

"It got on his God-Mark," Pel responded, not looking up from the injury.

Rictor spoke before anyone else could interject, "I-it still shouldn't burn. I've been compiling any and all m-mentions of uibixa in the temple library. No one has ever recorded that the blood r-reacts differently to God-Marks." His voice was scared, shaking, while his gaze darted from person to person.

"But other than in the last few weeks, how often do we see these them? Maybe it wouldn't be in the books?" Aubron pointed out.

Eton scoffed. "Most people also end up with their God-Mark covered by armour while fighting. Not everything can be learned from your tomes, Rictor."

Rictor opened his mouth to retort but instead let out a grunt and shifted as Pel—all focused precision—whipped out a cloth, wet it with water from a flask, and started wiping away the salve.

"Hold still," Pel commanded. "Normally, this stuff doesn't burn skin or anything else. It's like it's sticking to you, but only where the Mark is." He looked at Eton. "I'm going to take him back to town. I need something stronger to make sure this is cleaned properly."

Eton nodded and turned to Dakar. "Let's keep patrolling then."

The dwarf grinned. "I was hoping you'd say that." His gaze met Aubron's. "You and the caeles going to join us?"

Aubron turned to Soril to see her standing perfectly still, eyes focused on something in the distance across the valley of the dune.

He looked at where she was staring but couldn't see anything. "Soril?" Her eyes snapped to him, and he could see the panic, plain as day, on her face.

"Go on without me," she said, eyes straying back to where she'd been looking before.

"Are you sure?"

She nodded distractedly. "I will find you later. We need to talk anyway."

Rictor let out a low whistle and whispered, "You're in trouble."

Aubron shot him a glare and then looked back to Soril. "I'll see you later."

She nodded and strode down the dune, leaving the rest of the group behind.

"Can you walk?" Eton asked Rictor as Pel helped the Priest stand.

"Yes, my leg hurts, but I can walk."

Pel raised an eyebrow and then looked at Aubron. "Help me get him back to town, just in case. I don't know what the long-term effects of this will be."

Aubron nodded as Eton said, "Okay. We'll go on ahead and keep patrolling. I'll see if we can find one of the other teams."

"Let's get going," Pel said.

Aubron brought up the rear, staying a few paces behind Pel and Rictor to better keep an eye on them.

The group hadn't gone far when Aubron heard Rictor call back to him, "Aubron, can you go back and get a sample of the sand the uibixa disappeared into?"

"Sure," he answered with a faint smile and chuckle. *Even hurt and scared, Rictor is as dedicated to his research as ever.*

He turned and started heading back to the blackened ground where the monster had died. He stopped just before the dune's crest when he heard Soril's voice speaking in the language of the caeles. She'd taught him a small amount. However, her voice was so panicked and fast that his rudimentary knowledge of the tongue wasn't helping him pick up more than a few scattered words.

"Death. Uibixa. Burn."

Someone interrupted her, a deep male voice which sounded furious.

"Thoen. Home. Forget."

He risked a peek over the top of the dune and almost gasped. Down in the valley was another caeles. That wasn't surprising. No, what made panic thrum through his body were the giant scythe-like wings that spanned across the sand, erupting from the man's back. From what Soril had told him, only the most important caeles for each god were granted wings. The man's entire body was covered in Thoen's God-Mark. His Mark of the Maker shone brilliant gold upon his forehead. The one time Soril had described this man to Aubron didn't do him justice; the Arbiter was a force unto himself.

He ducked back down when Soril spoke again. Her voice was choked with tears, and it unsettled Aubron. She was often so controlled in her emotions, especially with others; it was unusual to hear her break down.

She stopped speaking and deafening silence overtook the night, oppressive in its weight.

After a few moments, Aubron cautiously looked to where they'd been standing. Worry warred with anger inside him when he saw they were both gone.

He gave his head a shake and headed down the dune. The last thing he needed to do was let his guard down out here. *Get back to Rictor first. I can't help Soril now, and worrying doesn't change that.*

The patch of blackened sand where the uibixa had disappeared was still there, and he scooped some carefully into an empty cloth pouch.

Task complete, he turned around and headed back to the village.

* * *

Aubron had arrived at the temple of Niphia, Goddess of Medicine, and immediately rushed to where Pel was caring for Rictor. The healer had confirmed the Knowledge Priest would be fine—as only a tiny amount of blood had gotten onto the God-Mark—and that was the only place his skin had burned. Most of the blood had wiped away under the careful application of tonics the healer had made himself.

Now, with the panic over Rictor's injury abated, Aubron sat on the coast and stared at the waves lapping angrily against the shore. Dark gray clouds hung in the sky, lending everything a dreary, flat look.

He heard the crunching of sand underfoot and turned his head to see Rictor settling down beside him.

"Is there a reason you're out here moping?" Rictor said, the easy smile on his face belying his eyes, pained and angry like the ocean.

Aubron leaned back on his hands, "I wouldn't exactly say I'm moping."

"I haven't seen Soril since the fight." There was a knowing look on the man's face.

Right for the throat. Aubron slumped, curling in on himself. "Another caeles showed up and took her away, or she went with him. I'm not really sure."

"Think she'll come back again? I have a question about my God-Mark for her. I've never been able to talk to a caeles freely before."

"I'm not sure." He pushed the worry for her down. "What do you have to ask about your Mark? Pel said most of it was untouched."

Rictor pulled his pant leg from his boots and rolled it up, turning his body so Aubron could see his God-Mark. The deep green swirl of books, scrolls, and ink blots that made up his Mark was marred on the left side by a gray stain, the flesh around it red and irritated.

"Pel did what he could, but some of my Mark is just gone with that splotch in its place."

"I've never seen anything like that," Aubron mused.

Rictor slid closer and said in a whisper, "Me either. But that's not all, Aubron. I heard a voice. As it was burning me, I could hear a voice that ebbed and flowed with the pain from the blood."

Aubron shifted in discomfort at the notion. "What did the voice say?"

"It was strange. I understood it, but it wasn't speaking any language I've ever encountered before." Rictor's voice had become so quiet that Aubron had to strain to hear him.

"But what did it say?"

Rictor closed his eyes with a deep sigh and lay down on the sand, face turned to the sky. "It was commanding me to kill Pel."

Ice flooded Aubron's veins. "It wanted you to kill him?"

"It demanded," Rictor trailed off, and silence overcame the two for a few minutes.

Finally, Rictor spoke again, "It told me to use its power. And I felt it. I could've tasted it, Aubron. It was calling to me. I felt so strong in that moment, like I could crush anyone, do anything."

Fear like freezing fingers skittered down Aubron's spine at Rictor's words. "Is it," he paused, swallowing a lump in his throat, "is it still talking to you?"

"No," the Priest's voice was quiet. "It stopped when Pel healed me, once all the uibixa blood was gone."

"That's good, I guess. But I didn't know they could communicate like that."

"I didn't either."

The two sat in silence for a few minutes. Aubron's mind raced as terror turned his stomach. *So, the uibixa can burn off God-Marks and feed on magic. How are they able to talk? Has anyone spoken with one before now? Just what are they?*

The last thought reminded Aubron. "By the way, I got that bag of sand you asked for." He reached into his pocket and pulled it out, setting it between himself and Rictor.

"Thank you," Rictor said as he picked up the bag. "I'd like to study it. Maybe it will reveal something about what they are or how to fight them more effectively. If these attacks are going to continue and their blood is corrosive to our God-Marks, we need to be as prepared as possible."

Aubron nodded in agreement even as he bit his tongue to keep from spilling his fears evoked by what Soril had told him. "Alright, but you should rest first. Eton told me you weren't to patrol tonight, but–"

"Like I'm not going to help tonight. I'll be there, and if Eton has an issue with it, I'll tell him where his opinion can go."

Aubron grinned at his friend. "I told him you'd say that."

"One more thing," Rictor pulled out a small bundle wrapped in yellow and blue cloth from a pouch on his belt. "This was left in my temple with a note that said, 'Use this to save your home.' I'm unsure what exactly it means, but we could use any advantage we can get right now."

"What is it?"

"It's just a blue candle," Rictor said with a laugh and a shrug.

* * *

The sun sank across the horizon, scattering golden rays of light into Thoen's temple through the few open curtains. Aubron knelt at the base of the statue, the god's impassive face looking down on him. He grabbed one of the already-burning candles and held it against the top of the incense before blowing out the fire, leaving the ember to smoulder and smoke. He placed both back into their proper spots.

The sickly-sweet smell of goldweed reached his nostrils, and he wrinkled his nose. "Protect us from the unjust," he muttered as he moved away.

A chuckle came from the dark corner of the temple by the entrance. "How interesting," said the voice of dozens of people speaking all at once.

Aubron whirled around to see a figure who was completely draped in multicoloured cloth–predominantly shades of blue and yellow–towering over him. All he could see of their face was one glowing gold eye that peered out from under the fabric. It stared at him, unblinking, unwavering. Aubron had never before felt so unnerved by the gaze of a caeles.

"Who are you?" His voice was shaky, his heart racing from being startled.

"We are the Harlequin," the voices responded. There was a pause as they moved closer to Aubron. The fabric in which they were draped shifted and revealed more bright colours underneath. The golden eye never left his face. "Curious, is it not?"

"W-what?" Aubron cursed his response.

"That you would light an offering for one God such as Thoen."

"I'm praying we will be protected if a patrol finds any uibixa tonight." He paused and then remembered what Soril said about the Harlequin. "What do you want?" He had no interest in playing whatever game the caeles was up to.

"We thought it was best to pose a question to you. Is it not curious that Thoen would pull all the caeles away when you need them most? Moreover, is it not suspicious how Soril has disappeared again?" There was an unnerving glint in the bright eye.

"Another caeles showed up–"

"And she left with him," the voices cut him off.

"I'm not sure she wanted to leave, though. She sounded upset."

"Ah yes, a consequence of going against Thoen's wishes, or would it be a punishment created and executed by the Arbiter? Funny how that works; how power can blur the lines of those making decisions."

"Did you come here just to talk in riddles?"

The laughs of dozens of voices came from underneath the cloth. "Possibly. Possibly we are here to make you think. Possibly we are here to suggest you make a decision. Or possibly we are just here because mortals are forever a source of entertainment for us. We would never tell." Their head tilted to the side, cloth sliding over the shining eye as they began to circle Aubron.

Aubron rolled his eyes. "Is what you said about Thoen and the uibixa true?"

"Possibly. Or possibly not."

"That's unhelpful," he muttered.

The Harlequin laughed again. "You do not need answers from us, mortal. You need answers from yourself."

"Then why even come here and talk to me?"

"'Why?' will be the question of the night. If we were you, we would focus on the *how*."

With that final statement, the Harlequin went utterly motionless in concentration the way Soril did when she was about to Realm-Step. Then, the next second, they stepped forward and disappeared into a ripple of air.

Aubron stood still for a moment, discomfort swirling in his stomach. Looking around, he tried to see any sign that the Harlequin hadn't actually left the temple, but the air was still and silent. He slumped onto a stone bench and let his head drop into his hands.

He wasn't sure how long he sat there, mind racing, sucking in deep breaths as if that could make the last month disappear if he tried hard enough. The rustling of the entrance to the temple made him look up just as Soril stepped inside, letting the curtain fall shut behind her.

"Are you hurt?" Soril's voice was laced with worry, a wan frown on her face.

"You're back again," Aubron tried to keep his voice even as he brushed off her question.

"It was urgent. I apologize."

She moved closer to him. As she did, Aubron caught sight of her tinted blue cheek and the cuts along her now bare arms. Dirt marred her white dress, and Aubron didn't think he'd ever seen her look so dishevelled.

"Are you alright?" he asked, concern for her overshadowing the hurt and anger at her leaving again, for the moment.

"Of course." She paused. "You did not answer my question."

"I'm fine, I just thought I saw something strange earlier, but I was wrong." He hated lying to her, but the exhaustion on her face made him unwilling to burden her with the caeles' odd visit. They could discuss it later.

Aubron stood and reached out to rest a hand on her non-injured cheek. She leaned into his hand, and they stood together for a second.

"Did the Arbiter do this to you?" he asked, gesturing to her injured arm.

Soril sharply pulled away. "How do you know–"

"I saw you two talking in the dunes, and then you left again."

Her shoulders hunched and she moved to take a heavy seat on the bench he'd just vacated. "He was angry that I disobeyed direct orders. I told him where to shove his orders." She let out a wry laugh. "I heard Rictor use that phrase once. Hopefully, he understood the meaning. I left immediately after."

"Are you allowed to do that?"

"No. But I did not want to leave you again. I want to help you protect the people here. I am unsure if I will be welcome in Thoen's village again."

"For disobeying orders?"

She paused for a moment. "The Arbiter did not like me talking back to him while others watched. I would not be surprised if he retaliated. The man is," she paused as if rolling the word around her tongue, "unpleasant, I would say. He is not very well-liked by the other caeles."

Aubron sat down beside her. There was no room between them as his thigh pressed tight to her own and their shoulders brushed.

He let loose a breath and leaned forward, arms resting on his thighs. He could see Soril out of the corner of his eye. "I'm sorry," he said.

"For what?"

"Making you choose between the other caeles and us mortals."

She rested a hand on his head and gently stroked his hair. "You are not forcing me to choose. I am choosing." She was silent for a moment and then continued, voice barely above a whisper, "I do not wholly believe Thoen is making these decisions. The Arbiter has been speaking on Thoen's behalf, and that is not a man I wish to follow. Furthermore, if these are Thoen's wants and commands, I am not okay with his choice either."

His shoulders slumped. "Still—"

He cut off at her hand moving from his head to brush along his arm, delicate fingers skimming across his skin, and Aubron felt his body tense, any leftover anger fizzling out. He always craved her touch and, even after everything, now was no different.

"Aubron," her voice was soft, and he couldn't stop himself from looking at her. "I am sorry I left. I should have ignored Thoen the first time and come back immediately. I have made my intentions known to the Arbiter. I promise you I am here now. Whatever comes next, we will face it together."

The Priest let out a breath at her reassurance. "I appreciate that more than you know."

She smiled weakly and wrapped her arm around his shoulders. "I have missed this," she murmured into his hair.

He wrapped his arms around her and let himself rest against her, finding solace in her embrace. "I've missed you, too," he responded.

He glanced up to see her looking down at him, a gentle expression that he'd only ever seen her send his way.

Aubron wasn't sure who moved first, but their lips brushed, and at that moment, he swore he felt sparks. Peace he'd only felt in her presence filled him, and she seemed to feel the same way as her hold on him tightened.

She broke the kiss and rested her chin on top of his head. "Aubron," she whispered. He hummed in response, and she giggled, a sound he hadn't heard from her in a long time. "Rictor is coming."

The linen parted and they moved away from each other as Rictor entered the room. He looked between the two of them and then laughed. "Need me to go find someone else to patrol with?"

Aubron could see a blue blush rise on the caeles' face, and he shook his head at his friend. "No, let's go." He stood and Soril followed suit.

"I am coming with you."

* * *

Aubron crept through the sparse brush of dead, withered trees that shot up from the white, sandy ground. He was trying not to make too much noise. Behind him, he heard Rictor trip on a root and swear quietly. Even farther back was Soril, who moved so fluidly her feet barely touched the ground, utterly silent as always.

Eton had, with a raised eyebrow, sent the three of them to patrol the northeastern section. They'd cleared the area faster than expected, and Rictor had suggested they continue a little farther out to where a scout had caught a lone uibixa emerging from the ground last night.

As they moved through the brush, Aubron wondered if they should've stayed closer to the town walls instead.

"Aubron!" Soril hissed.

He stopped walking and felt Rictor crash into his back with another curse.

"What?"

"I can hear them," she whispered. "The uibixa, they are coming closer."

Aubron crept farther and peered through the trees. His stomach lurched and he swore he could taste the fear that flooded his body.

A sea of darkness streaked with silver emerged from a dip in the ground. All grouped together, the uibixa moved like water across the sand.

"You have got to be joking," Rictor breathed from beside him.

Aubron looked to his other side to see Soril staring at the uibixa. Her eyes were wide, and her face drained of blue blood.

"I have never seen that many before," she whispered, despair heavy in her voice.

"I didn't even know there could be that many," Aubron said.

Rictor agreed, saying, "We can't take them all on by ourselves."

Aubron nodded. "We need to warn Eton. They're heading straight for the village."

"It'll be a siege," Rictor said.

Soril spoke up, "I will go to where Eton is supposed to be patrolling. You two head back to the village and warn them."

Aubron turned to Soril. "We'll see you back at the village."

She nodded and moved forward as if to embrace him before pulling back. "Stay safe, I will find Eton and we *will* beat these creatures back."

A moment later, she was gone.

Aubron looked back at the uibixa and saw they were getting closer; soon, they'd surely catch sight of the two men.

"We need to go," he said, urgency colouring his tone.

Rictor hummed his agreement before breaking into a sprint toward the village. Aubron's feet pounded against the sand, slipping out from under him more than once. Fear-fueled adrenaline filled him, and his lungs burned, a fiery sensation travelling through his body.

The moon was full and sent pale light through the sky, illuminating the dunes and reflecting off the silver streaks in the uibixa heading toward the town.

By the time the two men reached the walls, they could hear warning drumbeats; Soril and Eton had made it back already.

This was further confirmed by the man in question approaching them. "Good, you two are back," Eton said. "Get to the walls. We have archers up there. We'll close the gate and hopefully take them out before they get through."

Aubron started for the stairs that led up the wall with Rictor at his heels. When he reached the top, he peered out only to see the black mass of uibixa emerging from the rise of a large sand dune. They blended into the night sky, save for the pearlescent strands shimmering in the moonlight.

Dakar, readied with a bow, stepped up beside Aubron and whistled. "Now that's a sight fit to give me nightmares."

"You and me both," Rictor said from the other side of Aubron.

As the uibixa approached, a few started to break away from the wriggling mass. Then, just like the one last night, they began to take the shape of large birds and launched into the sky, shooting toward the town.

"Here they come!" Eton's voice boomed. "Archers! Draw!" A flurry of movement and then a pause. "Release!"

Bowstrings snapping in unison cut through the air as arrows whistled toward the flying uibixa. Aubron could even make out a few tips glowing different colours, telling him some people had been able to imbue a few with magic before the fight.

The first bolts connected, and the creatures shrieked as Eton called for another volley that loosed rapidly.

More cries echoed through the night. Aubron saw the mass of uibixa on the ground continue to break apart and turn into different beasts he couldn't make out.

A salvo of snapping bowstrings rang out just as the bird-like uibixa—that the arrows hadn't hindered—reached the wall. They started diving toward the archers as many of the fighters dropped their bows in favour of swords to slice at the creatures dipping into range.

Airy power filled Aubron's hand, and he shot a small blast of wind at one of the uibixa that was aiming for the archer next to him. The magic went wide and whooshed past the bird.

"Get down!" Aubron shouted, panic filling his chest.

The archer—who'd been scrambling to unsheathe her sword after dropping her bow—looked up just in time for the uibixa to collide with her. She toppled over backwards, falling off the wall with a scream that ended abruptly as her body hit the ground.

A choked shriek of terror from one of the other archers became a pained gurgle. Aubron looked farther down the wall to see another fighter with a black tentacle that had lashed out from the tail of a different uibixa-bird sticking out of his chest. It slid backwards and he slumped to the ground, blood pooling around him.

All along the bulwark, others were faring much the same, and for a moment, despair threatened to overwhelm Aubron.

The uibixa on the ground had reached the gate and were throwing themselves at it, black tentacles and claws beating on the metal-banded wood. Arrows, rocks, and magic were aimed by the defenders at the creatures below, even as the flying ones continued to attack from above.

A bird aimed at Aubron and he readied his sword. A second before he swung, a lance made of pure, glistening ice shot through the uibixa closest to him. A split second later, the ice exploded into shards that tore the monster's head apart but melted before they could reach anyone else. It let out an unearthly screech and dropped from the sky, crashing to the ground as dead weight. Immediately, it started to sink into the already blood-stained dirt.

He glanced down to see Soril standing there, one hand encrusted with ice while the other held her glaive.

Aubron didn't have more than a moment to look at her before, out of the corner of his eye, he saw another creature diving at him. "Dakar, on your right!" he called out, catching the man's attention. Aubron then shot a small jet of wind at the monster, pushing it toward the dwarf.

Dakar let out a grunt and he took a swing at the beast Aubron's wind had pushed. The club made a sick, squishing noise, and the uibixa let out a scream, black blood spraying as it tried to take flight. Before it could, flame erupted from Eton's sword and the creature fell to the ground where it lay—a wing twitching. It started to ripple and lost its shape, reverting to a black blob. Eton approached it. His flaming sword mercilessly cut through the air, slicing into the uibixa, killing it.

Just then, Aubron heard the crack of the gate collapsing under the onslaught of the living mass outside the walls and screams of the villagers-turned-fighters filled the air.

He looked to see the gate crushed under the wave of darkness spilling into the town. All around, combat had begun in earnest as many people were battling with makeshift weapons, ready to defend their homes and families.

Now that they were within the gate, Aubron could make out individual shapes of large panther-like creatures, giant spiders the size of horses, and a few that seemed to be never-ending masses of wriggling, tangled tentacles. All of them possessed striking silver pinpricks for eyes that shone like the stars.

He clutched his sword tighter and headed down the wall. As soon as he reached the bottom, he moved off to the side and found himself squaring off with one of the giant spiders.

The creature lashed out with its two front appendages. The Priest dodged and thrust out his sword, a shallow slice on its leg the reward. Quickly, Aubron realized he'd overextended and stumbled forward. He started to fall headfirst into the spider, catching his footing and righting himself at the last second.

It struck out with one of its spindly extremities—a wicked-looking claw tipping it—which pierced Aubron's leg. The limb buckled and gave out. Icy pain travelled from the wound, through his body, and he fell to the ground.

The uibixa turned to face him again but was blasted by a stream of colourful magic. It stopped and skittered away, heading to where the sorcery had originated. Aubron watched the creature move toward the edge of the battle and saw the spider focus on a flash of kaleidoscopic cloth.

The Harlequin stood with their arms outstretched, sporting massive, cloth-draped wings that shimmered and sparked yellow and blue. A spell, more powerful this time, erupted from them in a flurry of hues that matched the wings and a wail that made Aubron cover his ears in agony.

The spider-like creature dropped to the ground with a yawp as the sorcery engulfed it. Then, just as soon as the Harlequin and the magic appeared, both vanished into the night.

The spider stood up, but Aubron could see its limbs shaking. *Why didn't it die?* He wondered, confusion fogging his brain. *Where did the Harlequin go?*

The uibixa shook itself, darkness and silver roiling across its body as it started toward a closer target.

Rictor.

The Knowledge Priest was slicing with his sword at one of the panther-like uibixa even as the spider headed right for him.

"Rictor!" Aubron called, panic suffocating him as the sounds of battle drowned out his voice.

Fiery pain raced through his body as Aubron pushed himself off the ground and, in a limping run, took off toward the Priest.

Adrenaline replaced the pain, and he willed his legs to move faster. He stretched out his sword, needing to get there in time. He thought of the incense burning in Thoen's temple, the wish for protection for his village and his loved ones.

Closer, he could see the terror on Rictor's face. His peaceful, knowledge-loving friend was still learning how to wield his sword.

Ice that Aubron would recognize anywhere speared straight through the panther-uibixa and it dropped to the ground.

He glanced behind him and caught Soril's nod. She was fighting a different panther-uibixa, one hand wielding the glaive and the other shooting icicles into the creature. A bird dove for her and she broke eye contact to swing at it with her weapon.

Aubron turned back just in time to see the spider-uibixa bearing down upon Rictor. He dashed, falling into the Priest, taking them both to the ground just as it slashed through the air above them. Immediately, he leapt back up, his knees screaming and the wound in his leg pulsing in blinding flashes of pain. He turned to face the creature, determination burning through his body.

From the corner of his eye, he saw Rictor struggling to his feet, squeezing the hilt of his sword, knuckles white.

Aubron's sword hand shook, and he steeled himself with a deep breath and then lunged, letting a small amount of magic loose to make his feet lighter.

The uibixa started to move to the side in a dodge, but he caught the creature's appendage with his blade and sliced it deep. It screeched in fury as the limb knocked into his hand with enough force to make him lose his grip on his sword as black blood sprayed.

Rictor took that moment to attack, but the spider's leg struck out simultaneously and caught him in the stomach, sending him sprawling backward and tearing at the leather armour covering his chest.

Aubron looked where his weapon had fallen and lunged for it, ducking under the spider's other limbs. He rolled to the side as a claw stabbed down where his head had been seconds before. He scrambled for his sword and felt his palm slice open on its edge. Biting his tongue, he found the handle and grasped it. He swung wildly upwards and struck another leg, cutting it clean off.

While the uibixa was reeling from the blow, he crawled out from under it and stood just in time for it to lurch forward and whip a spiked tentacle at him.

Aubron jumped unsteadily to the side and then sprang forward, swinging for the uibixa's silver eyes at the front of its body.

He got it with a shallow cut right across its eyes but realized as he did that, he'd made a mistake. The creature, while irate at his latest attack, had rippled and healed the appendage he'd sliced first. He felt something strike his back, tearing into the skin.

Blinding pain tore through him and the world went white. He pitched forward and could hear the creature screeching although it was garbled, as if he was underwater. Someone else's voice called out in fear.

Aubron rolled over, feeling disoriented as his vision swam. The detachment, as if he wasn't quite there, intensified as he took in the scene in front of him.

Rictor had gotten up and stood, body swaying, between Aubron and the uibixa. His sword was lifted in a defensive position even as his arms shook with exertion.

A leg struck out, and Rictor deflected it, landing a glancing blow on the uibixa. Immediately, another claw was streaking toward the Priest.

Aubron struggled to stand and get to his friend, but the pain won out and he collapsed back to the ground.

The world seemed to slow for a moment as Aubron watched a tentacle tipped with a silver claw stab straight through Rictor's chest. Blood sprayed from the wound as the uibixa lifted him off the ground and brought him up to where its eyes glinted.

Aubron's fingers, slick with sweat and blood, scrabbled at the hilt of his sword until he grasped it and pushed himself up with a cry.

The silver in the uibixa seemed to shine brighter momentarily before it swung Rictor's body, sending him flying. He hit the ground with a thump that made Aubron flinch.

Fear and anger collided within him, filling his limbs with rage. He charged the spider, sword aiming right for its eyes. He stabbed it right between the twin pinpricks and then twisted the blade as best he could. It was like trying to cut through water.

The uibixa let out a high-pitched wail, shuddered, and collapsed.

He checked to ensure it wasn't moving before he rushed to where Rictor was lying motionless. His knees hit the sand as he dropped beside his friend.

"Rictor," he choked out.

Rictor's eyelids fluttered for a moment. "Genae," he whispered.

Aubron felt his eyes burn with tears. "Pel!" He shouted around a lump in his throat. He knew the healer would never hear him with the sounds of battle raging between them. "Pel!"

Rictor made a whimpering noise and Aubron looked down at him. He gripped his friend's hand. It was ice cold, and the colour had drained from his face. Through a new tear in his pant leg, Aubron could see the Priest's God-Mark was devoid of all hue and lustre.

"Genae," Rictor murmured again, "It's... you..." A wet cough wracked his body as blood bubbled from his mouth.

Aubron felt the moment the last of Rictor's strength fled and the life left his body. Still, he cried out for Pel, screaming in a broken voice that tore at his throat. Tears burned in his eyes, and he looked up to see more uibixa swarming through the gates and more taking to the sky.

He caught sight of Soril, wielding her glaive with both hands and sparking with less ice than he was used to seeing.

We're all going to die.

With one last squeeze of Rictor's lifeless hand, he forced himself to stand. As he was doing so, he caught sight of a small pouch with a piece of coloured cloth sticking out. *Worthless. It didn't save him.*

"Take it," a crooning instruction, forged by many voices, whispered in his ear. "Save yourself."

Heeding the Harlequin's directive, Aubron grabbed the bundle and stuffed it into his pocket.

He would end this before he lost anyone else.

He was barely able to stagger over to where the uibixa was still disappearing into the ground. Tearing off his bracer and then the sleeve of his shirt to reveal his God-Mark, he took a deep breath before plunging his hand into the black, blood-soaked sand and scooping some up.

He immediately slapped it on his God-Mark and rubbed it in. The coarse sand scraped along his skin as he ground the inky substance into his arm. He couldn't bite back his scream as the searing sting made his vision go white. Through the pain, unlike anything he'd ever felt, he managed to grab another handful and continue to rub it into the burning Mark.

Fire raced through his veins, spreading everywhere within his body. Even his bones hurt, but he didn't let himself wipe the sand away.

The shifting ground made him look up to see another uibixa shaped like a panther stalking toward him.

With strength that felt at odds with the agony consuming his body, Aubron grasped his sword that was lying in the sand and stood on shaky legs to face the uibixa.

The creature's surface glistened like silver jewels as it leapt at him with a yowl.

Aubron dodged to the side, striking out with his sword to connect with the beast's flank. The uibixa turned around and charged at him once more. He dropped to the ground with his sword pointed up to scrape along the panther's belly. It let out a roar and began to stalk around him.

He got to his feet again and felt a flicker of fire within his chest. A voice he didn't recognize spoke in a language he'd never heard. Yet, he could understand the words. **You have made a foolish mistake, mortal. Whatever you think you may get out of this, I assure you, you are dead wrong.**

He could feel the power inside him pulsing, warring to get out, wanting to tear him apart. *Is this what Rictor was talking about?* Something was inside him, breathing, coiled, ready to strike; the uibixa.

He blinked a few times to clear his head just as the panther rushed at him. This time, he stood firm and let the sword sink deep into the creature's shoulder.

Black blood poured from the wound, and he stepped back, ripping his blade away and enlarging the hole.

The monster screamed, louder this time, and Aubron fought not to drop his sword at the noise. Instead, he swung again, straight for the head and the silver, glinting eyes. It jumped away from his blade, leaving the weapon to whistle through empty air.

The pulse from the uibixa inside him grew and, in desperation, he let the feeling take over his body. Pure, unadulterated energy ripped through his limbs and bright silver magic sparked from his fingertips. He dropped his sword as the sorcery pulsated within him.

Aubron focused on forcing the magic out of his fingers, as he would with his boon, and toward the uibixa. This time, it didn't even cry out as it was filled with silver light and collapsed before him.

He heard the voice again, reverberating inside his head. **Insolent mortal. You dare to wield my own power against my kin? You will pay.**

He could feel the voice rebelling against him, trying to take control of the magic, trying to take control of him. His vision filled with white, blocking out the rest of the world.

Give yourself over to me.

He thought of Rictor's body and pain shredded his heart with grief so thick he felt like he could choke on it. "Shove it," he grunted and blinked hard. His vision cleared and he looked around at the battle raging in front of him.

Nearby, Pel was desperately trying to move an injured man away from the active fighting so he could heal him even as an uibixa bore down on them both.

Eton arrived just in time and stabbed his burning sword through the creature. It died with a howl. Before he could so much as take a breath, another spider-uibixa took the last one's place. A gangly limb thrust at him, and he moved to put himself between Pel and the monster.

The uibixa were fighting with a single-minded brutality that'd been missing when patrols would encounter one on their own.

Whatever game the uibixa have been playing, they are done. Purpose burned through Aubron as he looked at the whole village who'd rallied but were being beaten down. The struggle of the uibixa's magic rose to a fever pitch inside of him.

He knew, somewhere deep inside—as assuredly as the knowledge the sun would rise in the morning—that they wouldn't see daylight again if something didn't change soon.

Soril and Dakar were fighting off a panther-uibixa between him and Eton, so he grabbed his sword, sheathed it, and ran toward them.

She stabbed it right through the head with her glaive just as he reached Soril. The caeles took one look at him and let out a breathless shriek. "What did you do?" was all she had time to say before a flying uibixa dove at them.

Aubron tugged at the power, feeling it fight him for a moment before, like a dam bursting, it spread through him in a rush of cold. He sent a jet of pulsing silver sorcery straight at the uibixa, the light leaping from his fingertips. The creature broke apart in a burst of black blood that rained down on them.

Dakar looked up, sweat and blood running down his face. "Where in Aeppia have you been hiding that boon?" he panted.

"It's the uibixa's blood," Aubron explained. "I rubbed it on my God-Mark, and I think part of it, or at least its magic, is in me now."

Soril let out a strangled gasp. "Aubron... that is rejecting Thoen's boon, his favour. You cannot do such a thing."

"It's a little late now. Besides, I don't see a whole lot of other options to get us out of this," he snapped.

Dakar stood still for a moment, staring at him, before doing a doubletake when his eyes met Aubron's own.

"Your eyes..." he said, trailing off. "You really did it."

Before Aubron could ask what he meant, Dakar unlaced his leather gorget, scooped up some blood from the ground, and rubbed it against his God-Mark on the side of his neck.

The dwarf grunted and let out a haggard breath, brow furrowed in pain.

Three panther-uibixa were coming their way. Aubron and Soril moved simultaneously to intercept them and protect Dakar as he struggled to remain upright.

Aubron reached for the magic again, even as it kicked and bucked. It was like the power, despite wanting to be used, did not want to be used by him. He gritted his teeth and pushed harder, daring it to deny him.

Finally, it poured from his fingers and shot straight toward the enemy while Soril swung her glaive at another. The lack of preternatural ice shooting out of her hand or the weapon itself was a sign she was running out of stamina and magic.

The uibixa Aubron was fighting had just burst apart when the third exploded in a mess of black gore and silver light.

Aubron looked over his shoulder to see Dakar standing straight with a pained grin contorting his face. His once brown eyes were glowing the exact shade of silver as the uibixa.

"Wish I knew this worked before. Although, it'd be nice if the asshole I can hear would shut its trap," Dakar said. He paused for a moment and then picked up his club, hoisting it onto his shoulder.

An idea took root within Aubron and, pushing away all doubts, he called to Dakar and Soril, "We need to tell the others! We can win this! Let's go!"

"No!" Soril argued. "It is inviting your own death. Thoen and the other gods will never stand for this! The consequences—"

"They can try to stop us," he argued back. "They aren't here helping, so I don't care if they like my choice. If we're going to die here, at least we die knowing we did everything in our power to survive."

Soril was silent, so he turned around and sprinted toward Eton, who was fighting two uibixa by himself. They seemed to be trying to get to Pel, who was flitting between three people in need of healing.

The fire that had once engulfed the Priest of Hemi's sword had gone out and Aubron could tell his reaction time was slowing.

"Eton!" Aubron called. "We'll hold them off. Rub the black blood on your God-Mark!"

At Eton's incredulous look, Aubron let the power flow through him again, with greater ease this time, and shot the silver sorcery toward one of the uibixa. Shortly after, Dakar's newly coloured magic joined in, and the creature broke apart with a splatter.

Eton looked between them briefly before his gaze flicked over their heads. Aubron turned to see Soril standing there. She held some of the bloody sand in her hand.

"No one is coming to save us," she said. She reached up with the sand and pressed it to the Mark of the Maker on her forehead. A flash of brilliant silver light erupted from her, and she screamed, a booming sound that made the ground shake beneath Aubron's feet.

Ink-black wings streaked with shimmering pearlescent strands unfurled from her back. As she pulled her hand away from her forehead, Aubron could see her once golden eyes had changed to shining silver, and the blue veins that once covered her face had turned black. Her Mark was gone, burnt flesh left in its wake.

"Soril…" Aubron found himself at a loss for words.

She smiled at him although tears ran down her face. "I am with you."

"I can't believe this," Eton muttered from behind him.

Aubron turned to see Eton pulling his armour off, opening his shirt, and smearing bloody sand against his chest.

His lips pursed and his eyes squeezed shut as he let out a grunt of pain. Seconds later, he stepped up beside Aubron, alight with silver magic.

"We'd better win," was all Eton said before stepping forward to swing his sword—now glistening and sparking with power—at an uibixa approaching them.

We might just make it, Aubron thought, despair and relief warring within him.

The earth began rumbling and the airborne uibixa started flying toward the front gate. Many of the other creatures began heading in that direction as well and, without another thought, Aubron took off running in pursuit.

He reached the gate to see the uibixa converging into a massive beast taller than the village walls. Six powerful-looking legs, curved at random angles, sprouted from a body wriggling with tentacles that reached into the night. The creature's head was that of a thin dog with silver eyes and matching fangs that dripped with darkness.

You know not with what you are messing, mortal, the voice said inside his head. **We will not bow to you or that caeles. We will crush this whole town just like I did to your friend.**

"Fuck. Off." Aubron seethed before pulling at the magic. It was sluggish to respond and the uibixa fought back within him. He felt the now familiar race of power in his veins and his vision went white with pain.

He grunted and fell to his knees as silver light shot out from his body. He heard it connect with the uibixa in a shriek.

Aubron poured every bit of magic he could feel within him into the stream of energy pulsing into the creature. All his rage, despair, and hope kept him steady even as he drained the uibixa's sorcery and every bit of his own strength.

After a moment, he cracked an eye open and saw his spell had been joined by two more jets of silver and one of pure darkness, all flooding into the monster. His jaw dropped in sheer awe as the night sky lit up with magic taken from these creatures.

The uibixa itself was thrashing, tentacles flying in every direction, attempting to strike the townspeople who were rallied around Aubron, Eton, Dakar, and Soril, protecting them.

He dug deeper, imagining grabbing the power with both hands, ripping it from his body, and letting it free into the night sky. Shadows started to creep into the edge of his vision, and it was all he could do to keep his eyes open.

There was a chilling wail that Aubron felt deep within his bones, drowning out all other noise. The uibixa froze and then started to collapse. Its legs gave out, the body hitting the packed sand so hard the ground shook. The head let out another cry before it stopped moving altogether.

The wailing ceased and silence, oppressive and in stark contrast to the previous cacophony, settled over them.

Aubron's vision continued to blur, and he fell forward just as the silence broke into screams and cheers.

* * *

Aubron awoke in his bed with a splitting headache and a throb in his chest he couldn't place. It took a few moments for the battle to come back to him.

He focused but couldn't feel more than a pitiful ember of the magic within him, and the voice was silent.

"Take it easy," Soril said from beside his bed.

He tried to mutter something in response but only managed a weak groan.

He finally cracked one eye open and turned his head to where Soril was sitting, her face creased in worry. She looked much like the last time he'd seen her, minus the wings.

"How are you feeling?" she asked quietly, reaching out to run a hand through his hair, untangling it as she went.

"Pain," he groaned. "Rictor," he trailed off, his throat clogging with emotions as he thought of his friend.

Her voice was sorrowful in response. "I am sorry. He was a good man." She hesitated for a moment before continuing. "I can confirm his soul at least made it to the afterlife. Another soul came to guide him."

"Genae," he supplied. His eyes closed of their own accord. "His wife."

"The uibixa almost took him. But you killed it before it could completely consume him."

Aubron couldn't respond as his throat constricted and tears rolled down his cheeks. They sat silently for a moment, Soril gently rubbing his shoulder in comfort as a sob bubbled up.

"I am sorry," she whispered, her own voice choked with emotion.

Finally, he opened his eyes and blinked away the last of his tears. Soril's fingers left his shoulder, brushed over his arm, and clutched his hand. "What came over us?" her voice broke at the question.

"We were all going to die."

Her hand gripped him tighter. "Do you realize what you have done? What I have done?" When he didn't respond, she continued, voice rising in pitch as she spoke, "We have forsaken Thoen and encouraged others to do the same to their gods."

He saw the fear in her eyes and tried to keep his voice soft, "Is that not unlike what you did before when you spoke to the Arbiter?"

She shook her head. "I would have paid for that, I am sure. Now," she gestured to the bandage wrapped around her forehead, "I cannot even begin to consider the punishment that awaits me."

"I won't let anything happen to you."

She kissed his cheek, barely a brush of lips. "It may not be something you can prevent."

Silence fell over them, and Aubron took a moment to get his bearings and steel himself before he looked at his arm. It had been bandaged with white strips of linen, soaked in a tincture that he couldn't place, with a smell reminded him of the cold wind that blew in from the ocean.

Breaking the quiet, a voice called out, "Can I enter?"

Soril hummed in response and the linen parted to admit Pel.

His steely gaze met Aubron's own momentarily before he moved closer and started to check the bandages. "How're you feeling?"

Aubron tried to shrug and then hissed in pain as a burning sensation flared in his arm. "I'm…" he trailed off with a sigh.

Pel inclined his head in understanding; the pale tint of his skin and large bags under his eyes made him look as if he'd aged ten years in the last few weeks. "I'm sorry I couldn't save Rictor."

Hot tears he'd thought were all gone blurred Aubron's vision and rolled down his face. He tried to blink them back. "I need to address the village." He couldn't continue to think of Rictor lest he break down again.

Pel let out a scoff. "You need to rest. Let Eton handle it." Displeasure flashed across his face as he spoke.

"It's better if *he* speaks to everyone," Eton said, stepping into the room. "Speaking of people who should be resting," he shot a glare at his husband.

Pel glared right back. "Aubron needs to rest. I figured you could reassure them since you're apparently fine after removing your God-Mark," he snapped.

Eton seemed to ignore the displeasure in the other man's voice. "He's still the Keyholder; it's only right he address the village."

Aubron cut in, "If someone can help me stand, I'll go speak to them. Eton's right. It's my job, at least for now."

Pel made an annoyed sound in the back of his throat, followed by a muttering of, "Why do I even bother?"

Aubron started to swing his legs over the side of the bed and groaned as his leg jostled; the wound from the uibixa was still painful–even with what he assumed was a large amount of healing from Pel. Soril stood quickly and wrapped an arm around his back to help him stand.

He thanked her quietly and received a sad smile in return. "You mortals are always pushing yourselves so hard," she said.

"What else are we supposed to do?"

She shook her head, hair swirling around her face. "I am not sure, but it is truly awe-inspiring."

For a moment, neither of them breathed, two pairs of newly turned, silver eyes meeting. A soft brush of lips feathered across his own before pulling away.

Eton coughed. "That explains a lot," he muttered, and Pel cleared his throat to, poorly, disguise a laugh and then went to support Aubron from the other side.

As the caeles and the healer helped Aubron through the temple, he noticed a lone incense pot, coloured blue and yellow, burning at the base of the statue.

They passed through the curtain that went out to the dais and Eton spoke from behind him, "Your parents would be proud of you." A pause. "So would your uncle."

Aubron's heart clenched, and he nodded. "Thank you." *I'm not so sure about that,* he thought bitterly. The incense lit something inside him. Anger had been kindled in his stomach, fanned by the sickly-sweet smell that permeated the temple.

Once at the railing, he gripped it tight until his knuckles turned white.

When Eton and Pel seemed satisfied Aubron wouldn't fall over, they left him standing there and went down the small stairs to the street. The Priest of Hemi pulled a long rope connected to a large bell that sent a low ringing noise across the village, calling the people to gather.

It had only been about a day since the battle and torches lit up the street below him. To his left, a sconce cast flickering fire and dancing shadows across his face.

Aubron took a deep breath, trying to center himself and figure out what he was going to say. Something felt heavy in his pocket, and he reached in to pull out the bundle of colourful cloth he'd grabbed from Rictor. At Soril's sharp intake of breath, he opened it to reveal the blue candle and a match.

He wanted to ask her about it—he'd never gotten a proper chance to speak with her about the Harlequin talking to him—but already villagers were gathering in the street. He clutched the items tight as a plan formed in his mind.

Only a few minutes passed before Eton and Pel returned and nodded at Aubron to speak.

He felt lightheaded for a moment. The weight of everyone's gaze pinned him to the spot. He recalled listening to his uncle speak and how the man had sounded genuine in every address he gave.

"Friends, I stand before you today to thank you for your unwavering dedication in fighting the uibixa. Last night was a shock to us all, yet we triumphed against unmitigated evil. However, in that victory, we did lose loved ones. We must mourn and celebrate in equal measure. Every life lost is a testament to their love for us. Those we had to say goodbye to will never be forgotten or have their sacrifice taken in vain."

Aubron set the candle on the railing and struck the match. As it burned, he continued, "it is imperative I address the other event that happened last night. In an attempt to turn the tide of the battle, I, and a few others, chose to burn off our God-Marks."

At Aubron's words, surprised and fearful shouts erupted from the crowd. A few people covered their own Marks with their hands while some turned away from him entirely.

"Please," he called out, trying to quell the anxious voices in the crowd, "we did this in the heat of the moment in order to use the uibixa's magic to turn the tide. We are forever indebted to all of you who defended us while we were vulnerable."

He lit the wick with the match and then stepped on the stick to put out the fire, leaving the flame quivering. Indecision of how much information to tell them flickered within him like the blaze of the candle.

"I do not know what the gods were thinking, allowing this to happen to our village, whose entire existence is taking care of their sacred statues. But it did happen, and at the end of the day, it was our decisions and resourcefulness that allowed us to prevail."

He paused to unwrap the bandages on his arm, wincing in pain as he did so. Finished, he held his arm out so everyone could see. The skin where his God-Mark used to be, was mottled pink and streaked with black and silver. It throbbed a little in the open air, but he bit his lip and let the crowd look. Murmurs from the villagers sounded from below and the ones who had turned away started to face him again.

Something wrathful and dark began to unfurl deep within his chest.

"And so, for all we are, we have submitted to the gods. They claimed creation and demanded servitude, but we received nothing in return the moment it truly mattered." Flashes of Rictor's broken body filled his mind, and he choked back a sob.

Soril squeezed his shoulder, and he took a shuddering breath before continuing, "All our lives were on the line and yet none of them helped. Their boons? A pitiful attempt at making us feel less alone. I reject them. I reject all of it. I will no longer worship gods who care so little for me and my kin! With that in mind, I take the next true step to ending my association with them!"

Aubron grabbed the candle and held it up to ensure the crowd could see it. Then, he turned to face the temple and, being careful not to move too fast, walked toward the entrance.

"What are you doing?" Soril hissed at him.

"The right thing," he replied.

The candle flickered but didn't go out as he walked, and he felt the heat of the fire on his face.

He held it against the cloth for a few moments before the fabric caught and slow flames started to lick up the entrance.

The crowd started to call out, but Aubron couldn't make out their words over the roaring in his ears, pulsing with the anger spreading through his chest.

The fire continued to spread. First to the other pieces of cloth, then to the pole holding the curtain up. Once it caught the dry wood, it quickly overtook the temple's structure.

"Aubron," Soril cried out, her voice breaking his concentration on the fire. Aubron turned slowly to see her face twisted in fear. "He is here for me."

"Who?" Aubron asked, his voice flat even though all he wanted to do was wrap her in an embrace. He shook his head for a moment and then moved toward her. "What's going on?"

"The Arbiter is here. The consequences for disobeying." Her voice was shaking, a whisper against the crackling of the flames.

"I won't let him near you."

"You do not understand. There is no running. If I go, he may leave you and the rest of the village alone."

"I can't ask you to do that."

"You are not asking me to do anything." She moved closer to him and kissed his cheek before pulling away. "Keep fighting, and I will do the same. We will resist the gods and fight the uibixa ourselves."

The question burst out before he could stop it, "Will I see you again?"

"Mortal lifespans are short compared to ours, but I will always care for you."

"That doesn't–" Aubron started, but she'd begun walking away, leaving the dais and heading to the end of the street. The villagers ignored her; their eyes focused on the temple.

"Soril!" He called, but she didn't turn to look back at him.

The old, dry wood was catching fast, and flames started to flicker against the sky, bathing the night and village in a sickly orange glow.

Gritting his teeth, Aubron got ready to run after her when the sound of the Harlequin laughing chimed beside his ear, and he stopped dead.

"Coincidences and consequences," the voices of the Harlequin whispered from beside him on the dais. He glanced over to see no one was there.

Aubron looked back to where Soril had gone and felt his heart drop into his stomach as ice-cold fear gripped his chest. Her head turned and he caught a glimpse of her tear-streaked face, silver eyes shining as she stared at him. She mouthed something he couldn't make out as the stark shape of sharp wings spread across the street behind her.

A flash of fire, that only added to the orange glow of the night, flared, leaping from the Arbiter's outstretched hand and engulfing Soril.

Aubron heard himself screaming and, at that moment, he felt his heart fully shatter. His parents, his uncle, Rictor, and now Soril, all gone, with him left alone to deal with the blazing, incandescent anger that raged like an ocean storm inside him.

"Such an unfortunate outcome for you, and yet we are getting everything we want," dozens of voices spoke in unison, "and it cost us so very little. A few illusions, a bit of sorcery, and worthless mortal lives."

The sharp knife of betrayal stabbed through him, and the rage continued to build. Tears slipped down his cheek as the heat of the burning building warmed his back in a mockery of comfort.

Aubron strode closer to the railing—eyes unable to focus on the crowd in his grief. "Friends, I stand before you, humbly asking you to take your freedom back from the gods. You are the only person you offer yourself to. Let the temples burn, topple the statues, and we will rebuild our destiny from the ashes!"

As smoke swirled into the sky, blocking out the rising moon, he called out, "We can be free!"

Cheers and calls from the crowd rang out, muffled to his ears, as he raised his hands to the sky, feeling the silver magic start to swirl inside him once again, pulsing with wrath.

"Let the uibixa come. We are Unbound!"

L. A. Nights

Chenise Puchailo
Art by
Amy Gerein

There is a lot that could be said to describe a city at night.

From a distance it glows, a beacon to a weary traveller, or a marker for the average passerby. At times, a welcome refuge for those who are lost.

Scott thought it would be a good long while before he found himself looking upon the lights of Los Angeles again. The foggy haze they cast bled into the night sky as a stubborn benchmark in an otherwise barren topography.

He leaned up against the door panel of a mid-sixties Mercury Comet Cyclone and held his breath to contain the acrid burn of nicotine and tar. A cigarette hung between artist's fingers, casting a reedy trail of smoke in answer to the robust expanse of the city. The nicotine was a sad attempt to fix a much deeper craving, but it eased some of the tension in Scott's jaw and took the tremor out of his hands.

Like his vehicle, he felt he belonged to a different era. A stiff black leather jacket gave way to a white T-shirt, tucked neatly into the waistband of faded and worn jeans. The style appeared to be an intentional choice and not born of carelessness. He tied it together with a pair of simple black dress shoes that were of enough quality to imply class and average enough to complement instead of standing out.

His hair, in contrast to the rest of him, was unkempt. It hung in tight auburn ringlets about his head and neck in silent mockery of his overall grooming. If he had bothered to rein in the curly mop, he could have matched the car better as a proper greaser stereotype.

Smoke wreathed around his face with his next breath, cutting the image of a cartoon bull. From behind its rapidly dispersing veil, his viridescent eyes peered out towards the radiance of city lights. Silence kept him company and was only disturbed by the occasional draw of the smouldering cigarette.

Scott could confidently say that he did not startle at the scuff of a footstep off to his right. His next draw came deeper. The tempo and force of his inhale spiked, and he became heady from the rush of nicotine. It took a modicum of self-control to keep from turning his head and observing the newcomer, and only the desire to play it cool held him in check.

"Put that out." The voice was a smooth purr that sidled up next to him. As soon as it crested, Scott's tension ebbed and he was comforted by its familiarity. "Don't you know how awful that smells?"

A smirk tugged at Scott's lips. He neither changed his position nor extinguished his vice. "If you don't like it, then don't stand close to me," he suggested.

Another scuff of shoes on gravel, accompanied by a wry snort, indicated that the other man had not taken his suggestion. He came abreast of Scott to lean against the car, mirroring the redhead's nonchalance.

Scott extended his next exhale until his lungs ached from depleting themselves. When he inhaled, it was to take in the residual aroma through his nose and savour it. He would never admit his intention was to provoke the other man, and neither would he share his disappointment when his childish display went unanswered and unaddressed. "It's a nice view..." Scott offered, and only then did he turn his head to study his company. He had expected the man to be suited.

Instead, he wore a fitted black button up, tucked into equally black and immaculately pressed slacks. His shoes reflected the distant hazy lights with a polished shine. Scott was reminded of some kind of pressed-perfect serving staff or urban ninja. In the theme of lacking variance, the man's also black hair was pulled away from his narrow face to fasten tightly at the nape of his neck, showing off the wings of peppery white at his temples.

He looked out over the city. His only acknowledgment that Scott had even said anything was a non-committal *humph* which announced his intent to speak. "What are you calling yourself these days?" he asked and folded his arms across his chest. His lashes drooped so that he appeared to be dozing in their scenic environment.

For a moment, Scott thought of lying. For a brief interlude, a number of answers jumped into his mind. He could not say why he decided on the truth. Another long quiet draw gave him space to decide if he was at peace with his decision. "Scott. And you?"

"Damian," came the response, by way of introduction, as if this was their first time meeting one another.

Scott wrinkled his nose and squinted. A feeling that was not quite suspicion but was akin to incredulity leaked into his tone while he processed the answer. "What kind of name is that?"

A sharp look from Damian served as his response. A force Scott could not put into words stilled his next breath as a dying whisper in his throat. He could not explain the dread that wove in between each individual rib and cinched his chest tight.

"What kind of name is Scott?" Damian asked in kind. He did not smile. His expression remained a mask of neutrality, and yet Scott felt the atmosphere ease with the question. A physical force lifted from around his head and shoulders and let him breathe again. The redhead found himself smiling in spite of the brief catch in his chest. Damian always seemed to have that effect on him.

Having found some equitable ground, the men removed their attention from one another to bask in the luminescence of city lights. "Touché," was all Scott said in response to kick off their almost companionable silence. Scott took the time to finish his cigarette. Given long enough, he wondered if he could pretend that no time passed during his extended absence, and things could continue as they had always been.

He dropped the remnants of the filtered butt to the gravel and ground it beneath his fine shoe. From the corner of his eye, he noted that Damian had not taken the initiative to scout what he was wearing. He felt a small touch of disappointment that it did not warrant the other man's notice.

Cued by the completion of the cigarette, Damian straightened himself to continue the conversation. "We're still trying to figure out if it's a good thing that you came," he said, his tone more subdued. The bite his earlier question had carried was stifled by a cautious and husky whisper.

The shift in tone left Scott on edge. He felt his fingers itch and barely resisted the urge to stretch them out. His eyes roamed over the gradient of the city and wondered what strange things were happening in L.A.

that resulted in his summons. "That makes two of us," he said. It would have been just as easy to pretend the request to come had never reached him. That trail of thought brought up another question. "How did you find me anyway?"

Damian's smile as Scott shifted to look at him was both teasing and infuriating. He shook his head with a scolding little tut of "Ah-ah. You should know by now. I have my ways." The remark was punctuated by the sly tap of a finger against his own nose like he meant to scold the redhead for even asking.

Scott knew better than to pursue. Even if he got an answer out of Damian, the chances of it actually being true were slim at best. Instead, he reached for the pack in his coat pocket so he could flip open the lid and obtain another cigarette. He should not have been surprised by the hand that clamped down on his wrist, effectively stopping him from grabbing the new smoke. He had not even seen Damian move to apprehend him. The grip was iron. The fingers themselves were cold, as if the evening temperature had lowered a few extra degrees. Scott wisely loosened his hold on the cigarette, with the pack still held in his off hand.

"It offends me," Damian said cordially, completely belying the vice grip on Scott's wrist.

"Sensitive," Scott responded stiffly. With one of the fingers on his captured hand, he tapped the cigarette back into place. "But very well." In his free hand he adjusted his grip on the pack so that it was held to his palm via his thumb and in plain sight. With a flourish of his fingers, he tucked the pack up into his sleeve. "I wouldn't want to *offend* your poor nose."

The smile Damian graced him with left Scott feeling like a shared joke passed between them. He rolled his eyes at the dramatics and pulled his previously trapped hand back to massage his fingers over the wrist.

"You really think he's here?" Scott asked next, to pretend their altercation never happened.

Damian nodded and looked back to the city. His lips thinned into a pale line and his discomfort, tangible and impervious, spread as an infectious miasma. "It is not a matter of thinking, Scott," he put emphasis on the name. "He's not exactly hiding his presence in L.A." The bite had returned to Damian's tone, a reminder to the more serious nature of their visit.

When Scott spoke, there was a tightness in his voice that he controlled just well enough to keep a squeak from forcing its way out. "How do you know?" Absently, he reached up his sleeve again for the offending pack, Damian's warning already forgotten. He feared this was going to be a much harder conversation.

Damian kept his silence as Scott collected his next cigarette. He did sneer as the object of vice was lit, and the first few puffs of stimulating nicotine battled with the wariness Damian cast off. His next breath was an audible knife, cutting through the hiss of Scott's inhale.

Anxiety, it seemed, did have a sound and it made a pin cushion of Scott's nerves. He wondered if he truly wanted the answer.

"Flowers."

The simple response caused Scott's throat to tighten against the burn of the smoke. He lifted a hand to cover his mouth and stifle the tickle that swelled in his chest. Soft plumes of smoke escaped past the closed fist he coughed into. His voice was strained as he looked at Damian. "You think he's here for her?"

A clap on his back settled him, at the same time it almost knocked him off his feet. Scott fixed Damian with a warning look for the excessive force disguised as help to catch his breath and settled himself with a couple more hiccupping coughs for good measure.

"Know," Damian reiterated. His one-word answer managed to make those pinpricks of unease travel up Scott's arms and crawl down his back at a snail's pace. "Why else would he announce himself so blatantly?"

Scott's snort did not cover how uncomfortable the news made him. "Maybe he's just dropping by. You know, he fancied Claudia once. It's not out of the realm of possibility that he'll drop in with some nice gifts and nicer words to endear himself, and then be on his way," he added hopefully. The sinking feeling in his stomach became painfully real. He wanted to deny it, but flowers were as potent a calling card as any. *He* had always brought flowers as a greeting and a gift, and only for the woman in question.

"Sarah," Damian corrected. His eyes bore into Scott like he meant to burn the name into the other man's memory. "Her name is Sarah now."

A scoff. "Yes, yes. And you are Damian. And I am Scott. I'm betting he's picked something particularly awful to go by like Trent... or Troy," he added as an afterthought and earnestly tried to think of a more offensive name to lighten the air.

"This is serious," Damian scolded.

"Excuse me?" Scott said, his eyebrows raising. He stood from the car so he could face up to Damian. "Mister *I am the night himself*, telling *me* I need to be serious?" Another scoff. Another draw from the cigarette. "*He* must have really done something to rattle you if that's the case. Good old Catholic Incarnate coming to tell you to repent your sins or he'll..." Scott shrugged and let the sentence trail off as a mumble into his cigarette. Anything he could have said in that moment felt too grim to give voice.

The pressure of Damian's scrutiny dissipated and chased the vanishing smoke into the atmosphere. "This isn't a conversation we should be having here," he said, his tone more restrained. He gave a roll of his shoulders, both to square his posture and force it to relax. Whether the gesture was deliberate or subconscious, Scott could only guess. His bet was on the former in an attempt to offer both of them a semblance of reassurance as Damian stepped away from the vehicle.

It was as good a cue as any. Scott half turned to nod at the pristine beast and grasp the door handle. "Should we head over for a drink or two at the usual place?" he queried, hoping for a glimmer of better humour between them. His other hand tossed the unfinished end of his cigarette down to squash it out under foot. "Then we can talk it out with everyone present."

Damian designated his refusal by a single shake of his head. "You won't be meeting with anyone else. At least not yet." He reached into his pocket to produce a hotel key card envelope and held it up, secured between two fingers for display. Under Scott's observance, he turned the envelope over to reveal the name of some less than average dive downtown. Damian chose to ignore the dissatisfied scrunch of Scott's face upon accepting the envelope.

Scott flipped the package over and back again to ensure he saw the hotel details correctly, including the address that sprawled in Damian's notoriously perfect and flowing handwriting. "Hotel Silver Lake?" he asked aloud and fixed Damian with a flat look. "That's the plan? You're just going to hide me away?"

"For now, that may be best," Damian confirmed. "The longer you are in our back pocket, the more of an advantage we'll hold when we have need of you. Or maybe we'll just use you as bait."

The information was unsatisfying. Scott's expression remained unchanged.

"Consider it a detox holiday," Damian instructed and stepped around Scott to open the door the rest of the way and hold it open. Scott tried to ignore the barb and took the invitation to get into the car. The insult sunk in a little too deep.

"Hah. Hah." The expression of his satirical mirth was a sharp staccato and only served to draw a mocking but pleasant smile across Damian's face.

"I mean it, Scott. You stay clean while you're here, or you're going to know exactly what the inside of your anal cavity looks like, after I finish shoving your head up your own ass," Damian warned.

Scott took a momentary pause and looked up at Damian, his expression caught somewhere between suspicion and mirth. "You wouldn't actually," he decided, but his conviction did not stop him from adjusting the cuffs of his leather coat to keep his sleeves pulled down.

"I can, and I would," Damian responded and leaned against the open door to hold it in position. "So, unless you want to know what life is like as a self-contained pretzel, I suggest you accept the hospitality that's been extended and be on your best behaviour."

"That's gross, Damian," Scott rebutted in an attempt to disarm the threat. "And, frankly, an abuse of your talent and ability."

"I abuse what I wish, when I wish." The statement was punctuated by the abrupt closing of the car door. Scott leaned forward so he could hastily crank the window down with the intent to continue their bickering.

"So, what happens when you have need of me?" he queried, leaning his arm on the open sill of the car's door frame so he could look imploringly up at the other man.

Damian stuffed his hands in the pockets of his slacks and offered a noncommittal shrug. "Then we come get you, or we call you on your cell. Really, Scott, I thought by now you'd have a semblance of a working brain."

The eye roll Scott treated Damian with would have been better suited to a teenager. Even given Scott's youthful appearance, the gesture made him feel childish. He hoped Damian picked up on his lightheartedness. "Whatever," he said to double down on the immaturity. "Do you want a ride downtown at least?"

"No," Damian huffed. "It would be best not to associate with one another."

Scott mused and withdrew his arm back into the car so he could give the stick shift a rattle and set his foot on the clutch. "How are you getting back then?"

Damian's smile was positively wolfish. The glint in the man's eyes was more coy than informative as he turned away. "I don't think I have to remind you, Scott. Try to stay out of trouble while you're here, would you?"

As Damian turned his back on Scott in the vehicle, Scott likewise turned the key so the car could rumble into life with its rich, assaulting vibrato. When Scott looked up from his steering wheel to where Damian had been standing the man was already absent.

He was as alone as he was at the start of his evening.

* * *

It was another two hours before Scott meandered to the hotel. He had given Damian his personal information in an earlier correspondence so he could be checked in ahead of time. Scott took the liberty to skip the front desk and ventured straight to his ground floor room upon arrival. He adhered to the request to stay clean, mostly, in that he avoided purchasing anything that was not legal.

He used the credit card he found nestled in the key card envelope to purchase a fine bottle of Macallan whiskey and some takeout from the most hole in the wall place he could find. It had been a sight for him to show up with bouncing red curls and pale freckled skin in a place where the menu had not a word of English. With fluent greetings and compliments, he ordered a braised pork rice dish, complemented by an order of Taiwanese sausages. The smell of it left his mouth watering the entire drive to the hotel.

He set up the television to the local news and ate straight from the take-out container with the pair of provided wooden chopsticks. The single queen bed in the room had become a nest of pillows and blankets to ensure his complete comfort.

Within arms-reach, on the nightstand, was his precious bottle of whiskey, half empty and enjoyed as if it were water. If he was told to stay put for goodness knows how long in some mid-range hotel room—and what an insult it was for it to be mid-range—then he was going to enjoy being trash to the fullest.

Truly, the hotel was a step up. Scott had been in the slums of Manshiyat Naser, in Cairo, when he received his summons. It was a peculiar individual that approached him; a peculiar person who had drug his delirious and stupefied self through those slums to a hostel that, to this day, Scott still could not remember the name of. They stayed with him through a brief detox period and once he was coherent enough, shoved a phone to his ear and told him it was important. Scott still recalled very little of this person and knew even less about them. He assumed it was someone Damian or Claudia, Sarah as she was being called now, had at their disposal.

You should come, said the voice over the phone. *We think he is here.*

The news sobered him in a way the detox could not. Darkness overwhelmed and swarmed him at the thought of what that missive implied. He initially said no, and that they were on their own. His gutter life was simple and kept him content, but Sarah had asked him kindly. Out of emotions that were more guilt and duty than they were affection, Scott packed up and accepted the small allowance that would get him cleaned up and to North America. Loyal and stupid to the end, he answered the call.

Though it would have been easiest to land in California, he chose Houston and consoled himself with a couple of cabarets here and western bars there. Any excuse was a reason to delay. He procured the funds to purchase the Comet through mostly legitimate means and, after a few more days of indecision, decided to make the long Northwesterly drive.

So much as sharing a continent with *him* was an offence of the highest order.

In all of Scott's history with Damian, Sarah, and the many in-betweens, he had thankfully been able to avoid further altercations with the particular *him* in question. The last time they encountered one another lived in Scott's memories and prowled his nightmares with more frequency than Scott cared to admit. Everyone avoided *his* name as though it would summon him, even though they were fairly certain it was not an ability *he* possessed. Scott learned well in his younger years, and more than once throughout his older ones, that there seemed to be very little that Catholic Incarnate was not capable of.

He called himself Triton. It was the name Scott always knew him by, but whether or not it was his true title remained in debate. Like a story book villain, Triton left them all with the scars of his presence. He was the force that drew them all together as victims of his ethics and beliefs. Their greatest crimes had always been that they were not what the man hoped or wanted them to be.

Scott could have left Sarah to address the matter on her own and pretend their shared friendship and experience was a matter of another life. With Damian at her back, he was sure his own usefulness would be minimal. He was no better than an extra target between Triton and his goal, and perhaps that was the real motive for his presence in America. True, Triton terrified him. He dreaded the thought of Triton hurting someone else even more.

All of that was what led him here, so he could eat cheap take out and attempt to drink his weight in overpriced whiskey. All this just to prepare for an encounter that, at this point, he felt was inevitable. He had never been any kind of match for Triton in the past, and it had always been wiser to run. He was sure as soon as Triton caught his scent in L.A. the man would be on him like a hound.

Scott could not say with certainty that he would survive his little Western foray. The smile that touched his features at the thought was bittersweet. He wondered why he ever entertained his dismal running and hiding. At least, that's what he told himself it was. He could not fool himself into believing it. Not when the very thing he spent years trying to avoid was the reason he had come traipsing back to Los Angeles at Sarah's beck and call. The knowledge left his stomach hollow in a way that no amount of rice or alcohol could fill, and yet he ate to ease the queasiness of the unknown and lubricated it with whiskey.

As meagre as it was, Scott was mildly grateful that Damian and Sarah at least provided for him. He had suspicions of who the anonymous credit card belonged to, and enjoyed thinking about the reprimand he was likely in line for due to frivolous spending. As long as he did not withdraw money to cater to the depravity of his other habits, a scolding was all he would suffer for the indulgences he did enjoy.

The television interrupted his thoughts with some sort of feel-good community story about a senior's complex receiving an anonymous donation to build a community garden area, but that was the extent of what he caught. His head was spinning, and the whiskey was an excellent dance partner for his woes. A shower would help clear his thoughts and refresh him from the long drive. He set the food containers aside and pushed off from the bed, rubbing his hand over his face to try and clear his alcohol infested sight.

He stumbled once or twice on the way to the bathroom. Every few steps, he lost another piece of clothing and left them unceremoniously strewn as a trail behind him. At the door of the bathroom, he patted himself down in search of his bottle and took longer than it should have to recall that it still sat on the nightstand next to the queen size bed. Scott debated with himself where he stood, and it was truly a riveting discussion, on whether crossing the room was worth his implied prize.

The seconds of indecision passed only because the promise of another drink lingered after he cleaned himself up. With resolve, he set a hand on the door frame of the washroom and guided himself inside. He hopped once or twice as he fought with his last sock and tossed it aside to stand only in a pair of boxer briefs.

He fumbled around the bathroom inefficiently, drawing the curtain of the shower bath closed and muddling with the faucet dial until a steady stream of water began to flow. The temperature was set to what he assumed would be comfortable, and he turned away so he could brace his hands on the sink and try to steady himself after so much exertion. The television warbled on in the distance.

Motionless, he listened to the steady stream from the showerhead and felt the temperature gradually warm in the bathroom despite the open door. He looked up to watch condensation fog the mirror, and through it he could see his face. Caught somewhere between boyhood and maturity, his cheekbones had only started to sculpt from a childish roundness. It seemed no matter how hard he fell into addiction, the mask of youth clung to him to take the cutting edge of undernourishment and struggle from his appearance.

A few seconds longer and he began to grow uncomfortable with the self-scrutiny. He pushed the observations aside and likewise thrust himself away from the sink.

Scott was half a step away from the hotel room mirror when he first felt it. The initial drop in temperature wafted as a soft draft through the thickening steam. The barest of shivers coursed through his body and directed his attention to the thickening condensation in the air. Steam became mist, became vapour. In any other circumstance, in any other city, with any other context, he might have ignored it.

Today, the draft sent a chill up his back and birthed a cold sweat that had little to do with the encroaching chill. He forced his breathing level and swivelled his head to take a quick survey of the bathroom. He looked from the edge of the shower, back around to the mirror. The open doorway remained in his peripheral vision.

At the corner of the mirror, a spider web of frost began to form, travelling up from the bottom edges to creep upwards. Frozen branches continued to spread and thicken to choke out his foggy reflection. As frost climbed the reflective pane, terror formed hardened knots in Scott's stomach. There was not enough whiskey in the world for what he knew would come next.

The first pounding knock on the door of the hotel room made him jump. The lump that developed in his throat was the only thing that stopped the cry that wanted to leap out of him. His skin crawled and his hair stood on end, raising goose pimples all along his body. He had been found, and a bathroom of running water was the last place he wanted to be.

Another resounding knock rattled him into motion. He felt his mouth run dry and launched himself the rest of the way across the bathroom, tangling with the curtain as he reached desperately to turn the water off. He did not know why he thought it would do him any good. The room was filled with moisture. The pipes in the walls were full of water. The human body was primarily water, yet he still knew a moment's satisfaction when his shaking hands turned off the tap and the shower gave a dying squeal as the flow ceased.

The pounding on the door stopped, but his relief was short-lived as a deafening bang shocked a scream out of him. Out of the corner of Scott's eye, he saw the blur of the room's door fly off its hinges and heard it obliterate the desk and entertainment section. The ruckus continued in a chaos of thuds and crashes and finally ended when the news went silent.

Scott's chest heaved. He groped at the shower curtain both to draw him back up to his proper height and to keep himself from staggering. The curtain frosted in his grip, leaving steaming handprints where he clutched it, in his mad scramble to get aloft. The effort put too much weight on the bar. His only warning was a sharp snap before the support gave out. With a clatter of the curtain rod, as it rapped him on the head, Scott lost his balance and ungraciously deposited himself into the tub.

His tailbone, and a spot on his thigh, ached from the impact. As quickly as he settled into his fall, he found stillness and grasped the curtain to him as though he could hide behind it.

He could hear doors opening and raised voices calling out in concern and confusion from the hallway. He thought of shouting for them to go back to their rooms, that this was no place for them. He found his tongue held tight, paralyzed to the roof of his mouth. His eyes began to sting from the effort it took not to blink. Terror replaced the bliss of alcohol, and he could not tell if that was the source of his light headedness or if that was because he had not drawn breath.

The metronome thud of booted feet matched the tempo of his thundering pulse. The first step in the doorway of the bathroom announced the entrance of ankle high leather boots. The next was a deliberately shortened stride, more for formality and positioning, as the intruder squared up to look in the room. The pointed stare from cold, blue eyes homed in on Scott and held him motionless. He hoped the wetness he could feel staining his boxers was from the water that had yet to drain from the tub.

Soft brown boots gave way to a dark blue, perfectly pleated, pair of dress pants. The look was completed with an off-grey dress shirt, buttoned with the collar slightly undone, and the sleeves rolled up. The man himself carried a sport coat slung over one shoulder. Scott might have laughed at the pretentiousness of it all, if he did not feel his stomach clench at the tilt of a crisply shaved jaw. Scott got the impression that he was being looked at with the same distaste reserved for the vilest of cockroaches.

After all these years, his face was unchanged and hard. His expression was intense, and his eyes were still vacant. The corners of those eyes creased in a display of mirth, but there was a noted lack of warmth in the rest of his countenance. All of this was framed by dirty blonde hair, slicked back with volume, and buzzed short sides.

Every inch of him was perfectly manicured and was a blatant contrast to the rumpled T-shirt and dark denim jeans Scott left discarded on the floor. It was not hard to embrace the feeling of feebleness that resin stare inflicted, made colder by the ice and frost that now encompassed the bathroom. They remained in that tableau, watching each other. One took in the other's measure, while the other was immobile—a hare beholden by a wolf.

Triton.

"Proteus," the man began to speak. He adjusted his stance so that his unencumbered hand could reach out to the prone redhead, as though he meant to lift Scott out of his stupor by the gesture alone.

The shock of the word, of the name, struck Scott and spurred him into movement. He threw out a hand to mirror the man's offered one, but no hospitality came from the gesture. Heat spread from Scott's fingertips, distorting the air immediately in front of him.

It was all the visible indication Triton needed. At the last second, he crossed his arms protectively before his face and chest to accept the impact of the sudden change in temperature and pressure. It struck squarely, staggering Triton with enough force that his back collided with the wall behind him. His legs buckled, forcing him to lean heavier into the drywall, but he was not without retaliation.

The sound of creaking metal was all too close to Scott. A line of water hit him in the face, most of which he swallowed in the shock of the moment. The fixtures burst throughout the bathroom, from the faucet of the sink and most evidently to Scott, the shower bath. A great font rose from the porcelain toilet, further drenching the entire room. The water was frigid and left Scott shivering within seconds.

His scramble out of the bathtub was hindered by the soaked curtain. He had to roll out of the tub before he could scramble to his feet and dash for the now vacant doorway. Scott led the charge with his shoulder and slammed into Triton, flattening him back into the wall with enough force to bust the flimsy drywall.

"Really, man?" he cried out in the confusion of trying to separate himself from the tangle before Triton could get hands on him. "The fucking toilet, too?"

He shoved off in the few confusing seconds it took for Triton to recover. The once immaculate sport coat Triton hauled over his shoulder was thrown to the floor. The perfection of the blonde's expressionless mask was gone, and his face erupted into a mix of shock and fury.

Scott made it a step before one of Triton's booted feet tangled in his ankles, turning his lunge for freedom into a clumsy fumble and a hard fall. He threw his hands out just in time to keep himself from losing teeth on the edge of the door that demolished the entertainment area, and once on all fours he launched himself over the door, desk, and ruined television. His target was the pair of discarded jeans left carelessly on the floor. He scooped them up in one hand and continued his momentum to get back up on his feet so he could both turn and create distance from his attacker.

Thrusting his hand into the pants pocket, Scott dug for the phone he had been so careless with. The lifeline given to him back in Cairo also happened to be his only link to Damian. He fished the phone free and looked up to see Triton straightening out the collar of his shirt, a sight that left him regretting every decision he had made that brought him to this hotel room.

"After all these years," Triton remarked, each step was deliberate as he navigated the mess between them. He took a moment to brush his fingers over a reddened cheek to inspect Scott's handiwork. His face was scalded and started to puff in some spots as blisters began to form. "You don't even have a spark. You're still as useless as the day I found you."

Scott tried not to let the words find purchase. His hands, made clumsy by his panic and inebriation, fumbled to unlock the device. It was a fool's hope to believe he would actually use it in time. He could have run but suspected that he would not get far. He dreaded the thought of cutting Triton loose amid civilians.

Triton closed in faster than Scott expected. One hand knocked the phone clear out of Scott's grip. The second hand caught him in a solid blow to his jaw. He staggered back, tripping over his feet and landing heavily in one of the cushioned hotel chairs that thumped into the far wall under the assault of his weight.

"How do you expect to defend yourself," the monologue continued, "when you can't even handle the gifts you were born with?" Triton straightened out his sleeves, made crooked and charred in the heat wave and tackle. The manner in which he did so implied he blamed Scott for delaying the process of tidying himself back up. His hair was out of place, but he did not seem as concerned by it as he stood before the chair in a wide stance.

Triton's teal gaze flicked once to the discarded phone, resting face down on the floor, at the foot of the bed. A sneer started to tug at one end of his mouth. "Don't call them into this," he scolded. "This has nothing to do with them."

Scott brought a hand up to feel his jaw, where an immediate ache had begun. He tried to even the rate of his breathing so he could respond to his attacker. In his memory, Triton had always been a talker. "Triton..." he grunted out, voice hoarser than he expected. "Or are you going by something else nowadays?"

Past the man, and in the hallway, Scott could see people gathering and milling about. They handled the identification of the problem room with all the efficiency of a herd of livestock. Water continued to soak into the carpeted entryway where the rush of its escape echoed from the bathroom. The rest of the room and surrounding area seemed unaffected by the plumbing malfunction.

Triton smiled amicably, in a way that did not reach his eyes, and was stalled by Scott's willingness to talk. "Triton suits me just fine between the two of us, brother," he informed. Scott forced a smile as he ran his tongue over the inside of his cheek to find where the taste of copper was coming from.

The commotion was building in the hallway. Scott thought he heard someone on the phone with 9-1-1, or perhaps he was being hopeful, and it was actually the hotel front desk. It was enough of an indicator that they would not have this time to themselves for long; a fact Scott punctuated as he asked, "You sure know how to make an entrance, don't you?"

Triton grunted in answer and relaxed his stance enough to hold out a hand once again, palm open, to help Scott up. "There was a time you would have greeted me with more warmth," he pointed out, his voice cold.

Scott felt his skin crawl at the gesture and chose instead to stand on his own. He was only a little surprised that his brother shifted back to allow him, but their proximity was still too close and too uncomfortable. The smile Scott maintained was forced and left his stomach doing backflips.

"I fear now, if I am to have any conversation with you, I must force it." The tone was accusatory. Scott thought he could feel the temperature in the room lower again. He had half a mind to see if frost was building on the windows, but he dared not look away from the cause.

"We have always been brothers," Triton continued. "We used to be friends once." He remained close enough to Scott, that the redhead was kept pinned between him and the chair.

"Enemies, too," Scott recalled, without really thinking until after the words had left his mouth. He stiffened and glanced back to see how Triton had taken the slight and saw that his expression remained unchanged. It was neither a relief nor an indication of Triton's mood.

"You wore a different name back then, Proteus," he said. Scott did his best not to flinch from the ancient name spoken aloud. That existence, that life, felt like a completely other entity at this point. He knew Triton's intent was to goad him.

Scott's voice was more subdued, fearing offence as he said, "It was a different time."

Triton's quiet *humph* left ambiguity as an uncomfortable current between them. Scott swallowed to try and work enough moisture back into his mouth to speak again. He was treading the knife edge of potentially offending his brother and wanted to do his best to not be cut.

"Why are you here, Triton?" he asked, turning his shoulder to try and slip past. If he could not flee his brother then he might as well try to find out something useful. Triton held his ground which left Scott to stand awkwardly in place, unable to move without physically shoving past.

There was little interest in answering Scott's question. It seemed Triton had his own intentions as he reached out and grasped Scott's bare arm in a bruising grip. When Scott tried to resist, the withering look he received stilled the fight in him. It was a look he knew well. It catapulted him into that other life, where Proteus would have acquiesced to any command, spoken or implied. He stood unmoving for the inspection. Triton's authority was once again absolute.

Scott swore he could feel Triton's gaze on his forearm and inner elbow. The distaste from the blonde bled into vapid disgust and threatened to smother Scott. Triton twisted and manoeuvred the arm to allow for the most thorough assessment. "I see things haven't changed," he said stiffly.

Scott responded with a placating, but uneasy, smile. His face began to hurt from the strain of maintaining it.

The map of scars on Scott's arms were the pathways to Triton's ire. Fading bruises marked the spots of old injection sites. Parts of his arm had become so toughened and marred, from the careless application of a syringe, that he was sure the scars would never go away. Displeasure radiated from his brother, and when Triton's gaze rose to meet his own, a queasiness born of terror made Scott's vision blur. Perspiration lined his forehead, and he wondered if Triton was going to kill him then and there. Who in the world could possibly stop him?

"It's a pity," Triton began, jolting Scott from a fear born spiral. He paused as though looking for engagement from the captive sibling and, when none came, he decided to start anew.

"It's a pity that creatures like you and I were born into such feebleminded bodies." He spat the words as if they carried physical weight. Scott tried not to flinch and looked away as they descended on him. When Triton's fingers dug into his forearm, demanding his attention back, he looked up and did his best not to wither under the baleful stare that met him.

"You didn't answer my question," Scott deflected half-heartedly. He knew better than to look away again.

"I could say the same," Triton countered, releasing Scott's arm. The gesture was akin to a discard of something offensive to him. Scott drew his limb back to himself, wrapping his fingers around old scars as if to hide them and tried to bring back his wan smile.

"I asked first," Scott ventured. His tone accompanied his strained expression in an attempt at lightheartedness. It did not have the effect Scott hoped for but had the one he expected as Triton's lips thinned into something sour.

Triton crossed his arms over his chest to look down on him. The height difference was sparse, but Scott certainly felt it. The glassy-eyed stare did little to reassure or warm Scott. "I'm finishing some business I should have done years ago," Triton said sagely. There was a power and self-righteousness in his voice that caused Scott's scalp to prickle.

"Oh, yeah?" Scott managed with feigned curiosity. He just had to keep Triton talking. "Business with Claudia?" Damian implied the man had already been to see her, after all. Scott was not sure if Triton knew the name she went by now but decided it was not his place to betray her.

"Business with all of you," Triton explained. If words could crackle with energy, Scott was expecting some strike to come from it. He knew some reprieve as Triton turned away to take a step back from Scott and look towards the busted doorway. In the length of their conversation, hotel staff had come to join the gathering spectators. They could both hear the exclamations of confusion and dismay at the worsening flood, but, as of yet, nobody thought to enter.

It was not the break in their conversation that stopped Triton. A call from the doorway did. A man in the hotel's uniform addressed them, though Scott could not make out what he said, and Triton appeared to have little ear for it. He did register the cell phones that were out, some recording, others on calls. A shout came from another hotel employee who held a radio near his mouth.

He thought, again, of calling for help. He clamped down on the urge before it could fully surface, and the words "Get out! Run!" passed over his lips instead.

This was between Triton and him, and the former demonstrated as much by lifting a hand towards the doorway, startling the hotel staff into taking a step back. The temperature in the room dropped rapidly. Scott could see the newly formed vapours of his breath drift past Triton's shoulder to follow the flow of his outstretched hand. Gasps and exclamations erupted from the hallway as ice began to form at the threshold of the entryway. It was only a matter of seconds before the gap that would have led to some kind of safety was closed off. Seconds was too short a time for anyone to act or prevent the marvel they witnessed.

The sounds of the hallway became muffled behind the sheet of ice. Triton's back was to Scott and his voice was the only thing Scott could focus on. "It just so happened to be my luck that you'd already come to Los Angeles."

"What business is this?" The words were as tentative as the shift of weight he took in preparation to move. His eyes locked on the phone, for just a second, before returning to his brother at such an angle that the device remained in his periphery.

Satisfied with his work to isolate them, Triton turned back to Scott. The renewed distance between them did nothing to provide a reprieve from Triton's presence. Scott kept his eyes fixed on the man, knowing reprimand could come if he looked away for even an instant. It was vaguely reminiscent of a time when Triton was once brother and tutor.

A friendly smile, too wide at its edges, split Triton's face as he squared up to Scott. The expression could have been sincere if Scott did not know better, so the impersonation of a good nature set him even further on edge.

"You have always been troubled. Between your addiction and whatever other depravity you've thrown yourself into..." He listed off the offence like a hangman tying his knots. His voice was low, so much so that Scott had to struggle to hear him. "I think it's time to put an end to that."

Scott had to blink a few times to register the words spoken to him. His mouth opened, and his thoughts jumbled in a short circuit. Even as he tried to make sense of what Triton told him, he was dumbstruck. "An end to what?"

The smile on Triton's mouth twisted to something truly vicious, and his eyes brightened with intent. He moved in a sudden burst of motion that startled Scott in its abruptness. Triton's hands went for his throat, but when the redhead dropped to his knees to evade the offending grip, there was nothing for Triton to latch onto.

A couple fingers hooked into a small chunk of Scott's hair, which ripped free in his drop. Scott hissed but forced himself to keep moving. His eyes locked on the phone and he sprang for where it lay beside the bed. He did not know what he would do with it once he got it, but having it felt like a good idea.

He avoided Triton's clawing hand, but he had not escaped the swift toe kick that bludgeoned his ribs and blasted the air out of him. He landed just out of reach from the phone and curled around his midsection to frantically suck in a breath past his protesting ribs.

"What about Claudia?" He coughed, as if talking could stop his brother now. His curled body allowed him a view of Triton adjusting his stance to stand over him. From the new vantage point, Triton reached a hand down to grasp a handful of Scott's curls. It was a grip he never obtained. Flipping onto his back, Scott gave a roar that was equal parts panic and desperation. He drew his knees to his chest and kangaroo-kicked up at Triton.

His brother tried to block, but the force of the kick unbalanced him. He staggered back and into the chair that previously trapped Scott.

"What happens to Claudia is none of your business," Triton snarled. He sprang to his feet as quickly as he had stumbled. Scott continued to scramble.

Scott rolled onto his stomach and propped a foot underneath him in order to lunge the last bit of distance for the phone. He was just about to leap when a blinding flash of pain lanced up his back and spasmed his fingers. He cried out, and the phone mocked him, remaining just out of reach.

The heel of Triton's boot stomped down a second time, a little higher up on Scott's back to prolong the momentary paralysis of the first and keep Scott prone on the floor. "You should be more worried about yourself," Triton said. Scott struggled to bring his arms underneath him to push himself up, but the strain of Triton's weighted heel digging into his back brought tears to his eyes. He mewled a pitiful sound in response.

He was not given long to wallow. Triton tangled his fingers in a handful of hair. The force with which Triton hauled Scott's head back cut off the cry that would have emerged. Scott found himself gasping around the roaring ache that lanced up his back.

A knee settled beside him as Triton came to crouch over him and wrap an arm around his throat. The grip on Scott's hair was released only so he could further cinch the choke hold in place. Where Scott's breathing was already stunted for the agony it brought to his back and ribs, it was now completely cut off. Scott was oblivious that their position changed until he was lying on his back with Triton below him, and a hooked leg restrained his own.

Desperate, Scott brought a hand up to rake his fingers over Triton's forearm, trying to gain purchase so that he could dislodge the crushing grip. He met the resistance of flexed tendons and muscles. Tears stung in his eyes, and, when he could not claw his way free, he vainly balled a fist and struck the offending arm instead.

Terror welled in him, starting as a hot bubbling in his chest. The warmth overrode any chill that lingered. He barely heard the words,

"Give in. Go quietly," whispered in his ear as the heat built to a blaring roar in his skull. His vision started to blur, though he could not tell if it was from hysteria or lack of air.

Scott had felt this warmth before. The building of pressure, the herald of his birthright. He knew that his skin began to feel hot to the touch. It was once described to him as resting a hand upon sun baked metal. Unlike in the bathroom, he could feel the atmosphere around him this time, the carbon, the oxygen, the combustible energy. Triton said he could not make a spark, but Scott knew he would make a flame.

He focused less on his struggle to breathe and instead threw himself into the blindness of the heat surging in him. His organs felt like they were blistering. His head continued to spin, and the energy continued to build and gather. He was a container under pressure. He was a charge about to burst. Triton must have felt the shift and the urgency in the air. His grip adjusted and tightened. Scott's lungs filled with a different kind of burning. He wondered if he would draw breath again.

As the pressure reached its peak, Scott dug his fingers back into Triton's arm. He opened his mouth for a breathless, wordless, soundless scream. He felt the rush of heat dive out of his body, to be eaten by his surroundings. He opened his eyes, expecting the orange and yellow of angry flames to lick at the corners of his vision and… there was nothing.

There was no expected conflagration. No grand eruptions. Scott heard Triton's growl in his ear as though the other man was in pain, but the choke hold remained intact. Scott was losing focus, his access to air still denied.

"Pathetic, brother," Triton hissed. There was tightness in his voice, an acknowledgment of hurt, but his grip held strong. The scalding of his own face made Scott very aware of the tears that were cutting tracks down his skin.

Sirens howled in the distance.

He wanted to scream with them.

He wanted to breathe.

"You could have been something," Triton's guilt trip continued. "Look how far you've fallen."

Scott had no defence with which to block the words out. They landed on him, leaving scorches as falling cinders do. They burned into the window of his resolve and invited darkness to creep at the edges of his vision. The sweet coals of consciousness were slowly being doused by the resounding chill that replaced the burn. Triton was right. He should give in.

This was not the first time that the heat, the fire, Scott's birthright, the domain he was supposed to find mastery in, had failed him. The effort to combat the seeds of self-doubt Triton had long since planted in him was astronomical and far above his ability. He could not resist the rapidly approaching void that promised to swallow him.

"You're done, Proteus."

The words both stung and assured him. An aching and empty chill took the place of the warmth that failed him. It seeped into his bones, like a creeping spill, oozing to claim and stain every inch of him so he would stop fighting. His body began to sag. His eyes fluttered, the weight of their lids unbearable, losing the struggle to stay open.

The fire of life became a dying ember. It could not hold oblivion at bay. It barely stayed the encroaching blackness. Smoke threatened at its edges, waiting to signify an end.

All was gone.

A spark—small and persistent flared once in the dark. The dying pieces of his soul stirred just a little, as a gentle breath goads a dying flame into one last hot angry burst of defiance. It was comforting as Scott sunk beyond pain to feel his consciousness fade deeper.

It came again, another spark flashing in the depths of him, begging him to hold on in a world his vision had abandoned. What was left of his mind danced and basked in it as shadow puppets on a wall. The ember of the remains of him pulsed in mimicry of a heartbeat.

The third spark held a voice, a soft purr. Scott thought he was imagining things. He could not grasp what it said. It lingered as the softest cry, just out of reach from the sanctuary of fleeting thoughts. The voice was gentle, but clear, probing softly into the depths of his remaining soul to cup and envelope him. It lifted the dying coals of him to bring them into better light. The voice enveloped him, repeating the same words over and over until they became a cacophony of whispered sounds.

Where before he had resisted his strangulation, he now resisted this warmth. He was so close. Better to just die.

not yet.

Though whispered, the voice struck him as a hammer on an anvil. The words branded him, clashing with the leftover coal and forcing it beyond its means into a heat once abandoned. The air of a bellows rushed into him, flooding him, fighting back the cold with a warmth that was blazing and all encompassing.

It hurt. It was an agony he had never experienced before. A fever that could end worlds raged through him.

Scott did not know where he found the breath to cry out. The sound that came from him was primal and suffering. Heat continued to fill him. It poured off him in a roiling haze, filling the room, and, when he thought he was at his brim, it just kept *coming*.

He was distantly aware of another scream that joined his own. When he opened his eyes, he found he was still in the hotel room, but the room itself was a hellscape.

Blue flame had taken over the entirety of his surroundings, blackening all of it as the firestorm not so much spread as it engulfed. Scott was dimly aware that the sprinklers had burst at the rapid flare, for what good they did. The heat ate the moisture before it could even come free and stunted any reprieve. Through it all, he was warm, but he could not feel the fire. It had never been blue before.

Scott slowly rolled onto his side and pushed himself up to his hands and knees. He looked down at himself, his skin raw but otherwise untouched by the fire. He looked around for Triton in the raging conflagration and saw only the crumbling furniture instead.

He was alone. Triton was gone.

As soon as the thought hit him, as quickly as consciousness had been thrust on him, the fire snuffed out. It was a marvel, and frightening, as a world filtered in blue flames became normal in the time it took Scott to blink. He might have admired the phenomenon had he not been so aware that it was not his doing. He was never given the time to process it.

The absence of flames also meant the sudden absence of heat. The clarity he had maintained as he scanned the room, quickly dispersed, snuffed out like a candle. His questions of how the fire did not touch him were lost to the vertigo and confusion that crashed through him and caused him to waver.

Lacking the strength in arms and legs, Scott crumpled to the floor. The movement stirred ashes into a whirlwind of disruption around him which was quelled by the steady spray of water from the sprinklers. His entire body plunged into shock. He felt as though he had been thrown into snow. He tried to wrap his shaking hands around himself to conserve warmth as his body trembled like a leaf.

That was when he began to feel again. Every nerve in his body screamed at him. Each breath felt as if he was breathing through a layer of cloth. His throat ached and sent him into a fit of spluttering coughs he was too weak to commit to.

He was not aware that the ice wall Triton erected came down nor was he alert enough to register the stunned faces of the people who entered. They found him whole, miraculously alive, and in his boxers amidst the pasty ashes and unidentifiable charred lumps that were once furniture.

He did not have the strength to do much else beyond lay on the floor and shiver. He was submerged back into delirium by the time he felt hands on him. There was now talking, and so much of it. Scott wanted to beg for silence and some kind of peace, but people kept filtering into the room that should have been his tomb.

Mired in confusion, he was only partly aware that he was coaxed to his feet. Something, perhaps a blanket, had been thrown over his shoulders which he clutched at gratefully. His fingers were desperate claws, craving the heat he had been sucked dry of even as the provided material itched and irritated his skin.

There was shouting now. An arm wrapped around his lower back, strong and secure, that goaded him into walking. He did not have the faculty or the will to resist, and so Scott shuffled where he was led. He lost track of his progress when he became aware of the voice that was mumbling in his ear.

"That's it. One foot in front of the other. Come on, shake it off, hothead. I've seen you live through worse." There was such care in the tone. Assurances wove themselves into the words, and all Scott wanted to do was believe them.

His vision blurred as he lifted his head. It took a couple blinks, and a few extra seconds, to focus his attention from his shuffled steps to the face of the man who walked alongside him.

Damian was dressed in a firefighter's uniform. Thick, rough gloves chafed on Scott's arms where the man's grip tried to secure him. Scott opened his mouth to object, but a gasping squawk was all that came out of him. It was enough. Damian slowed his stride so he could likewise turn his head and study Scott from beneath the flipped-up visor. His eyes, deep and striking, actually looked like they held something akin to concern.

"Shh," Damian cut in before Scott could form the words, not that he thought his voice was likely to cooperate. "Keep walking." It was a command that Scott's body followed without any more conscious thought.

He had so many questions, none of which he could sort out, all of which were stifled by the overwhelming relief at seeing a familiar face that he was sure would not try to kill him. His eyes stung. He reached his shaking arms up to latch his fingers into the rough, fireproof coat Damian was wearing. The blanket was discarded and forgotten as an ache filled his chest, only to burst with a ragged sob that caused its own brand of agony for his abused throat.

His knees weakened and he pressed his face into the coat, smelling of char and chemical. He might have fallen right back to the floor had Damian not caught him and wrapped him in a protective hold. "Scott," Damian scolded, but there was no real reprimand in his words. "You're making a scene."

The statement made no impact on the now weeping Scott. He clung to the coat. His fingers dug for purchase. He shook so hard his teeth rattled, and gods... *everything* hurt.

They stood for a few moments like that, painting an awkward picture, as Scott did not so much heave with sobs as he awkwardly squeaked and chirped his distress and his relief into the other man. Damian seemed to believe that leaving the situation was better than dealing with the demonstration, and so while Scott wept, he was effortlessly scooped up into a bridal style hold.

That suited him well.

He was unaware of the trek through the hotel. He vaguely knew he had been lowered carefully into the back seat of a vehicle and covered with a blanket that smelled and felt fresher. He was unconscious before the door shut.

* * *

When he woke, he could barely open his eyes for the crustiness of them almost sealed his lashes shut. He was in a windowless room with concrete walls and dark oak furnishings. There was a dim bedside lamp beside him, just bright enough to illuminate the majority of the room. It let his eyes settle and relax, though it did not negate the piercing spike of pain through his temples that pulsed deeper with each hammer blow of discomfort.

Silk sheets rustled as he freed an arm and attempted to rub his eyes clear. It was enough to stir the other entity in the room, alerting Scott that he was not alone. He froze. His body seized and straightened, causing an electric pulse to rip through his nerves and remind him of the beating he had taken.

His unease was short lived as Damian, immaculately groomed and dressed again in his formal shirt and slacks stepped into the dim light. He came to sit on the edge of the bed and, without asking, lifted a hand to press against Scott's forehead. The chill of his palm sent a shiver through Scott. Unsteady hands sought the edge of the blanket to try and pull it up around himself.

"Your fever has gone down," Damian soothed and leaned across the bed so he could reach for a glass of water on the nightstand. "Sit up and drink. You're going to have company as soon as the sun goes down." Damian punctuated the news with a playful wink, like nothing had happened, as he waited for Scott to painstakingly ease his way to sit up. His back protested and he knew relief when Damian stepped in to help him. It felt as though a familiar setting had rekindled some of Damian's rare, good nature. "I managed to buy you at least that much time before Sarah comes to fuss over you."

Scott took his time shifting into a position that would let him relax against the headboard behind him. Sitting up left him short of breath and he forgot all about the water he had been told to drink. Damian reminded him by tipping the cup up to his lips so the first brush of it could ease his cracked and irritated skin.

Silence sat between them save for the laborious sound of Scott's attempt to drink. The water eased some of the pain in his throat. He had forgotten what being strangled was like. He drank in sparse sips, mostly to keep himself from overdoing it and breaking into another coughing fit.

When he was done, he tilted his head away from the glass and firmed his lips. Damian took the hint and withdrew to set it aside on the nightstand. His dark eyes bore into Scott, waiting for him to finish swallowing before pressing him for answers.

"What happened?" he asked, though the conversation was waylaid momentarily as Scott wordlessly reached for the blanket folded at the foot of the bed in a silent plea for Damian's pity. He was no longer shivering, but it felt as if cold made a permanent home of his body, and his fingers numbly obeyed him. Damian looked at him sceptically but obediently stood to shake out the blanket and further tuck Scott in before taking a seat.

"Triton," Scott croaked and was shocked that his voice was reduced to a wheezing rasp. He noticed that when he breathed a soft whistle accompanied each inhale.

The news was not a shock to Damian. His impatience showed in the pinch of his brow. "I got that part," he said simply. "I didn't think you'd really blow up a hotel room because you just *felt* like it."

The reminder made Scott run his tongue over the inside of his cheek where his teeth had been rattled by Triton's punch. He carefully shook his head, slowly, so that when the room spun, he could catch back up with it before he spoke again. "Wasn't me," he said again, gulping for air in between each strained word.

Scott could feel the questioning look he earned from Damian. He felt just as suspicious of the statement as he tried to parse what exactly happened.

"If not you, then who?" Came the bald question. "Unless you've got little minions or sidekicks running around like their own little fire starters, I don't see any other likely candidates."

Scott shook his head again with more emphasis. "Not me," he said, making each word its own statement. He dared not lend his voice more strength than that, lest he start coughing. "Someone else... there." The answer had not pleased or convinced Damian.

"Fine, don't tell me," Damian said, conceding the point, for now. He crossed the room to the darkest corner where he had been sitting and came back with a digital tablet in hand. By the time he settled himself next to Scott, the screen was on and he was searching for something. "You're all over the news, you know. You... or whoever it was could have been a lot more subtle."

Scott wanted to tune Damian out in the worst of ways, to give himself time to think through what happened. He knew better than to invite that argument. Instead, he tilted his chin up to rest his head back and close his eyes, trying to find the best position to absolve some of the ache in his throat. "Triton wasn't subtle," he rasped.

He was surprised to find the glass of water pressed into his hand. Damian stared at him; his previous sympathy gone in favour of impatience as he nodded at the beverage. The gesture was nice and, Scott hoped, done out of care.

The conversation broke long enough to allow Scott another sip of water. Damian gracefully ignored it when he tipped the glass too far and dribbled a mouthful down his chin. When he lowered the water, Damian turned the tablet to face him, a finger hovering over the play button on the screen. "Watch this," he instructed. His charity had come to an end, and Scott had to helplessly dab his own chin with the back of his hand to clean up the mess.

Tired, hurting, and frustrated, Scott obeyed and held the glass in both of his hands to wait for Damian to start the video.

It was taken with a cell phone. The camera jigged and jumped as the person holding it tried to divide their attention between the goings on, and making sure they captured it. The doorway Triton had broken down was already sealed in the ice he erected, thick enough that the only indication anything was even happening on the other side was the barely perceivable shadows of their figures fighting.

Scott found himself squinting, trying to make out the flow of action. In the video, he could hear the faint blare of sirens. People marvelled, cried out, and crowded. It made hearing anything through the ice barrier impossible, though Scott was sure the bystanders had not heard anything to begin with.

It started so subtly that Scott hardly saw it in the choppy video. He could hear the exclamations of the spectators, though, and it was the only reason his focus centred on the ice as it came back into frame and the camera zoomed in. There, where he could just dimly make out his and Triton's dull figures—that is, the shapes serving as visual placeholders of where Scott knew Triton had been strangling him on the floor—he could see the faintest glow starting.

It became white hot, like the flash of an arc welder. Scott assumed the shield of ice was what protected the eyes of those observing. Within seconds the light grew both in size and brightness until, even with the ice as a barricade, he saw people shielding their eyes in the periphery of the camera.

There was one panicked cry of, "**Get down!**" before the blast of an explosion rattled the camera and drowned out all other sounds. For a dizzying moment, the footage itself was spinning rapidly, focusing on nothing. Scott had to look away to avoid vertigo as the person filming likely hit the floor and then had to sort themselves out. Fire alarms started blaring instantaneously.

The screaming came next, though Scott did not remember hearing any as it happened. The time it took the camera person, and the people around them, to settle was painstakingly long as Scott found his gaze drawn back to the video account of his own suffering.

Flames, white hot and blue, roared at the edge of the doorway, spreading no farther than that. The heat of it began to scorch and discolour the floor and walls in its proximity. The brightness of it filled the camera and chaos, once again, erupted amidst the screams and panicked cries while the field of vision became jumbled and scattered.

Scott looked up at Damian, speechless, and swallowed hard through his discomfort. He knew it was not his doing. He knew for a fact he had never been capable of such a raw and wild feat, but whatever could be, was downright terrifying.

Damian's eyes were not on him, but he seemed to be aware of the split in attention. He shook his head subtly and nodded back to the screen. "Keep watching."

Seconds of confusion stretched on for an eternity in which the camera continued to film. People started to account for themselves and others, and then, finally, whoever was in possession of the phone found the courage to approach the scorched door. The suddenness of the fire's disappearance was as astounding as it was startling.

He saw himself in the midst of it all. There was no lingering smoke or embers in the room. Small clouds of ash rose from where he'd disturbed them by falling to the floor, and the rippling of a lingering heat signature showed up on camera. The entire room was black with charred remains and had quickly become a mucky mess due to the running sprinklers. Then there was Scott, beginning to acquire a dim coat of wet ash.

What was most startling was the realisation that, in a room completely blackened by such a primal arson, he was intact and untouched. His skin tone was an angry red, but outside of that, the fire had left him be. It was one thing to live through the ordeal, it was another to see it, and even worse to know it was immortalised in film.

Seeing the full impact of the situation acknowledged, Damian removed his tablet and folded the case over it. He let the growing and foreboding silence hang before drawing in a quiet breath. "It seems, old friend, that we now have bigger problems."

Scott found himself nodding numbly. After keeping such a low profile in the obscurest of slums, having not only his image but his ability broadcasted so openly, drained the blood from his face. He was not aware his tremors had begun anew until moisture splashed onto his hands and the blanket. It was Damian who saved him from soaking himself anymore as, with a swift movement, he reclaimed the glass to set aside.

The image of him in the footage was blurred as the camera zoomed in, but clear enough to identify him. Scott knew a tiny portion of relief that he had already fallen, and his hair obscured his face. He was glad it was a struggle to speak, for he did not know what he could say at that moment.

His attention was only diverted from his personal crises by Damian standing up from the bed so he could cross the room and tuck the tablet away for safekeeping. When he turned to face Scott, he was wearing a smile that lacked any kind of sincerity, made menacing by the shadows that played across his face. "Welcome to Los Angeles, Scott," he said simply, placing emphasis on the name and reminding both of them what a flimsy cover it was now.

"Looks like you couldn't resist making one hell of an entrance."

Perry Främling's Desert Dangers

Donald Gaitens
Art by
Shaan Khan

1

"**D**anger!" A scuffed and stinky, standard issue, size 14, desert combat boot pushed against my face and jiggled my head in cadence with my nickname.

"Danger! Perry, C'mon Sergeant, wake up." Kahele kept nudging my face while clinging to the rear crossbar of our Polaris DAGOR ultra-light combat vehicle. It's basically an armored ATV and hella fun to roam around in when you're not being shot at.

Sleep dodged away behind a sand dune, and I blinked myself awake, batting away the reeking boot. "Dear gods, Flower, your foot smells worse than a skunk's ass!" I hit his nickname with extra emphasis and pushed Kahele's stinking boot away. "We're having another chat about basic foot care when we get back to base."

I rubbed the grit out of my eyes and looked up at the tanned, grinning hulk of a man with the soft-pink, Hawaiian, hibiscus tattoo under his ear. I had initially thought that his nickname came from the tattoo, but he'd woken me up with his stinking sock more than once and I learned the horrible, horrible truth. We'd been working as a team under the Combined Special Operations Force for months, and I enjoyed his bad puns and ability to stay positive in the worst circumstances enough to forgive the occasional stinky prank.

Sinead O'Leary, the petite Sergeant in the driver's seat, kept her eyes forward and scanned the sandy hills of the expansive desert the whole time as she teased, "You boys and your nicknames. Främling, did you really think you could introduce yourself to me as Perry Louis," she ran my names together so they sounded like one word, "and not get nicknamed Stranger Danger?"

Kahele snorted, "I thought it was his pedo-stache!" Sinead snapped her fingers in appreciation and pointed blindly over her shoulder at the muscle-bound Corporal.

I winced at the double shots and picked my battle. I nudged the back of her seat with my knee, "Cute, little, freckle-faced, shaved-headed, science-fiction fans have no business throwing shade, but I'll take it over what they *were* calling me before I cut that monstrosity. Do you feel left out that we've been stuck in this oven for six months and no one's roasted you with a spicy nickname yet?"

"My head is shaved and my name is Sinead; you lot just aren't creative enough to move past the obvious."

I leaned forward and teasingly stage-whispered, "I've seen your So-Me feed, Sinead Marie. I know you're a cosplayer; should we work with that?"

Kahele chortled deep in his chest. "So, you're creeping her So-Me fan site, are you, Danger? Do you STAN? I'm gonna tell her girlfriend!"

I sighed and looked into the mirror to see how much of an apology I owed her for outing her hobby.

O'Leary met my gaze in the mirror and her eyes sparkled, "Oh, he's done more than creep me Kahele; the young buck practically threw himself at my feet when we met. Cheryl was there for it and she wasn't mad about it." Her eyebrows waggled lecherously in emphasis.

Kahele slapped me on the shoulder, grinning. "Danger, you motherfucker. I knew you were lucky, but I didn't know you were *that* lucky."

O'Leary made a snorting sound, "He really is. If I'd have known I was going to have to look at his face every day for the last six months, I'd have never gotten off of it."

I nudged the back of her seat, "You know nothing compares to you, Sinead."

She nodded, "Yeah, yeah. Keep it in your pants, lover-boy; I have to focus on the road, not your ego."

Sanchez made gagging sounds from the front passenger seat. His large Adam's apple bobbed up and down emphasizing the sound. "Keep it discreet there, you two. I get that y'all are bi and poly and ethical and whatnot, but not everyone is as understanding as us two corporals."

Kahele grunted and replied in a cartoonishly simple voice, "News to me. Wink, wink. But then I'm just The Muscle." He actually said the winks out loud and then flexed, straining the sleeve of his top.

Sanchez blew a mustache-rattling raspberry at Kahele's tired old joke and went back to watching his section of road while commenting, "I didn't know about the cosplay thing, though."

Kahele whistled under his breath and muttered, "Never bet against Danger. Ridiculously lucky." He resumed scanning the horizon to the left and right. His back moved as he scanned, his thick neck and heavily muscled shoulders pivoting as a single unit. The sun beat straight down on top of him. Beads of sweat trickled down the side of his face cutting tracks into the road dust.

We were central in a little convoy traveling over packed sand and gravel to a designated "safe zone" and technically off-duty, but we rolled out armed, ready, and cautious despite the light-hearted banter.

I leaned forward off my pack to adjust it. I'd secured it to stick slightly forward of my seat on the left to provide a bit of a head rest. It's slightly bigger than my torso and heavy with medical supplies in addition to standard gear. My good luck charm was poking out of an extra tac pouch I'd added to the top, his little pointed cap slightly bent.

I responded to O'Leary pretending the other two hadn't added their two cents. "Tempting as I am, please do keep your hands on the wheel and your eyes on the road. If I'm gonna die out here in the dust I want it to be quiet and peaceful; in my sleep, just like my dad—not like his passengers."

O'Leary snorted from behind the wheel. She somehow made it cute. "And that's why we don't let you drive." I took a moment to admire her and let my face get soft in memories. Her red-orange hair had been shaved down to her scalp and the stubble shone like glitter in the sun. When standing, the top of her head was just below my eyeline and I could slide my arm across her shoulders and snuggle her in comfortably. It made me feel tall even at 5'10.

I sighed again, more dramatically, and pitched my voice into the most annoying child-like whine I could, "Are we there yet?"

Kahele called out over the road noise, "Sandstorm brewing up. I can see the wall on our nine and there's some big dust-devils forming up in front of it. Weird."

O'Leary looked into the mirror at me and spoke up over the road noise. "Visibility is going to drop when that wall hits and we've got another couple miles of this bumpy shit to roll through. Is Gnorman going to be okay?" She drew out the vowels of his name in a mockingly long singsong.

I had caught a lot of shit over my little good luck charm, but we were allowed comfort items and Gnorman was the only one I had.

I straightened out his hat and turned him in the pouch to face front. "Dusty but fine, just like always. We should let him drive. He's never been in an accident as the driver. You two are practically the same height, but he's got the better track record."

Kahele cut in and nudged me with his boot again. "Stop playing with your dolly. How's the package?"

"For the last time Kahele, he's not a dolly, he's an action figure. That's why he's out here in the shit with us."

Gnorman had alternately been called a dolly, a plushy, a fantasy fetish stroker, and, though I wouldn't admit it out loud, my personal favorite: a beard barbie. He had been boxed up during the long weeks of Basic Training when I joined up. Afterwards, when we could have other items and civilian clothes, I'd hidden him in my favorite boots, but there's really no expectation of privacy and he'd been found. I'd taken the teasing as gracefully as possible and given as good as I got most days.

A couple guys tried to mess with me by stealing or trying to destroy Gnorman. It never went well for them. I had nothing to do with it, and had alibis that stood up, but it became common knowledge around the barracks that bad luck came to anyone that fucked with Gnorman or me. Laces broke. Straps slipped. Seams tore. Stains stuck.

Those might seem like minor things, but you try rucking 10k with one loose boot or showing up to formation with a stain on the crotch of your dress uniform and see how much fun you have.

Friends and squad mates that weren't shit bags also seemed to get choice assignments whenever luck-of-the-draw was involved. Soldiers are a superstitious lot, and Gnorman is kind of awesome, so he quickly became a mascot wherever I went.

The fact of the matter was that he was six inches of poseable, damn near indestructible, hard plastic and probably lead-based paint. I'd had him as long as I could remember and he still looked pretty good. He had a pointy red hat pulled down to eyebrow level, sunglasses that sat over a bulbous nose, and a beard that stretched halfway down the beige overcoat that covered the rest of him down to little black boots. Most of his clothes were removable, but I respected his privacy.

Mostly I just kept him around as someone to talk to when things were rough, and things were rough a lot when I was growing up. When my dad died, and took my mom with him, I bounced from a fucked-up family to foster care to a senile crone of a grandmother. Nothing was reliable except Gnorman. He was always there for me.

Kahele looked down at me from his wide-legged stance, hand resting on the back of his M240B machine gun secured on the roll bar. Sweat and road dust had caked onto his tan skin almost obscuring his tattoo. "Fine. Stop playing with your action figure, then. How's the package?"

I looked over at the large cooler strapped in next to me and lifted the lid a crack. A big smile crept over my face at the sight of the good-will gift we were going to share with some locals. Three dozen cans of beer nestled securely in ice. "The mountains are blue, I repeat, the mountains are blue." I was so looking forward to a little R&R and hoped the delivery, one of many, would help us make some local connections.

I pulled my helmet off and dipped my head rag into the ice water before resettling it over my close-cropped patchwork mess of hair. I was grateful for the regulation haircut as it kept the numerous calico cowlicks, dog-licks, and swirls under control; plus, it was easy to cool off my head. I resettled my helmet and strapped it back in place. "What are they cooking again, Sanchez?"

"There's a whole goat getting roasted, Little Buddy," Sanchez shouted from the shotgun seat without looking back. He called almost everybody

"Little Buddy", except Kahele. The lanky Latino signalman slouched in at 6'6" inches, sported a Texas drawl, and a mustache as large as regulations would allow. He'd shown us pictures of it pre-service where it was twice as large and, apparently, an award winner. I could hear the eagerness in his voice and started salivating at the thought of the delicious, spiced meat roasting on an open fire.

I heard an appreciative whistle from behind me and was nodding in agreement when the car in front of us exploded. My mind recalibrated as I watched it flip full over, back to front, and I realized the whistles were in no way, shape or form, a sign of appreciation.

Another whistle sounded and something zipped through the roll cage in front of my seat. Sand and rock blew up to my left. Our DAGOR slewed to a halt under O'Leary's expert hands. Sanchez radioed for help.

Trained procedures kicked in as I checked my M4 Carbine and slid my pack onto my back. I looked past O'Leary at the smoking wreck of the lead vehicle. Flames licked around its edges.

My brain was still focused on the promised relaxation and recreation. My mouth was still watering from the thought of the seasoned goat I had been expecting, but my stomach lurched uncomfortably when I actually smelled burnt meat. I knew what that meant. Images of the anticipated meal spliced together hideously with the scorched and smoking scene before me.

"Shit," I grunted as everyone rolled out of our ride taking what little cover they could. My seatbelt stuck. I slammed the release again and nothing.

"Fuck me," I swore again as the flames in the lead car jumped and another whine of a rocket propelled grenade preceded an explosion from behind us. Debris and shrapnel blew past my side of the DAGOR, but I was sheltered by my pack and the seat. I cut myself loose with my medic shears and darted past the burning metal, looking for somewhere safe to return fire.

The roar of heavy weapons kicked in as the rest of the squad engaged the hostiles. Kahele would be laying down a steady stream of suppressive shots from our position in the middle while O'Leary, our designated marksman, picked off targets.

The teams in the rear vehicle would be deploying and returning fire, too, if they could. Glancing back, I saw a smoking wreck instead of the flatbed carrying crates of supplies.

I felt the surge of adrenaline pushing me toward panic, and the spike of despair that I'd already lost people, but I pushed those feelings aside and I did my job as Line Medic.

"One problem at a time. Feelings later, work now," I muttered to myself. Weapon ready, I scuttled toward the overturned DAGOR, in the front, to save who I could.

The desert road provided no cover, but I knew I could safely follow the tire tracks of the vehicle in front of me. If they hadn't set off a mine I surely wouldn't. I could hear some screams coming from within the cab and hustled to a trot. Survivors!

I was almost at the lead car when I saw Sanchez's skinny ass backing out from the rear driver's side of the overturned wreckage. He must have sprinted there while I was stuck. He was hauling out our squad leader, Staff Sergeant Sioux. I could easily make out Sioux's stern profile even with the lowered visibility. His face was scorched and bloody.

I squinted into the blowing sand and blistering sun at the passenger's side of the burning DAGOR. A movement in the sand dunes drew my attention, and I spotted a dusty figure hefting an RPG launcher to his shoulder. It was aimed at Sanchez and the DAGOR I was hustling toward.

"Down, down, down!" I screamed. I dropped to one knee and started firing at the man with the launcher. Everything slowed down and I was treated to an excruciatingly slow, frame by frame, moment.

My first shot took him in the leg.

The second took him just below the belt.

He folded around it, dropping the empty launcher.

I was too late.

The rocket propelled grenade flew right at our DAGOR where O'Leary and Kahele sheltered.

O'Leary was looking at me.

Kahele was firing at another group. He didn't see it.

The world went red and black.

My ears rang from the explosion and the world sped up again. Everything moved too fast. I was thrown to the ground, bounced and rolled. Gunfire and explosions and shouts and screaming wind sounded all around me.

Something heavy slammed into my pack and pushed me deep into the sand, knocking the wind out of me. I couldn't get a breath in and started seeing bright dots on the insides of my eyelids, then gray, then black.

* * *

I slowly crawled my way back from the edge of darkness into a dim world of whispering sand and screaming pain. All I could hear was the low, hungry sound of crackling fires. There was no gunfire, no shouts.

Did we win?

I couldn't see anything but beige. Sand was everywhere. It molded against me, coffin close. Something heavy was holding me down and making a sort of shelter over my head and back.

Everything was rubbed raw and sticky, bloody grit covered me everywhere. The left side of my face was disturbingly numb and I couldn't open that eye. The back of my head throbbed along with my racing heart. I pulled my knees up under me and pushed and heaved until something above me gave. Sand poured away and metal rang against metal as the hood of the transport truck slid off my back.

Light speared into my right eye. I blinked at it, and something slid across the left side of my face. I clawed at it in panic and peeled a large chunk of charred, rubbery something from my face. I realized I was looking at a chunk of ear and neck covered with a colorful pink hibiscus tattoo.

I hurled my breakfast onto the sand. Pain exploded in my head and face as the world faded away.

2

My mind lit up in neon-bright, chaotic animation that shattered the darkness that followed.

Scintillating, silver pages swirled around in tiny tornadoes. They burst into butane blue flames and roared. I didn't know why the wind was angry at me.

A goat flew by, lifted by one of the whirlwinds, bleating in distress. Its eyes stared at me accusingly as it exploded into shrapnel kebabs that speared into the ground and vibrated with the wind.

I was buffeted by the blast and slid across the sand. Gnorman stood on my back with bent knees and sunglasses. He was wearing board shorts and a Hawaiian shirt covered in bloody hibiscus flowers. He surfed me down the slope until we beached at the bottom, and a wave of sand rolled over my face.

Bronze blades slashed at my hands and head, their edges blackened by burned blood. Silvery pages slid into a shield above me whirling into a wall of text; a contract thousands of lines long with hundreds of names signed at the bottom.

The words twisted around on the paper and in my eyes. Semiotic sorcery twisted the symbols into images that leapt from the page. Stick men made of bramble words and thorny ideas grabbed my arms, threatening to drag me into the dark to lay before their cold Queen. A leathery hand pulled me back into the sun by a single finger.

I blinked and was back in the convoy looking out at the mixed palette of crimson and ochre at our nine o'clock position. Beer and roasted goat filled my mind. The sandstorm was approaching, and it had knives enough to carve meals for an army. The explosions and gunfire tried to distract me, but the flashing, slashing sand held my attention.

I could see through the veil of storm to lemon yellow robes over crimson-coloured arms, coal black beards spiraled into thick cones wicking toward butane blue flames where eyes are supposed to be. The cartoon colors twisted and tumbled in a vertigo-inducing refraction from the disco ball bronze blades edged in darkness.

I clung to my pack, a life raft on a sandy ocean. Bandages spooled out from my fingertips in anticipation of the blood that was to come. They burned before they reached my comrades. Fire and smoke and blood flooded my vision. Hands as large as pillows pushed me into the ground and piled sand and debris over my head.

I heard voices in the distance, but they didn't make sense. My ears were ringing from explosions and gunfire. Everything was muffled by sand. All I could make out were the craggy outlines of conversation.

Whispering winds with slithering, sibilant consonants and harsh, biting edges shivered into submissive apology at tectonic, basso growls and granite hard declarations.

Then, the mental equivalent of a calm, comforting, favorite blanket and a bedtime story, well told, fell over me. I took a breath to relax, but the winds spun up and my head exploded into flickering, buzzing, too bright agony.

It started all over.

3

I don't know how long I was lost in that neon nightmare, but it finally ended when I heard a clear voice call my name.

"Främling! We've got a survivor over here! Främling! Are you with us?" Rough hands shook my shoulder. They stopped but I kept shaking, shivering, and twitching uncontrollably. It felt like there was ice in my veins.

Something sharp jabbed into my leg. Everything stopped hurting and warmth ran through my muscles. Water trickled across my face.

I blinked my eyes and something felt wrong. My right eye focused but I only got dancing lights from my left. I reached for my face and hands held mine down. I gasped and choked on sand, then coughed, spat, and managed some words, "Where… who else?"

The medic bandaging me, a blonde-haired, blue-eyed farm-boy named Cooper, just shook his head and kept working. He shoved cooling packs into every crease of my body and put my hands on an IV bag as he set the needle.

It was several minutes more before I was allowed to sit up, and only because I agreed to stop "helping" Corporal Cooper bandage me. Head injuries are a serious thing and he was being diligent, but I was me and hated being taken care of. There were probably others worse off that needed attention. Honestly, other than the pain in my face and a huge headache, I felt largely OK. I was sore all over, but I was the lucky one, again.

Fresh dunes pressed up against the smoking wreckage of our little good-will convoy and across where the 'road' was supposed to be. New, heavily armored vehicles had taken up sheltering positions on either side of the road as teams were deployed for rescue and recovery. Soldiers swarmed all over the area taking pictures and gathering debris and bodies and information. Most moved in angry silence while others muttered curses about the people who did this or cast sideways glances in my direction.

Not the R&R I was hoping for.

The sun was farther across the horizon than I would have expected and gloomy, stretched out, stickman shadows followed everyone around. From the less than frantic pace I could tell that someone considered the area 'secured.' I was lifted onto a stretcher and hauled into the shadow of one of the Guardian armored personnel carriers where Cooper continued to look me over. Once he was certain I wouldn't fall over, he propped me up against the knobby, oversized wheel of the APC. He wouldn't leave despite my repeated assurances that he could see to the others. In painful, stuttering steps, with long awkward pauses, Cooper eventually informed me that he wasn't going to leave my side because I was the only person in the convoy left alive.

I muttered, "Why does this shit keep happening to me?"

I held one hand to the thick bandages that looped around my skull to cover the left side of my face and slowly crawled myself up the Guardian until I was standing. I was shaky and full of painkillers, and knew better, but us medics make terrible patients. Cooper complained, but I outranked him.

I needed to see the aftermath. My brain froze at the line of bodies waiting to be bagged for transport. I tried to make sense of it but, as the meds worked deeper into my system, things took on the fuzzy edges that I hated so much. Every one of them was wrong. It was like a dollar store jigsaw puzzle after a week-long hitch in a daycare. I swooned a bit, but Cooper had my shoulder.

I looked again as he tried to lower me back down. Heads and hands were gone, just gone, from my fallen friends. Sand and blood had crusted together along the edges of the cuts into a thick, brownish paste that smeared on the uniforms of the soldiers gathering my friends. I felt up to my own face in slowly dawning horror, remembering the thick sandy brownish paste under my left eye.

Cooper pushed with more insistence on my shoulder, and I shoved hard against him as rage filled me. I turned to look for a senior officer; too fast. The world tilted punishingly, and I slipped down into the sand.

4

Hands were holding me down, burying me. I thrashed around in the black and fought back.

"Främling. Främling. Wake up, soldier!"

I struck out and woke up shouting, ready to fight. Junior medics were holding me down and the shift doctor, Captain Sveinbjorn, was holding a hand to his mouth. A loose restraint strap dangled at the edge of the bed. Bandages and light sheets flapped around as I slowly realized I was in a hospital bed, in a familiar tent, back at base.

"It's just a dream, lad. Calm down now. You're safe." He spoke slowly and carefully while holding his quickly swelling lower lip.

I snorted, but relaxed and waited for the strong men to let go of my arms and legs. "I'm awake. I'm sorry, sir. Vivid dreams and all."

"Must have been quite vivid. You were screaming for Kahele and trying to rip the bandages off your eye." He daubed at the corner of his mouth with a fresh chunk of gauze. It came away bloody and he glared at one of the junior medics, "I don't know how, because you were supposed to be *properly* restrained until conscious."

"Sorry, sir, yes sir. Too vivid. I'll put it in the after-action report. There were pieces of him… on my face… after it went wrong."

His face softened. "I'll read your reports later, lad, no need to rehash it just now. I've already seen Cooper's notes. I just came back to talk to you about the eye and a good thing I did. The way you were digging at those bandages you could have done yourself some *serious* damage and complicated the surgery."

I raised an eyebrow in question. It was the one above my left eye and I could feel the empty socket open with the muscles. I gagged a bit but managed to reply, "The surgery?"

He scowled at the junior medics and they filed away. He bent and picked up a sturdy tablet in a hard-case and began scrolling through it. "As it turns out you were more lucky than we thought. That horseshoe tattoo of yours and the shamrock are for luck, aren't they? I'd say they worked!"

I choked back a sarcastic laugh, took a breath, and managed to minimize the bitterness of my response, "How so, sir?"

"You could have died about a dozen different ways out there, but you only lost the front half of one eye, received a minor concussion and a slight case of heat exhaustion, despite being in the middle of multiple explosions. The exploded vehicle and blowing sand all but created a tent over you and protected you from the sun and, from what I've read, extensive gunfire. Your pack had some shrapnel in it, but you didn't. Again, extremely lucky." He waved a hand at my hip and left wrist.

Technically, the horseshoe was on my ass, but it wouldn't have been professional of him to comment and he exuded professionalism. Everything about him seemed curated toward that image. His beard was an immaculate golden line from ear lobes to the corner of his tidy, slightly darker, mustache. His hair was cut in a high fade but left enough length on top to require a bit of product to maintain a dirty blonde Clark Kent curl in the front. His lab coat looked recently pressed and tailored just enough to highlight a marathon runner's physique. He even spoke with radio-perfect elocution. It made me hate him a little.

He continued without noticing that my mind had drifted. Doctors will do that, assume you're hanging on every word, while somehow also assuming you couldn't possibly understand them. Captain Sveinbjorn kept his words simple though, a professional courtesy to those of us less gifted no doubt.

"Now that you're conscious, we can do a proper assessment. As for your eye, I don't know what did it, but it was a near surgically precise removal of your cornea. You are almost unbelievably lucky. The optic nerve is still fully functional, as is your retina. We are going to be able to provide you with a functional prosthetic instead of a decorative one."

That got my attention. "I'll be able to see?" I could hear the hope in my own voice and cringed at how pathetic it sounded. I didn't deserve hope. I didn't deserve to be the lucky one.

"Possibly better than you do now."

I tried to look at the silver lining, but it was hard to do with just the one eye. I steeled myself, locking my feelings inside a mental box, and responded the way he would expect from me: cheered and curious. "That is actually pretty cool sir. It's a cybernetic implant? Does that mean that I'm going to be a cyborg?"

He dipped his head in acknowledgement of the geeky reference. "It is very cool, but is mostly cultured tissue and plastics so... no. The cloned tissue will, however, replace the front half of your eye and should outlast the real one if you... stay out of combat." His salesman's voice faltered a bit at the end, but this was good news. He continued on, trying to add a bit of playfulness to a dark situation, "Public Affairs has decided that science-fiction words send the wrong signals to the civilians. Sorry, Främling; while you will technically be a cyborg, you won't be able to *say* you're one."

I nodded, showing acceptance and gratitude, but winced at the pain in my head and neck.

He continued, "It won't happen until you're back home. Are you going to go with its original brown or a blue to match the other one?"

I paused for a second and considered. The Captain was a good one. We'd only met a couple times, but he remembered my heterochromia. I'd been born with one brown eye, one blue. You'd be surprised by the number of people that don't notice but he had and remembered. "No. I think it would be nice to have them match for a change. I always felt like I stood out with the two colors and not always in a good way. I'd like to blend in for a while."

He nodded absently and added some notes to the tablet in his hand. "Fair enough. Once you've rested a bit more, I'm going to give you a local and ensure we keep that orbit healthy for the surgery. We'll get you scheduled for replacement stateside when we can get a flight out. Keep your fingers crossed, but with that horseshoe you're sitting on I'd bet on sooner rather than later." He paused and smiled at his own joke when I didn't laugh.

He left me with a negligent wave at my attempted salute and I sunk back into the pillows and closed my eye.

Let me tell you something, pretending to be OK is exhausting.

I stayed in the combination of shipping containers and heavy-duty tents that comprised our Combat Support Hospital, the 42nd, for five more days. It was stationed next to the airfield, allowing for injured soldiers to be treated immediately upon arrival but was crap for sleeping.

I was grateful for that. My dreams became less blindingly colorful and frantic while I recovered, but I woke up more than once screaming for a fallen comrade or with the single thin blanket twisted around me or on the floor. I couldn't bear the weight of anything pressing down on top of me anymore.

Worst of all, I'd lost the one thing that had always helped me center and calm myself when life was out of control. I'd lost Gnorman. He wasn't where he was supposed to be, and everything felt even more out of order because of it. I couldn't settle.

I spent those days of mandatory rest hopelessly searching for him in the sheets and pestering the nurses to check for a little red cap in the laundry or another bed or in my gear, anywhere nearby really.

I did my best to use as little of the painkillers as possible. I'd seen how easy it was to drift off and lose yourself in that fog, but I was determined to stay awake and suffer. I owed my friends that much, they were dead; and me? I was just lightly damaged.

I suffered through repeated assessments, head scans, substantial disbelief, and more comments about luck and horseshoes and asses than I believed was strictly necessary. They eventually deemed me fit to return to barracks, but not duty. Room was needed for more urgent cases.

I had two barely noticeable stitches on the back of my head, in the middle of a large, mottled bruise. I was fitted with a water and dust-proof bandage that covered the left side of my face from shaved eyebrow to just above my lip and stretched from the side of my nose to the edge of my cauliflower ear. It pulled when I spoke, or emoted, and I hated it. Lastly,

I was given a small prescription of pain meds and orders to follow the schedule on the label and to check in daily.

After days of nothing but washcloth wipe-downs and sweaty fever dreams it was a little piece of heaven to be able to use actual water. I was showered, shaved, and dressed in a fresh uniform in an hour, possibly the slowest it'd ever taken me since before basic training. To be fair, my mind kept wandering back to places I didn't want it to go, and I spent extra time trying to wash it all away.

5

I tried to tough it out, but the pain in my face was too much. I had to use the pills and suffer the dreams. I decided it was appropriate penance, but the knife-edged images cut deep and were bleeding into my everyday thoughts.

When I finally crashed down from my time on neon-clouds it was into a pile of paperwork in the form of after-action reports, incident response forms, and procedure release permits. The last one was the only form I didn't cringe at filling out. The procedure release was for me—my eye, specifically.

The Army was going to fix the damage done to my face and issue me a shiny new eye to replace the one lost in service. I had to laugh a bit at that. If I had lost my eye doing a keg-stand at the barbecue all I would have had to look forward to would have been a medical discharge and a jaunty eye-patch. But I lost it while crawling through fire and blood to save my friends, so I was going to get a "medical marvel" and a medal. As if making my injury go away would erase all that had happened.

I didn't believe it. I didn't want it. I would rather have been blinded completely and have living friends.

I shook my shoulders loose and refocused on the paperwork in front of me, trying to tune out the memories, would-haves, could-haves, and unattainable futures that died with my friends. I had some decisions to make. I looked over the Functionality Assessment Checklist and ticked off the boxes indicating a lost eye. Other columns existed for hands, arms, legs, testicles. No replacements for heads, though.

"Why were their heads missing?" I muttered as I signed the permission form.

"Sorry?" Captain Sveinbjorn stepped into my line of sight from my left—my blind spot.

I jumped... well, twitched violently, and lost my balance at the little desk in the medic tent and banged my knee against the sharp metal frame, knocking a couple pages and my pen to the ground. I tried to regain my composure and straighten the papers I still had.

"Hey, sir. Didn't see you there."

"Well, at least your sense of humor survived intact." He smiled down at me, completely missing the fact that I had not been making a joke. His smile was the type people gave you when they're trying to hide pity.

He bent down and picked up the papers and stood with something else in hand. A little pointy red hat stuck out of one end of his hand. He looked at the action figure, then at me, and propped Gnorman on the desk next to the coffee cup full of pens. He took the time to arrange him jauntily with one hand on the lip of the cup and a foot crossed.

I just sat there, stunned, staring at Gnorman.

"Looks like you found your good luck charm. Don't want to lose him again." He said gently and then started sorting the papers for me like I'd damaged more than just an eye. "It looks like you're making some good headway on the reports. No dizziness, nausea?" he asked.

Where the fuck did Gnorman come from? Had I taken a harder head hit than I thought?

I sat, mouth open, and staring until he put a gentle hand on my shoulder. I blinked and tried to put words into order. "No... some, my head is fine, sir, except for the missing bits."

"Oh, I wasn't asking about your injuries. Paperwork always makes me sick." He delivered the punchline like he'd practiced it. He probably had.

I reached out a shaky hand to touch Gnorman, then pulled it back short of contact.

Is this real? There's no neon. I'm not dreaming.

If I was hallucinating, I'd take it. I was glad to see him. I reached out again, paused, and remembered I was in a conversation.

I looked up at the Captain and covered with a weak chuckle. "If a papercut is all I have left to fear, I'll have the rest of these forms for you later today, sir." I reached out for the pile of papers in his hand. He took the hint and left me to the distraction of work.

I didn't want to think about anything anymore, but I shuffled the papers back into a stack. I stared at Gnorman. I rubbed my face. I needed a pen. There were papers to fill out. Gnorman was just… fucking standing there though. Responsibilities and duty and forms to finish, but…

"Where the hell have you been?" I muttered.

My brain was short-circuiting. There was no way I'd be able to finish these papers now. I'd only been deployed for six weeks and I was getting shipped back from a "safe" zone—broken.

Have I lost my damned mind?

I stood, took a deep breath, and picked him up. The solid weight of Gnorman felt right and real in my hand, but the situation didn't. I didn't understand where he came from or where he went. I was glad to have him back, but it felt surreal. I put him in his usual spot in my thigh pocket and stepped towards the barracks. I went back for the papers, then again for the pen, then changed directions and sought out the duty nurse to give me something extra because "reading with one eye is a headache." The joke didn't land, but I got some decent pain meds for the headache.

The Percocet made me sleepy, so I stopped for coffee on the way back to the barracks. I didn't want to dream so I tried to work on the forms. The letters swam together into fuzzy, silvery patterns. I fell asleep with Gnorman in one hand and a pen in the other.

6

My dreams were red and loud this time. There were still butane blue eyes and a wind that was full of knives, but it was a familiar face that stabbed me.

I was back in the dream of the convoy again. The glowing neon colors were washed out and more realistic. I knew it wasn't going to be beer and roasted goat filling my afternoon. The whispering sandstorm was approaching with blades to claim heads and hands and hearts. Blades enough to carve twenty goats. The insulating bandages of cartoon imagery provided by my rattled brain burned away. When I peeled the fresh cut chunk of Flower from my face, I saw things in a new and startling clarity.

Those burning eyes were set in a red brick colored face obscured by sandy beige cloth. The whispering winds wound around my head and resolved into a refined breathy tenor with a musical accent.

"Apologies. We serve, but had we known we would have refused."

A deep, gravelly, bass ground out in possessive protective tones, "He's fine. I have him covered."

The tenor urged, "No longer! He can't be here. The Great One cannot find out."

The bass again, black granite certainty edged in scarlet anger. "He's fine! I have him covered."

"He can't be fine. We were sent to reap and harvest. There was an explosion and other soldiers are coming soon." The tenor sounded apologetic but urgent as he continued, "There will be questions; you must tell him. Wake him and tell him and hide him!"

"I can't tell him," growled the bass voice. "I'm bound by my Queen to never speak to him of it, or in front of him, until he claims his power and birthright."

"But you speak of it now?" replied the tenor, his voice rising into a question.

"You see that? It's his back, and I am speaking to you." The bass voice had stretched out vowel sounds like the speaker was from Minnesota but spoke in a rush. "So, I will tell you this, but definitely not him. He is in great danger. You lesser djinn were sent at the behest of your Lord to kill him, were you not?"

A djinn? The tenor was a djinn, like in folklore? I rebelled at the thought.

"We were not. We were sent to kill the American soldiers and harvest trophies for display. A genie is involved. This one's presence was unexpected."

"That's because I've been hiding him his whole life and pretending to be an action figure."

My mind whirled... *GNORMAN was the bass voice? I thought djinn and genies were the same thing?! Is Gnorman a genie?*

I struggled to get up and turn to face him, but hands as large as pillows pushed me into the ground and piled sand and light debris over my head and back.

"This attack has made him aware of the real world and he may now learn, but I may not violate my commands. I only have time for one more question. Who holds the leash?"

The lesser djinn responded in sorrow, "I am forbidden to speak the name, but the uniform is the same as the man who lay here in the sand; whose name I do not know and face I have not seen. It is kept close at hand." It cut off suddenly, then resumed, but speaking much faster. "I sense The Great One. He is almost here. I must begin gathering trophies, your ward will be among them unless..."

"Unless what?" growled Gnorman.

Wind whipped up from nowhere, almost wailing as it formed words, "I will spread the word, but you must do something about his face, he cannot be a worthy trophy."

I struggled to my hands and knees, spitting out sand. Questions and curses percolated through my brain, ready to burst from my dusty lips. My skull felt loose on my neck. My vision swam.

I saw a flash of red from the corner of my eye and heard a tender apology in Gnorman's deep voice, "It hurts my heart to do this, but it is for his own good."

A wave of prickling energy washed over my body like a calming blanket and I lost control of my limbs, my breathing deepened. I was rolled onto my back, exposed, but somehow felt safe. My left eyelid peeled back and I caught a glimpse of a blurry, bearded face.

Pain exploded in my eye and my vision filled with stars. I was flipped face down in the sand. The grit filled the holes of my face, including the new one.

The wind whipped up and a new voice, a raspy voice, sliced through the air, all throat and no resonance but somehow carrying. "Trophies shall be collected. The contract requires it."

A chorus of "Yes, Great One," preceded the sound of blades slicing through thick meat, tendon, and MIL-SPEC armor.

I started to shake in pain and shock. Things blurred and the dream took on the edges of hyper-realism and hastily drawn outlines again. There wasn't any goat, but I could smell the meat. It smelled burnt and greasy. I was so confused.

A strong wind flipped me up into the air and spun me, dropping me onto my back amidst scorched olive drab rubble. "This one is ruined, Great One. It is not worthy," whispered the breathy tenor.

"We can take the hands," responded the raspy voice.

The tenor responded in worried tones. "Great One, more soldiers come. We have enough. The contract is satisfied."

Wind picked me up and tossed me. I landed in a boneless jumble against a slope. I curled into a ball and tumbled down over debris. Something metallic shifted, fell, and bashed me into the ground. I felt a sharp pain just below the lip of my helmet. Sand slithered down over me.

A small soft hand wiped it away from my nose and mouth, and I drew in a gasping breath.

The deep, gravelly bass spoke low, near but not to me. Gnorman's voice was full of sadness but with the rock-solid tones of promise, "The next bit will be hard for him, but I'll be around. He can sleep and heal for now; he has work to do soon."

The dream flowed from too-bright razor edges to comforting dull tones. The contrast dimmed, pain faded and so, too, my thoughts. I slipped from sepia sand into colorless oblivion.

7

My eyes opened slowly… correction, my *eye* opened slowly to the sound of a helicopter overhead. The lid on the empty side fluttered painfully under the bandage before I corrected and focused on my good side. I swallowed my scheduled meds and lay back on the pillow.

The details of my dream were razor sharp and filled with stunning clarity. I couldn't stop thinking about them and my lost eye and my lost friends. The thoughts whirled together, cutting at me from the inside.

I growled under my breath then patted around my single-sized bed until I felt the gnome shaped lump tucked under the sheets and pulled Gnorman into view. He was still dressed in his red hat, sunglasses, overcoat, and boots. His hands were behind his back and he stood in near perfect parade rest position—chest up, feet shoulder-width apart, head and eyes straight ahead.

My hand slid to my face where I had pulled a chunk of Kahele off me, a tear slipped down the un-bandaged side, and I gripped the little action figure harder.

I heard a faint intake of breath. Maybe it was the meds or head injury or the exhaustion or just all the shit, or maybe I was… no, I passed all the tests. No history of mental issues in my family, but I couldn't get the dream out of my head. Probably the meds, unless…

I looked around to see if I was alone. There were new people in the beds my squad mates had filled, and I hated them for that. Red lines pulsed in my vision as my heart rate and blood pressure rose. I rolled onto my side away from the others and held Gnorman in front of me. I dropped my voice into an angry whisper. "Are you real? I heard you. I heard you in the desert talking to the wind. What the fuck is going on?!" My voice had risen to a shout. I wasn't managing my emotions.

A voice called from behind me, "Trying to sleep here Främling. Dial it down!"

I glared down at him and squeezed. I swear I saw him brace against it. I shook him and growled, "Are you real?" I waited. Nothing happened.

"Are you REAL!?" My voice rose again.

"Yes, we're real! And we're trying to sleep. Knock it off, man,"

Another softly added, "Fucking nutbar."

I raised a weary hand in acknowledgment and pretended to try to settle in to sleep.

I blinked heavily as the meds kicked in. The super-saturated, high school, highlighter glow of the dream sequence started teasing around the edges of my vision. Flickering images spun up like the opening credits of a favorite movie, except I fucking hated this one and my brain didn't have a pause button. It rolled forward, trauma in high-def, but this time something stood out at me.

"Conditions. You have rules. Alright. Fine. Let's find out if my brain is broken or not." I looked the figure square in his dark sunglasses and spoke with careful deliberation. "I claim my birthright and my power."

I waited. Nothing happened. I repeated the words while staring at my dual reflection in his dark sunglasses. He remained silent and stationary. "Fine, fuck you!" I hissed at him and threw him at the wall. He hit the canvas with a dull thud and slid to the floor.

I looked at the silent little action figure and sighed, pulling myself together.

"Fuck... I'm so done." I laughed at myself and remembered my Grandmother's words after my parents' death. *Self-pity solves nothing. Stop complaining and do something about your situation!* I pushed thoughts of her back into their trauma box and steeled myself.

I got out of bed and bent down to pick the gnome up and the lid slipped off the trauma box. Everything spilled out and I started ranting. "Crazy or not, I'm going to find out why they died, who killed them, and put a stop to it. If you're real, you're going to help me because you took my fucking eye! You owe me, you piece of shit! I'll figure it out on my own if I have to. I'll stab you in your fucking glasses and see how you like it. You're going to find some way to tell me what the hell is going on or I'm going to toss your fake plastic ass into the first open fire I can find!"

A rolled-up sock hit me in the back. I turned to apologize and when I looked back at Gnorman one of his hands wasn't behind his back anymore. I suddenly felt dizzy and tired. I stumbled back to my bed and crumpled on top of it. The last thing I heard was the soft whoompf of my head hitting the pillow and muttered grumblings from the other end of the room.

8

I woke up to the heat of the morning and I couldn't find Gnorman. Again.

I was pulling my bed and footlocker apart for the third time when a harried looking Corporal arrived and let me know that our Commanding Officer wanted to see me that afternoon. I looked at the absolute disaster I had created, like a whirlwind had... nope, not going there. I clamped down on the lid inside my head again and focused on my next steps.

One problem at a time. Feelings later, work now.

Being called up in front of the CO usually only happens for two reasons: exceptional praise or devastating punishment. I'd been blown up in the line of duty, so I was hoping this was a meeting for debriefing, maybe praise for surviving. I had a chance to put my things in order, if not my thoughts, and grab some chow before I hustled over to the Command Complex.

The CC is a series of large, interconnected tents and sea-cans indistinguishable from the other groupings of unmarked tents and shipping containers unless you know what to look for. I wasn't in shape to move double-time, but I had thought ahead and was still arriving 10 minutes before my appointment. Soldiers wait on Colonels, not the other way around.

A burly Corporal with the distinctive military police armband around his bulging bicep sat just inside the door, a carbine within easy reach. He stood up and nodded as I approached. I presented my ID, which he checked against a clipboard, before waving me past with directions to the briefing room. I found the door along a section of sea-cans converted to office use and knocked. A low and husky feminine voice called out, "Enter."

I let myself in and saw a wide shouldered, olive-skinned woman filling a canteen from a water jug. Her name tag read 'Descharme' and the railroad tracks on her shoulders read Captain. She was in her middle years and had a sour cast to her face, maybe because she should have been higher rank by now. I saluted and introduced myself.

"Sergeant Främling reporting as ordered, ma'am." She nodded brusquely and tucked a long strand of dark hair back into her bun as she sat down at her desk. I deliberately looked around the room instead of at the generous curves highlighted by her movement.

The room was obviously set up for administrative and logistical work but could double as a briefing room. It looked like the side doors of two of the storage containers had been bolted together to make the twenty-foot-long room sixteen feet wide. There was a visible separation, but it worked as a single space.

There were several, heavy, lockable, filing cabinets visible along the far right wall with a stack of folding chairs in the corner. The near left wall had three large smartboard display screens, currently showing news tickers from across the world. Low, wide, filing cabinets sat under the screens to serve as a side table for a coffee machine and microwave. Her desk was wide and solid and set to the middle right against the partition so that the door to the Colonel's office was unobstructed. I could just make out another desk on the far side, but it seemed unoccupied.

A single, hard-plastic, folding chair sat open in front of her desk and I looked at it longingly.

She caught my glance and nodded. "Sit. He'll be a few minutes." She coughed slightly and drank from the canteen.

I relaxed from my At-Attention stance, thanked her, and took the seat.

I coughed and spoke up when her eyes met mine. "I wasn't told what this was about, could you give me any…"

She raised a single eyebrow, moved her head an inch left and right, and my question died on my lips. I pretended interest in the News tickers, but just stared sightlessly at the screens, reliving my dream and fuming. It was almost a half an hour before there was a ping on her computer that made her look at me again. She stood up and moved to the door.

I stood as she did and ran sweaty hands down my legs.

She opened the door and stepped inside saying, "The Colonel will see you now, Sergeant Främling." Her voice carried as she announced me.

I walked in and saluted as soon as the Colonel looked up from his seat. The span of his shoulders took up almost three quarters of the space behind his desk and his Pacific Islander features had me immediately thinking of Kahele. He waved the salute away and pointed me at one of a pair of large, padded, stacking chairs in front of his desk.

I took in the rest of the room, blinking my suddenly misty eye.

The Colonel's room was fifteen feet long, eight feet wide, and was obviously intended to be a private work area. There were two other doors exiting the room, one behind and one to the right. I assumed they led to his private bathroom, quarters, or an escape route. His desk took up the middle of the room with a laptop open on top. There was just enough space for someone to pass on either side.

There was a large map on the wall behind him above three filing cabinets that nestled next to a narrow sliding door. The left wall was bare except for a set of pull up bars bolted to the ceiling. I looked to the right where the other exit stood with a mini-fridge next to it. An old style, olive, drab, wind-up alarm clock sat on top of the fridge tick-tocking away in calming metronomic fashion.

The Captain nudged me forward and stayed at the entry door until I was seated, then asked, "Will there be anything else, sir?" Her voice was substantially softer than when she had addressed me. I looked over my shoulder and I could see that her face had softened as well. Her entire focus was on the man in the chair.

"No, thank you, Evelyn," responded the Colonel. She nodded her head and her cheeks visibly dimpled at his use of her first name.

The door closed and I noticed that the short wall behind me had a single floor-to-ceiling, shelving unit bolted in place. It was filled with an odd assortment of books, documents, and knicknacks, including an ornate antique hookah pipe. A familiar, red-pointed hat poked out from behind the hookah just enough to be seen.

What the actual fuck?

"Now then, Främling." I snapped my head around to focus on the Colonel and the room kept spinning as the implication of what I had just seen sunk in.

Gnorman is moving on his own! It's not a dream. I'm not crazy! Or I'm entirely crazy and hallucinating.

I grabbed the arms of the chair as vertigo hit me hard.

The words of the djinn in my dream started chugging toward the front of my brain, but the Colonel derailed my train of thought by turning the laptop to me and showing me an overhead picture of the scene of the attack. I felt a chill as my stomach twisted and sweat beaded on my forehead. My fingers started to tingle, and my hands got slippery as my mind filled in details that weren't captured in the on-screen image.

It showed sand, twisted metal, and surprisingly little evidence of any human remains. The wind had washed away so much. He spoke in a rich baritone, from the diaphragm, but not so loud as to sound like he was shouting, just serious. "I've read the after-action reports from yourself and the investigators, as well as the doctors' workups. You were remarkably lucky, son."

I winced. I hated it when people called me son.

He must have noticed the wince or the green tinge to my skin as he turned the screen back and continued as if it had hurt me to think of what happened, not his comment.

Honestly, it was both and the fact that, implausibly, Gnorman was on a shelf behind me.

His voice dropped a bit and gentled, "Can you go forward with a debrief? I've got some questions. Losing your team and friends is hard, but surviving like you did? Taking shelter while banged up and heavily concussed? You followed your training, son. That shows grit and skill. I want you to know I've recommended you for a…"

The door banged open and Captain Evelyn Descharme all but sprinted into the room. "Colonel, there's a broadcast you need to see! Someone has claimed responsibility for the attack." She caught the door without looking as it bounced and held it expectantly.

The Colonel got up and I stood as he did but wobbled and had to grab the chair for support. He waved me back into my seat as I struggled. "Stay there, son. I'll be back in a minute."

He moved in sprightly fashion across the room despite the years that showed clearly on his weathered face. I followed him with my eye. Despite the distraction of potentially relevant news, my gaze circled past him and settled on the red hat that was not quite hidden in the bookcase.

Descharme's eyes tracked in the same direction mine had started, but hers stayed on the Colonel. She didn't even spare me a glance as she pulled the door closed behind them.

I levered myself up out of the chair as fast as I could and, ignoring the dizziness, rushed over to the shelf. I caught myself against it and glared at my gnome. Gnorman was still behind the hookah but had poked his face and one arm out. He pointed at the hookah in comedic "action figure" fashion.

"Fucking, shit, liar, hiding, bullshit, can move!" I couldn't even make a coherent sentence. I was so furious at all the things and actively questioning my sanity.

I reached for Gnorman ready to wring his little neck, but with only the one good eye and feeling wobbly I missed and jostled the bottle. I shot both hands up to steady it and then brushed my sleeve along the side of the bottle where I had smudged it. I wiped my marks off the hookah, then went to grab that damned gnome, but he was gone. I swung my head from side to side until I saw him.

Gnorman was sitting on the front edge of the next shelf down with a self-satisfied tilt to his head and a thumb pointing back over one shoulder toward the hookah.

What the hell is going on? How is any of this possible?

The pipe rattled, burbled, and a thick purple smoke began to issue from it.

"This is not happening," I whispered. Kid's movies, hundreds of hours of horror films and thousands of pages of fantasy literature spiraled together in my head ready to cut my sanity to shreds.

The purple smoke continued to burble out of the hookah in a long, steady… look there's no polite way to say this… it rolled out of the bottle with the same, deep, and rumbling sound as a particularly vicious and soggy fart.

9

The smoke coalesced into the upper body of a pale and unsettlingly muscular man with the head and droopy ears of a shaggy donkey. A brown turban wound around the long, misshapen head, both under and over the ears. It ended up looking like nothing so much as a particularly ironic emoji, considering the sound that preceded his arrival.

A gaudy vest that matched the enamel of the hookah stretched over his bowling ball shoulders and lay open over a bare chest. Coarse, mousey, blonde hairs sprouted down the middle of his abdomen in a treasure trail that led to a broad embossed and bejeweled belt. Below the belt was nothing but purple smoke tapering down to anchor to the top of the hookah.

The genie didn't look down at me, but posed with arms wide and, to my gym-educated eye, flexed slightly to pop out his lats.

It suddenly made sense. Life is shit and my own brain is making fun of me. It's a random-ass hallucination. It's a giant joke. Could have been a white rabbit, or Robin Williams, but, no, it's a donkey-headed bodybuilder? Sure, cool. Let's get weird.

A cultured, but somewhat pompous and toothy, braying voice issued from oversized lips as the donkey-faced genie announced, "Greetings, oh thrice blind mortal. Know that even though you cannot perceive me I, the Genie of the Pipe, am here to grant your request. Speak it in my presence and, though it be great or small, it shall be granted. You have…"

"Hi!" I interrupted trying to keep myself from snickering.

He looked down at me in shock, dropping his arms from the pose and cocking his head to the side. "Oh, you're not… you're… new." His voice garbled as the huge lips stuck together with a zipping sound.

He sighed heavily, inhaled, and started over, bulging arms crossing over a barrel chest. His lips made an unzipping sound as he began, "Greetings, oh thrice blind mortal. Know that even though you cannot perceive me I, the Genie of the Pipe, am here to grant your request. Speak it in my presence and, though it be great or small, it shall be granted. You have summoned me and are therefore eligible for up to three requests."

I stared blankly at him, waiting for something else. Maybe little cartoon birds to start flying circles around my head. The silence stretched and suddenly my social reflexes kicked in, and the squirrel running the machinery of my brain cranked out words before I had fully thought through the situation. "What should I call you?"

He pulled his head back in shock and snapped his fingers. The steady tick-tock of the clock on top of the mini-fridge stopped, and the sound of the newsreel from the other room vanished. I could suddenly hear the lub-dub of my own beating heart.

"That," enunciated the genie, "is the first time someone has EVER asked me that particular question. You may call me Tailor, or Genie. My pronouns are he and him." His eyes sparkled as he breathed in and exhaled, "Request granted."

I stood shocked and looked at Gnorman who had one hand to his chest and the other tilting his sunglasses down to stare over them. My anger returned at full volume.

"That's some magical bullshit, Tailor. I was just being polite. And this guy," I pointed at Gnorman, "is apparently alive and has been stabbing me in the back... face. Fuck!" I paused, took a breath and shouted, "Is anyone else seeing this? There's some ass in a genie costume and a tiny spy disguised as a garden gnome in the Colonel's office!"

"I am here to grant your request," responded the genie. "Speak it in my presence and, though it be great or small, it shall be granted. You have summoned me and are therefore eligible for up to three requests. What is your next request?" He rolled his eyes and made a nodding motion toward my right.

Blood pulsed in my head, throbbing in the empty socket. Vertigo hit me again. It was all too much. *What if all this is just my brain running some Jacob's Ladder bullshit as I bleed out on the sand. What if it isn't and the genie and gnome are real? Oh gods. I'm so lost.*

I turned away from the brain boggling sight and muttered to myself, "I wish O'Leary were here to help. She knows so much more about this mythological shit than me."

Tailor hee-hawed and said, "Request granted. What is your next request?"

"I... but.. I didn't... I wasn't even talking to you. How the fuck am I... mmmfrrfmmm." I started to turn but found my feet locked in place and what felt like a giant hand wrapping around my entire head and holding my mouth shut.

A deep bass voice with a Minnesotan accent sounded from behind me. "It would be best if Perry did not turn around or assume that I am speaking to him, as I am not. I am speaking to you, Genie Tailor. He doesn't understand that questions, wishful statements, or even idle musing could be interpreted as a request by an indentured spirit. But what you, Genie, whom I am definitely addressing all my commentary to, don't understand is that this one-eyed child used to have eyes of two different hues. More than that, he is trying to correct a situation that none of us currently in this room would ever wish to have occurred, if we had any such agency."

There was a long and thoughtful silence from behind me. I glanced around with just my eye and found a blurry reflection from the door behind the Colonel's desk that showed the genie had turned and faced the little pointed red cap on the shelf.

"That is an accurate statement, noble Kabouter. Requests, questions, and the like all count. I am bound to fulfill up to three such requests from any individual that summons me. All such requests must be answered. I have no choice about that. Even the courtesy he exhibited in asking how to address me was, by Order of the Queen of the Summer Court, to be treated as a request."

I saw the reflected figures moving their hands in some sort of elaborate pantomime while the genie continued in his lecturing tone.

"I saw fit to provide us time and solitude with which to have this discussion. It was my hope that you would address me, because I am not permitted to initiate conversations. Worse, I may only speak ritual phrases to mortals."

There was a moment of silence. I'm not great at subtext, but I assumed all this exposition was for me. I mean, probably. I don't know what Gnorman knows. Hell, I didn't even believe Gnorman was sentient until, like, seconds ago. I still wasn't sure I wasn't in a psychiatric ward somewhere just drooling away my days.

I tried to turn but then thought back to Gorman's words from my dream. He wasn't allowed to speak in FRONT of me. I knew some guys in my old Dungeons and Dragons group that would have fit right in with these two. They were rules-lawyering their way clear of some fairly restrictive directions, finding loopholes in the tiniest of details and conditions.

I started racking my brain for all the lore I could come up with. I had no idea what a Kabouter was. I knew a bit about genies. D&D had them as mostly asshole monsters or trapped wish vendors that players would use to break the game. I had never used them, but someone in this office, who wore the same uniform as me, had been making wishes. My stomach twisted again at the implication.

Gnorman spoke up with a painfully familiar apologetic tone. "Convenient then that I have encountered you; it must have been very lonely these long years without the opportunity for proper conversation."

My attention split as I tried to piece my own thoughts together and make sense of their conversation.

Tailor responded with a noticeably sad and self-pitying tone. "Indeed, it has been. I've no idea how many years I've been trapped in this bottle, time and again forced through the humiliation of that excruciating entrance. I've only been allowed to come out to answer the requests of whatever small-minded, selfish, thrice-blind, idiots fumbled across my bottle and bothered to polish it."

His voice dropped to a more confidential volume and lost the posh accent. "Even when I'm inside, waiting for my next chance to get out and breathe fresh air, I'm not as graced as I once was. I'm stuck with this face, this damnable turban, and as extra punishment, it's just smoke below the waist. I don't even have the distraction of self-pleasure available to me. Genie of the Pipe, my cloudy ass! You can't stroke smoke." He sighed heavily and it whistled slightly between his oversized teeth. "So, I've been doing push-ups."

Gnorman spoke gently and with obvious consideration. "It shows. Truly you are an intimidating presence, and, as you may have noticed, this one is *not* blind in the least. I have a duty to this chimeric child, as my bloodline has had to his for ages past. He sees. He is recently aware. He may yet even come to understand. To the point, though, I don't know how often I'll be able to speak to you, Tailor, but I know your pain. *My Queen* bade me never to speak to him or in front of him until he finishes the quest to claim his power and birthright."

The donkey-headed genie chuckled ruefully, "The Royals are a fierce and fickle sort, but at least their laws are specific. My own tenure here began because of a misunderstanding with Queen Titania on a midsummer's day some long time past. It was complicated when I tried to gain some slight notoriety by telling the tale of my conquest in local taverns. She found me, bound me, and transformed me into *an appropriate form* and bade me only speak to mortals to fulfill their requests until someone showed me the kindness and discretion I had not shown her. She even inflicted this upon me." His hands waved through the smoke below his belt.

I burst out laughing as memories of high school Shakespeare surfaced and the pressure of my locked lips had me blowing snot all over myself. My knees buckled at the sudden pain in my eye and I would have fallen to the ground if not for the force holding my head in place.

Gnorman chuckled too, and I could see the blurry reflection of the genie stiffen. Gnorman waved his hands in apology and continued, "A cruel fate, considering how blind mortals can be, but your story is a famous one Tailor! The Bard of Avon himself put it to pen and it is remembered and performed even to this day. If we can resolve this untenable situation, and were I able to speak to my charge, I would encourage him to use his final request to free you from your penance."

A surprised grunt sounded from the genie. "That plagiarizing hack! I should have known better than to tell… well, it is what it was. I can but hope that someone will free me. Your human charge may be the one, or he may not. Now that you know my situation, perhaps you could help? Spread the word at least?" The last had the hopeful lilt of a favor being asked.

Gorman's bass voice started and paused several times before he finally said, "He may yet help. He's a good boy. I believe in him. As for myself, I will do what I may. Should the occasion permit, I will tell those that can listen."

Tailors voice warmed, the posh accent creeped back in and his volume rose with enthusiasm. "The same rule that requires me to interpret idle musing as a request provides me some latitude in how I fulfill it. I have granted him the ability to seek help from any spirit that has not yet moved on, rather than just the one he specifically identified. I fear that this *untenable situation*, as you call it, will draw the attention of the High Courts and Powers unless quickly resolved. *Laws* are being broken. I thank you for your conversation, noble Kabouter, and hope that we may all see our wishes fulfilled. I may not pause things longer than I have lest we draw unwanted attention. When the clock next ticks we will no longer be able to talk."

"I thank you for the opportunity to speak to you freely. My own work is lonely and there is no end in sight." The blurry figure of Gnorman bowed on the shelf and the clock started to tick. My head and mouth were suddenly free. I turned around to see the genie floating above the bottle, smaller and less imposing than before. I stepped forward to collect Gnorman and opened my mouth to make a request, but the door swung open and the Colonel barked from the other room.

"Främling! You need to see this."

I looked at the genie, nodded a silent promise to him, then turned toward the Colonel. My anger roared back to the front of my mind as I looked at his uniform, so very like my own. "Yes, sir! On my way, sir!"

10

"The following content may be disturbing to some viewers. American soldiers have been brutally..."

The screens in Captain Descharme's office were displaying four different news sources all running the same content with slightly different commentaries. I could only see the station identification bars above the screens because of the crowd that had gathered in the office. Officers stood shoulder-to-shoulder with soldiers in menacing silence. They seethed in unison. I could actually feel the scarlet heat of anger pulse in the room as the footage rolled. The MP at the door turned green and disappeared. I heard the sounds of violent vomiting a moment later. An ashen faced Major turned his back to the screens and stepped away shaking his head. I caught a glimpse of the screen through the opening no one stepped into, just as the image changed.

Driver's license photos of everyone in the convoy, myself included, showed on the screen with the caption, "Russian fringe group claims responsibility for decapitated soldiers."

I could see the flush of purple rage race up the Colonel's neck to his hairline as he took position in front of the screens and shouted, "I want drone operators working non-stop! Tactical teams on standby! Every admin, clerk and officer that had operational intelligence about this attack in my office now! Somebody leaked something and, by God, they will pay." His voice dropped into an animalistic snarl at the end. People started clearing the room, and I caught sight of the screens as another channel picked up the broadcast.

I don't want to get into the details, but the phrase, "American Pigs must die!" was used and the images were less than metaphorical.

I fell back against the door, causing it to slam against the wall like a gunshot. People leapt for cover, pistols cleared holsters, and the MP swung around the entrance with a carbine in hand and vomit on his shirt.

The Colonel took in my wobbly, pale, and snot covered face and waved the room to silence. "Stand down! Stand down! You've got orders, go!"

He approached me, visibly controlling his emotions. "Främling, I want you to know that this will not go unanswered. You look like shit. Go get yourself cleaned up and get some rest. You'll remain on medical leave until further notice. Eve... Captain, take a note."

Descharme's face was as pale as my own, her sharp features gone waxy, and she was looking anywhere but the screen, the Colonel, or me. I couldn't bear to look at the images anymore either.

I failed. The screens were too damned big and too damned vivid.

I did not faint. I just slid the rest of the way to the floor very quickly and may have closed my eye for a second while I thought very hard. The glass of water that hit me in the face was entirely unnecessary.

I refused a wheelchair but couldn't get out of being both ordered and escorted back to my barracks. The officer escorting me repeatedly assured me that everything was being done to deal with the situation. I had to laugh. He had no idea what situation I was dealing with.

I was dropped off at the commons near my barracks. The news was running there as well. I ignored it to replay the last hour over in my thoughts. A genie's lamp in the Colonel's office. Gnorman and the genie having a conversation while a clock stood still. The words "Request granted," echoed through my thoughts. I tried to think of some reason for this mess.

Maybe it was just some idle musing or random thing he said? Nobody would wish for this on purpose.

The images of my friends' heads and pigs' bodies filled my brain and I couldn't sit still any longer. I went for a walk around the camp. I moved purposefully away rather than toward anything in particular. I was trying to get the pictures out of my head, but they kept getting overlaid with the memories of Kahele's hibiscus tattoo, Sanchez's ridiculous mustache, and O'Leary's quirky smile and soft kisses.

I stumbled in my tracks as I realized that her girlfriend Cheryl was probably seeing this news as well and we had no way to comfort each other.

I turned down a narrow alley between tents and into a shaded square mostly used by smokers. I stood there in the middle of blowing sand, green canvas, the smell of diesel fuel and old tobacco, letting tears run down the unbandaged side of my face. A soft, cool hand rested on my shoulder. My skin tingled at the touch. I turned to see who it was and looked into the face of my friend, lover, and battle buddy: Sinead O'Leary.

I squeaked and my knees gave out. A wash of dizziness swept over me, and I sprawled in the dirt and sand. I closed my eye hard and shielded my head with my arms. The burbling sound of hushed, concerned voices brought me back to my senses.

"No! No touching. No need for medics. I'm good. I'm good!" I struggled to sit upright, facing a canvas wall and steadied myself with my hands. I could feel the pressure of people backing away. They knew trauma when they saw it here. Everyone had some of one shade or another, and I was full to overflowing. I took a breath and slowly opened my eye.

"Easy there, Little Buddy," said a comforting Texan drawl.

I froze.

I took a deep breath, reached back for balance, and slowly turned my shoulders.

I couldn't bring myself to turn my head.

Another voice, soft and playful, chimed in, "Is your plan to just keep throwing yourself at my feet until I take pity on you?"

My chin dropped to my chest and I sobbed.

"Fuck my life," I muttered to myself. "Now I see dead people."

11

I stared down at a smoldering cigarette exposed by blowing sand and considered taking up the habit. Nothing seemed to matter anymore. I was probably crazy. I stepped on the thought like someone should have the smoke. I'd had the idea before and it wasn't helpful. I said it out loud to ground myself and make it more true. "Crazy, or dreaming, or dying; it doesn't matter. The only reality I have is what I see and feel." Years of therapy from my teen years kicked in. I looked for three things I could see, two things I could feel. I clutched Gnorman.

A soft, teasing, tenor began singing. "Is this the real life, is this just fantasy, caught by a land mine, no escape from reality. Open your eyes, look up to the skies and see...."

My eyes started getting wet, but I couldn't help myself. I joined in, "I'm just a poor boy, I need no sympathy..." We sang through the first two verses as a drawling baritone and rumbling off-tune bass joined in and my voice died out on, "I sometimes wish I'd never been born at all."

I looked around. O'Leary and I weren't alone anymore, but none of the faces that joined us had the substance of a living person. Tears ran down my face in a steady stream. I sat on the ground, back against a post in the little unofficial smoking spot and let them flow. All around me, ghostly soldiers stood sentry over my pain, giving silent support. I dropped my chin to my chest and sobbed once. I stayed there, head down and quiet for a long time. When I finally looked up, it was just me and my squad sitting in the sand.

Sanchez was wearing a Stetson, jeans, a white t-shirt, and blunt tipped snakeskin boots. A stub of cigarette glowed a gentle blue between his thin lips. The tip was dangerously close to a mustache that was longer and more elegantly styled than I'd ever seen outside of pictures.

Kahele stood behind him, muscles bulging as if he'd just worked out. He sported sandals, shorts, and an unbuttoned Hawaiian shirt that showed the full scope of his tattoos.

I turned my head and, squatting in the sand within easy touching distance, was Sinead. She was wearing a sports bra, yoga pants, and jogging shoes. Her hair was in a punk, pixie cut, and she was hugging her knees.

I couldn't process what I was seeing and my mouth started without me, "You're all… out of uniform?"

Sinead smiled, "We're dead. May as well be comfortable."

Sanchez drew on the cigarette, his Adams-apple bobbed. "So, Little Buddy, you can see now?"

"Yeah," I laughed a little hysterically, "I met a genie and made a wish."

He took the cigarette out of his mouth and flicked it. The ash didn't budge. "Live long enough, you'll get to see all sorts of things."

"Genie, though," Kahele said, disbelievingly, "that's some weird shit."

"Lots of that going around these days," I muttered grimly.

I presented Gnorman and put him on the ground behind me where I couldn't see him. Kahele's hazel eyes widened a moment later, and I heard the now familiar bass voice from behind me. "Greetings, spirits."

Kahele rocked back on his heels, giggling, then pointed a meaty finger. "I fucking knew it!" he crowed.

I looked at him with my head cocked to one side. "You fucking did not!"

Kahele clapped his hands like a toddler that just found out there was extra candy. "I fucking did! I found him by my shoes every morning for like three days. It's when I stopped getting blisters and the fungus went away. I left out a jelly donut and it was gone the next morning!"

I stared at the ghostly gunner, "And you didn't tell me?"

He nodded. "I thought you knew! It's a secret, right?"

I scowled and nodded. "Yeah. A secret. Even from me. He can't talk directly to me because of *a Queen and her rules*. I'm getting the impression I'm not even supposed to know that he *can* talk, but here we all are!" I threw up my arms.

Sinead looked at me, then behind me. "So, you can't talk to him, and he can't talk to you, eh?"

Gnorman spoke from behind me, "Specifically, I'm bound by my Queen to never speak to him, nor in front of him, nor about certain topics, until he claims his power and birthright."

Sinead glanced back and forth. "So, even if I asked…"

Gnorman cut in, "I am not able to explain the specifics of his power or birthright or how he may quest to claim them. My Queen has prevented it. But I *am* here to help and I *do* have ears."

Sanchez picked up the conversational ball and looked at me, "So, Little Buddy. What do you need?"

I shook my head slowly and responded, "Assuming I'm not drugged up in a mental ward somewhere, or that my brain isn't otherwise broken and I'm hallucinating… I think you know all the things that I do; except maybe, that Russian radicals claimed responsibility and… well, they had your…" I couldn't finish explaining.

Sinead reached out, her hand passed through my sleeve and rested on my skin. It was chilly and tingled slightly. I reflexively moved my hand to rest on top of hers like I'd done a hundred times before. My breath caught in my chest.

"There's a reason we couldn't pass on. We know," she said softly.

I tried to relax into her touch but couldn't bear the tingling contact. I patted her hand twice before moving away, gently tapping out. My mind started racing as the words rolled out. "I thought the Colonel used the genie to try and murder us, but he's acting fully outraged and like he knows nothing about it. I don't know if it was *us* specifically, or just American soldiers, that were targeted, or why, but I need to stop it or fix it. I don't know what he might have said that made the genie do this. Can magic undo it?"

Sinead looked past me and asked hopefully, "Can magic bring back the dead?"

Gnorman considered and answered with regret tinging his voice, "Not in any way you'd want. Those Monkey's Paw stories are around for a reason. Wishes can be twisted to give you the worst version of what you ask for."

I shuddered at the memory of those horror stories. "No, no zombies; thanks. Could magic stop this war, win it for us, maybe?"

Sanchez nodded at my question and added, "It would be good to put an end to all these kids leaving home and dying in foreign sand, or being so broken they might as well be dead." He was looking at me as he finished and I felt anger building up inside me at the unfairness of it all.

Gnorman answered, weariness clear in his tone, "If it could, we wouldn't still be having wars, would we? There are wars deeper than this one that are being fought in places you've never dreamed of. We've... I've had to do things. Terrible things." He paused, then finished simply, "As above, so below."

I turned toward Gnorman, lungs full and ready to shout. I was still pissed that Kahele had known and I was just finding out. I was pissed that they were dead. I was pissed that I was half-blind and double traumatized.

The little action figure had his sunglasses off and a handkerchief wiped one side of his face. Tiny wet streaks had carried dust into his beard. My voice died in my throat and I reluctantly turned my back and focused on the cigarette held loosely in Sanchez's lips.

I looked around at everyone but Gnorman. "Okay, magic can't bring back the dead. Maybe it can't fix shit, but we can stop it being used to make this worse. We can find out why we were targeted. I just need to get my hands on that magic hookah pipe, then we can stop the Colonel. Maybe we can even stop this war."

Sinead snorted, "Magic hookah pipe. Maybe you *are* in wonderland, Danger." My heart ached at the familiar, adorable, sound.

Kahele cocked his head. "One white boy is going to solve all the world's problems, eh?"

I scowled at him. "C'mon, man. It's not like that. I'm no savior. I'm just trying to make things less shitty and maybe balance the scales a bit. Can you help? Gnorman, can you help?" I turned toward my little luck charm, but halted before I had my front toward him.

Kahele looked past me again. "*Can* you help, little red hat?"

Gnorman's bass voice deepened with pride, "I'm always helping this little chaos magnet and in ways he can't yet comprehend. Yes. I can help. I will direct some of the energy he leaks to our advantage and use what gifts I have, as well."

Kahele smirked. "Hey! He agrees that you radiate privilege, Danger. Of course we're gonna help. We've got unfinished business, but…" His smirk dropped and he uncrossed his arms. "It's more than just the three of us. They're keeping back right now, but there's so many other ghosts stuck out here. You gotta find a way to release us all."

My shoulders slumped with the weight of that. I had fled home because my Grandmother kept on about responsibility and duty and family and it was all too much. The Army seemed like a good idea. Someone else would do the thinking for me. All I had to do was show up and follow orders… and I ended up being a Combat Medic and a Sergeant and being responsible for life and death situations and the care of my team's health and… gods dammit! My whole fucking life keeps rolling back onto those two points: duty and responsibility.

I wiped a tear from my eye and laughed at myself muttering, "One problem at a time. Feelings later, work now."

I pushed myself to my feet and nodded. "Yeah, one more straw, sure, why not? I promise. I'll free you all somehow."

Kahele shook his head. "Too vague. You sound like a politician. You said there's a genie. Promise me you'll use a wish to free us spirits trapped here."

Gnorman started making noises, but they came out garbled and faded almost instantly to silence. I glanced over my shoulder at him and he was standing still, lips pressed together.

I looked the dead Corporal, my friend, in his ghostly eyes. "I promise you, Kahele. I will use a wish from the genie to free all of you. I will use everything in my power to put an end to this. Flower, I got you. I promise."

Something shivered through me at that moment. All the hairs on my arms and neck stood on end as a pulse of energy washed down over me into the ground. The sand at my feet shivered and fell into an odd smoothness.

A moment later the energy hit my team in a shimmering wave like heat haze over tarmac. There was more color to them when it passed, more substance.

Gnorman's voice projected from behind me, suddenly formal. "Corporal Kahele. My charge has spoken a promise three times to you and I am now bound to help him regardless of the consequences. He has invoked everything in his p…" Gnorman's voice was suddenly garbled and muted again. A moment later he clucked and spoke with the clipped tones of obvious frustration, "That of which I may not speak has been invoked, and, while he does not understand the breadth of that promise, it will be fulfilled."

He sighed gustily, and I felt tiny tugs on my pant leg for a moment. When I looked down, the pointed red hat of my "action figure" was tucked into my leg pocket.

I looked at Kahele, and he nodded to m., "We can't touch things, but we can see without being seen. The little guy is magic. You're magic. There's wind spirits and genies involved. What do we know about all this hocus-pocus stuff?"

I snorted, "Nothing! Dammit, Flower, I'm a medic not a wizard."

12

I spoke to the team for a few minutes more, but quickly found that I was, in fact, worn the hell out. Much as I wanted to, I couldn't just turn around and try to fix everything in double-quick time.

Sanchez and Kahele went to scout and gather intel. Sinead followed as I went back to my tent. All the events of the past few days ran around in my head and collided with each other like a particularly poorly played game of Tetris, or rubble after an explosion. I shook my head to reset my thoughts. I needed to start trying to make sense of all the parts.

"Three questions…" I started.

"Yes, no, maybe," she shot back, a crooked grin on her face.

A tear welled up, but I pressed on, "Is this real? Am I crazy? Are we going to get out of this?"

She shrugged. "It is what it is. I'll help how I can. What do you need to know?"

I nodded, "Genies, those wind spirit things, faeries. Also, what is a Kabouter?"

She told me about the differences between djinns and genies and the many courts of Faeryland— Summer and Winter, The Gleaming, The Gloaming, The Twixt, and The Tween. It was a lot, but not all of it immediately useful. For instance, it turns out Kabouters are just Dutch gnomes, but also a Danish absurdist philosophy. Actually, it totally tracked for how my life was working.

I laid down on one edge of my narrow bed, facing the wall, and she laid down on the other, not making a dent in the pillow. It was hard to see her and not be able to touch her. I cried as quietly as I could, and when she tried to comfort me the shivers from her touch turned it into silent, sobbing convulsions. I knew that anyone else in the tent would pretend they weren't seeing anything as long as I kept quiet, so I let it out. Sinead was my safe place.

Eventually, I stopped and slipped into an exhausted sleep. The last thing I saw as my eye closed was the soft, sad smile of my lost love watching over me.

I sighed in relief as I slipped into a mix of memories instead of neon-edged, black, and bloody dreams.

13

"Get this thing off my bar!" A dirty bar rag poked at a tiny pair of black enameled boots, smudging them ever so slightly.

"Gnorman? No! He's my drinking buddy." I moved the indicated statuette over an inch or two to make room for another pint of beer. The top of the little gnome's pointy, red hat was slightly higher than the five pint glasses crowding together on the bar top. It looked like he was hiding amongst them. "He goes with me everywhere. My mam got him for me when I was little."

"It looks like Boris Badenov had sex with a garden gnome."

"Hey now!" I raised my voice at the offending bartender and simultaneously reached out to cover Gnorman's ears. "Cool Bullwinkle reference notwithstanding, you'll kindly refrain from insulting my drinking companion." I took a twenty from the dwindling pile under Gnorman's booted feet, folded it, and put it back in my pocket significantly. "That was going to be a tip, but you were grouchy. You should have talked to the other bartender when you took over. She wasn't grouchy. She got a tip."

I heard a throaty chuckle from down the bar but was busy making bleary eye-contact with the bearded bartender.

The bartender scowled at me and dropped a fresh pint down in front of me, sloshing foam and dark brown porter onto the bar. I moved Gnorman away from the encroaching puddle and glared at the grumpy tapsman. I pulled another twenty from the pile as he sauntered away and patted Gnorman on the top of his pointy, little hat. His trench coat and dark glasses did make him look like a Cold-War era spy; his hands were shoved deep in his pockets, and I imagined he bore a fearsome scowl behind his beard, but he had always seemed protective rather than villainous.

"It's okay, buddy, he doesn't understand our history." I wiped a speck of beer foam from Gorman's bulbous nose and dusted the shoulders of his trench coat. I raised my glass. "To dear old Dad! Dying in a car crash was too good for you." I took a deep pull from the pint that had just arrived.

Gnorman was saluting with his middle finger by the time I put the pint glass down.

"Ha, ha. Funny." I pointed a bleary finger at the bartender. "Keep your hands off my gnome!"

A quiet conversation full of girlish giggles went on just at the edge of my hearing.

I leaned toward Gnorman and whispered conspiratorially, "That bartender's grouchy and sneaky. Dad used to do the same thing. Pose you around the house. He got the idea from those stupid elf-on-a-shelf books. You were the Gnome-in-the-Home. I love you, little dude."

I moved Gnorman's hand back into his pocket, picked him up, and dropped him into his regular spot in the left breast pocket of my oversized surplus combat jacket. I like pockets. Pockets are like bank accounts: you can never have too many or too big and mine always seem too few and too small.

I got up, checked myself in the mirror behind the bar, and straightened my gambler. Much as I love them, you can't wear a good fedora with a combat jacket. Fedora and combat jacket isn't cool; it's bad Indiana Jones cosplay. A leather gambler is okay; you look like a badass.

I think the only thing I have that doesn't look like thrift shop reject material is my hat and my boots: lovingly maintained and polished, square-toed, low-heeled ropers. I had hand-tooled the uppers with horseshoes, pentacles, shamrocks, and other symbols and sigils for luck. I was deploying to an active combat zone soon and needed all the luck I could get.

I got up and headed toward the bathroom. At the end of the bar sat a pair of stunningly fit women. The taller stood almost six feet in her heels and had pink and purple streaks in white-blonde hair, a lean profile that made me think of triathletes, and science-fiction tattoos over both arms and one leg. The shorter one stood maybe 5'5" in Doc Martens and had short, curly, strawberry-blonde hair, strong gymnast's shoulders, and bright pink panties that rode up out of her low-slung jeans to hook over sharply defined hipbones.

I got to the men's room and took care of what I needed to. I spent extra time washing my hands. They were out of paper towels, so I used my wet fingers to tidy the hair under my hat and wipe the bleariness from my eyes.

I pushed my back against the door to get out and was shaking my hands to dry them as I steeled myself to approach the girls. Maybe my luck would take a turn, and I could have some cute company.

A loud crack sounded from the pool table nearby and I jerked at the sound. The cue ball flew through the air toward my face, and I ducked to one side, straight into the waitress carrying a fresh round of drinks to the pool players.

She yelped and struggled to keep the glasses on her platter. I moved to grab at it, trying to help, and stepped onto the rogue pool ball. My feet flew out from under me and hit her in the thighs. She dropped the platter straight down and fell into the lap of some overly made-up goth kid.

I landed on my back, arms splayed across the floor, trying to absorb the impact, and the platter landed square on my chest. A little beer sloshed into my face, but all the mugs were standing up.

When I blinked my eyes clear, I was looking up at a circle of people, including the women I had hoped to meet. The short one cocked her head to one side and said, "Good catch. You can go to hell for spilling drinks. You're a lucky guy."

I laughed and stopped as the glasses tinkled together. "Oh, I'm the luckiest guy you'll meet; it's just usually bad."

She laughed. "Throwing yourself at my feet is a new move, though. Points for originality. Do you suppose I should take pity on you?" She wandered back to her companion and stared, a speculative look on her face.

The boys at the pool table helped themselves to their drinks from off my chest.

"Super helpful guys, thanks." I grimaced. They laughed.

The waitress scolded them, and they apologized for the errant ball and returned to their game. I handed the platter back to the waitress along with the money I had stuffed in my pocket earlier and turned toward the ginger and her friend, back at their drinks.

"Hi, I'm Perry. Perry Louis Främling."

The ginger sized me up with her emerald eyes and blinked golden lashes at me slowly. "Främling… as in stranger? Good girls aren't supposed to talk to strangers.""

I saw the mischievous glint in her eye and blushed, but I could play along. "Well now, that's why I went to all the trouble of introducing myself. We're hardly strangers. You already know so much about me, translating my name and all. Tell me, is it that you speak Swedish or are you just a big Orson Scott Card fan?"

"Oh, a reader, is it?" She leaned back against the heavily tattooed shoulder of the tall blonde, pulling her attention from the pool players. "Cheryl, we got us a reader."

Cheryl glanced over her head without standing up. "Is the reader bothering you, Sinead?"

Sinead shook her head, making her short-cropped curls sparkle in the lights of the bar. "I don't think he's going to throw himself at me again, love. No, not bothering me… just trying to get to know me."

Cheryl snorted, "Didn't your parents tell you about stranger danger?" She looked me over with a calculating eye. I stood up a little straighter and tried not to flex obviously. "Nice boots, though, could do without the porn-stache."

Sinead nodded, face mock serious. She looked at Cheryl, then at me. "Whatever shall I do?"

I took a deep breath, manned up as much as I could and took a gamble. "You should probably run away. Good girls don't talk to strangers and I am… Perry Louis." I ran my names together to make them sound like a single word.

She snorted at that, her nose wrinkling up and shoulders bouncing, and stuck out her hand. "If I was a good girl, I wouldn't be here. Everyone on base said this place was a shithole that no one interesting would be found dead in. I'm thinking they were wrong. I'm Sinead O'Leary. Nice to meet you, Stranger Danger." The way she inflected the last word, I knew I had just earned a nickname.

I winced and shook my head at it. "Ok, three questions…"

"Yes, no, maybe," she shot back.

I raised an eyebrow and reconsidered. She nodded encouragingly, and I grinned.

The three of us talked deep into the night. Sinead, like me, was about to be deployed and had planned on spending the last free night with her girlfriend and maybe someone fun. I asked if I could join them.

We drank, told stories, and made stupid bets all night. They got to shave my mustache off and I got to do body shots. When they decided they had to go home, I asked if they wanted me to stay behind.

They didn't.

We caught a cab back to Cheryl's apartment and tattoo studio. She gave me a shamrock tattoo on my throwing hand after I came from behind to beat them both at strip darts with three triple twenties, and they bet me I couldn't do it twice. I could not, but it was fun to try and the sight of them in just their underwear was worth the pain of the tattoo.

Sinead got a rainbow dropping into the front of her panties when she lost at Rock, Paper, Scissors the entire time I was getting inked.

Cheryl let me trace a star under her left ear because she didn't want to be left out. We debated which other lucky charms we should get, and I ended up getting a horseshoe tattooed on my ass after losing a series of coin flips with the rest of our clothes on the line.

I won the next head or tail bet, though.

The next morning, they let me know we'd all gotten lucky, and it wasn't bad at all. I asked if we could do it again sometime.

14

I woke up with a smile on my face the next morning. I think it might have been the first time since the explosion. The barracks were mostly empty.

I pulled Gnorman out from under my blankets and held him in front of my face.

"Alright, little dude, whether I have gone crazy or I haven't, whether this is real or not… my brain thinks it's real and I have to do something." I felt the truth of the statement settle into my bones and nodded to myself as much as to Gnorman. "Everything can kill you, may as well pick something fun. Let's try magic."

The little, red-hatted action figure stood at rigid attention in my hands. I manipulated his limbs, more gently than I ever had before, and put him in a relaxed sitting position on my chest as I leaned back and thought out loud. "Ok. Facts. Magic, ghosts, genies, and general storybook shit are real. My team was killed, and I lost an eye because the Colonel made a wish. Don't think I've forgotten about your part in that. I still don't know how to feel about it."

His head drooped a bit and his hands folded together into an apologetic prayer position.

I continued, "Genies can treat any request, question, or idle musing as a wish to be granted. Not everybody can see genies. Sinead and I don't know what the rules are around that, but I can see genies. Also, I have a *birthright* and *powers* waiting for me to claim, and there's a quest?"

I looked at my tiny, overcoat-wearing, gnomish action figure. "And you, my dear Guardian Idiot… You can't talk to me or in front of me, or about my *power*, until I somehow claim it and my birthright. Whatever that is."

I stopped and shook my head. "Fuck me, I sound like a young adult novel right after '*The Call*'. All I want is to make the world a less shitty place and to hook up with Cheryl and O'Leary again. I don't want power or a destiny."

The hairs on the back of my neck stood up, and I felt a cool tingle against my right ear.

"'*The Call*' is trying to contact you about your Destiny's extended warranty," whispered Sinead.

I jerked, and my back and ass muscles contracted so hard I bounced myself out of my bed and catapulted Gnorman into the air. When I crawled back up to blanket level, he was standing mid-bed, bent over at the waist and had a hand over his beard. The corners of his eyes were so crinkled up I could tell even around his dark glasses. Sinead was leaning against the head of my bed. Her lower body disappeared through the wall.

"Ha, ha," I enunciated slowly as I flopped across the bed.

She walked through the headboard and drew her legs up to sit on my pillow.

I stared, "How?" I waved my hand at her denial of physics as I knew it.

She smirked and shrugged. "I've read so many stories about what ghosts can and can't do and the learning curve and all that. I just skipped over all the trial-and-error bullshit. Physics is my bitch now."

I shook my head and laughed. "I wish it were that easy for me." I checked myself and looked around. "That doesn't count with the genie, does it?"

O'Leary shook her head. "I don't think so, you said his opening phrase was something about speaking in his presence, right? He's not here."

Her eyes glittered with thought. I swear I actually saw light shining.

"Would just saying that you claim your power and birthright make it happen?"

I shook my head. "I kind of already tried it and threatened to set Gnorman on fire. Sorry about that." I looked at Gnorman then back to O'Leary and rattled off, "I claim my power and my birthright. See, nothing. I'm pretty sure I heard him mention a quest."

Sinead stared at me with that look that says, 'You're not really trying.'

I nodded, pushed myself back a bit toward the foot of the bed, stood up, concentrated, and spoke slowly and deliberately, "I claim my power and my birthright."

A shiver of goosebumps ran down my arms and back. The canvas ceiling rippled as a gust of wind passed by. A door slammed. I jerked my head around to look, and when I looked back the ghosts of Sanchez and Kahele stood beside me.

I about shit myself.

"Ghost. Recon. Squad. Reporting in," said Kahele, striking a different pose with each exaggerated pause.

O'Leary rolled her eyes, and Sanchez just stood quietly, letting the big man have his moment.

"Guys. Seriously," I said as my heart started slowing down. "I am all kinds of traumatized after watching you all die. I have a head injury from which I have not fully recovered. Could you NOT fuck with me?"

Kahele broke from his pose and tilted his head. "Bruh, we're dead, not stiffs."

Sanchez's mustache quivered. The still lit, unchanged cigarette glowed and he slowly started talking, "Jokes aside, the recon was useful. I've got a route scouted and believe I can get you in with a minimum of fuss or witnesses. It may also be worth noting that the Colonel was not alone in his quarters last night."

My eyebrows went up and some puzzle pieces slid together. "The Captain? Gross. Such a cliché. She's his admin."

Sanchez nodded silently. I could see the disappointment in his eyes as well.

Rank has its privileges, but that's not supposed to be one of them. Rules are supposed to mean something. Power isn't supposed to be abused.

I felt my face set in a grimace, both at the information and as a way of mentally preparing myself for shit to go wrong. I shook my shoulders loose and nodded at Sanchez. "Let's do this. The worst that can happen is we'll all be hanging out in blue-light territory."

Sinead moved up with the rest of the team and held up a finger. "One second, I've got an idea I need to test." We all got quiet. "Gnorman, nod if I'm right. Is there a quest involved in Danger's power and birthright business?"

His head dipped.

She grinned. "This doesn't count as speaking, does it?"

One of his little hands shot out signaling a solid affirmative.

Her grin blossomed into a full smile and she shifted her eyes to me triumphantly. "When this is all said and done, you can play twenty questions with Gnorman. He doesn't have to talk to give a thumbs up."

I rocked back on my heels. "You are a goddamn genius O'Leary."

We didn't have to suit up or gather materials or any of that other clandestine shit to get into the offices. It was unnervingly easy. As an unarmed, injured soldier that had just been in the offices the previous day, I was waved into the command tent. The team scouted and guided me around problem areas, and we found ourselves outside the briefing room door in a few minutes.

Sanchez poked his face through the door then pulled back and gave me a thumbs up. "Ok, you're up, Little Buddy," he said, nodding to the gnome in my pocket.

I set Gnorman down and turned to watch the corridor. There was a click behind me and when I looked the little guy was standing there with his arm wedged into a slightly open door. I stepped in as quietly as I knew how, and we walked across the room to the Colonel's door and repeated the process.

That was all it took for us to get inside my CO's office and in front of the hookah pipe that contained the genie. I reached up and gave the lamp a quick polish. It was immediately answered with a long, soggy, flatulence and the appearance of Tailor, the donkey-faced genie.

"Greetings, mortal. Know that even though you cannot perceive me I, a powerful genie, am here to grant your request. Speak it in my presence and, though it be great or small, it shall be granted. What is your next request?" Tailor's words went up at the end, past question territory and into a panicked squeak. His eyes looked a little wild around the edges and he was repeatedly bucking his head toward Gnorman.

Gnorman's basso voice sounded from behind me, "Sanchez, Kahele, something is wrong. Watch the halls."

The guys faded through the walls in opposite directions. O'Leary came up beside me, eyes wide as she took in the spectacle.

The pitter-pat of tiny feet sounded, then a light weight landed on my shoulder. Gnorman spoke from behind my ear, "Tailor, what is wrong?"

The genie looked at him and his voice shuddered in terror, "I... I don't know how to count."

15

A sleepy female voice rose from behind one of the closed doors in the Colonel's office, "Hank, did you hear something?" A mumbled reply and heavy snoring followed. "Ugh, fine. I'll go look... *sir*." The sarcasm fairly scorched the air and I immediately knew who it was.

I stared at Tailor, then craned my head to look at O'Leary. I felt a light pressure on my shoulder and then heard a click and the sharp sound of Gorman's' boots hitting the floor as he hid. The handle of the door started to turn. I looked back at the genie. I tried to remember all the rules.

"Umm... I need to consider my request before I speak it," I said out loud.

Tailor snapped his fingers and I felt a shudder of power sweep over the room, but the handle on the door kept turning. It opened as I stood staring.

Captain Evelyn Descharme entered the room in a black silk nightgown and combat boots. Her long, ebony hair hung loose and tousled around her shoulders. The nightgown clung to her, highlighting her curvaceous figure. Her long legs and muscular thighs caught my attention but not as much as the pistol in her hand.

She swung the door closed behind her, but it stopped as soon as her fingers lost contact. She stared at me, then looked at the genie hovering over the hookah pipe. His eyes rolled in his head in fear and he pulled back but wasn't able to slip back into the pipe.

"You can't be here!" She shouted at me. "You'll ruin everything! The genie is MINE! MINE!!" She pulled the trigger three times in rapid succession, but the bullets stopped as soon as they left the barrel. We both looked at the bullets, then at each other.

I stepped to one side. She cocked her arm back as if to throw the pistol, then stopped, and looked at the genie.

"Make time resume in this room only until I say otherwise," she said.

Tailor looked at me apologetically and raised a hand. I dove behind the desk as he snapped his fingers. "Request granted."

Bullets whizzed over my head. Two more shots rang into the metal of the desk.

Tailor continued the ritual phrases. "What is your next request?"

"I wish to see everyone in this room," called out the Captain.

"Request granted," replied the genie. I slid across the floor, as if yanked, exposing me to the Captain and the Genie. He was weeping openly now. "What is your next request?"

I scrambled back towards cover and the gun sounded again. A bullet took me in the leg, and I rolled onto my back screaming in pain and reflexively reaching for the injury.

"I'll let you know," she said smugly, then yelped in shock as the ghost of Sinead O'Leary became visible in front of her. She was in uniform and showed the gruesome injuries she'd sustained before she became a trophy. I gagged and turned a little, my eyes fell on Gnorman. He stood silent and still on the bookshelf next to the hookah, concern plain on his face and a finger pointing at the genie.

"Tailor, I wish no violence could happen in this room," I called out.

"Request granted. What is your next request?" he responded. I thought I could hear a note of cheer in his voice, mixed with the desperation.

Captain Descharme pointed the pistol at Sinead and pulled the trigger, nothing happened. She screeched, "Genie, I wish…" and cut off suddenly.

Gnorman's voice boomed from somewhere in the room, interrupting, "Tailor, cut her off, she's obviously used more than three!"

"I don't know what that word means!" wailed Tailor.

Sinead stood between the Captain and me. One of her ghostly hands stuck inside Descharme's mouth, the other in her chest. Evelyn stood transfixed, mouth open, eyes wide, skin pale, and shivering as she stared at the apparition.

"Captain!" I called, slowly rising to my feet, leaning on the desk. "Captain... this isn't necessary. I wasn't going to steal him. I wanted to..." I looked at Tailor and let my sentence drop off before it became a request. I changed tactics. "You asked to see everyone in this room. Ghosts count. She's with me... and you should recognize her from the videos." I gritted my teeth and limped away from the desk, positioning myself between her and the hookah, putting my back to Gnorman.

Sinead stepped back in all her gruesome glory and pulled her hands out of the stunned Captain. She held a single finger pointed at her in warning.

Descharme split her focus, looking back and forth between us, as she recovered from her shock and O'Leary's chilling touch. She stepped to keep us both in view, pistol still up. "You wanted to make a wish, didn't you?"

"Please, Captain," I said, wobbling slightly and raising one hand to my bandaged head thinking furiously. "I had some thoughts about what I could maybe accomplish. I love..." My heart broke a bit as I corrected, "I loved her."

Descharme looked at me and I saw pity and anger and frustration dance across her face. "I had thoughts too, but you can't undo some things. I didn't mean for your team..." She stared at O'Leary. "I didn't mean to cause that harm. I just wanted to be with Hank!" Her eyes got visibly wetter and she wiped one of the sleeves across her face, never looking away from O'Leary. "I saw the newscast of the attack. I watched it over and over. That wasn't what I wished for." She looked past me toward the floating donkey-headed genie and screamed, "That wasn't what I wished for!"

Tailor jerked and recoiled, shaking his head and trying to speak.

She breathed heavily, tears racing down her face. "I just wished for him to have a reason to stay here with me and everything went wrong.

I've tried. I've tried so many times to fix it, but every wish I make just makes it worse."

"There are only supposed to be three requests," I said gently. "How?"

She laughed bitterly, "I used…" she stopped and looked at the genie, "I used my third request to make him forget how numbers work." She dropped the pistol to her side.

I shook my head, "You found a workaround. Why didn't you find a workaround to get magic of your own, too?"

She looked at me as if I were a simpleton. "I've seen the movie. I couldn't figure out the right words." She shrugged and raised the pistol again, aiming at my head. "But you just broke into the Colonel's office while I was working late and I had to defend him. You were raving." Her face softened a little. "If I could fix this with magic I would. I just want this to be over." She took a breath and her face fell flat. "Genie, I wish…"

"Request granted!" shouted Tailor into the room.

"… for violeeennnccceee!" Her words were drawn out as wind picked up in the room.

Papers rattled and items fell from shelves. A canteen dropped from on top of the mini-fridge, and the top unscrewed itself as it floated towards the Captain. Descharme was picked up by the wind and twisted like dark licorice. I winced in anticipation of popping noises as bone and sinew were torn apart, but her body stretched like taffy and spun into cotton candy as she was pulled, silk nightrobe, combat boots and all, into the canteen.

I dove for it and crammed the cap into place.

16

I laid on the floor for several seconds. Diving with a bullet in your leg is stupid and action movies lie!

I crawled to the desk and leaned against it, yanking my belt free to use as a tourniquet on the wound. I looked over to the little gnome next to the Hookah. Gnorman stood frozen in place with a stern finger pointing in my direction, his other hand was held against his chest with his thumb and first two fingers held up significantly.

I looked at Sinead and a tear rolled down my face. I turned my face to Tailor and spoke clearly, "I have no further requests. Thank you for your service, Tailor."

The smoky figure sighed in relief as he was sucked back into the hookah pipe. The sound of bullets ricocheting off metal outside the room was instantly followed by shouts and stomping boots. I sat on the ground, bleeding, as soldiers, ghosts, and the boxer-clad, fully armed Colonel stormed into the room.

There was a lot of shouting and confusion as more and more people entered the small space, but since I was already on the ground, shot and bleeding, unarmed, and holding only a canteen I wasn't subjected to further violence.

Military Police and medics showed up moments later, and I was cuffed and bandaged and questioned pretty much simultaneously. The ghosts of my squad hung back and watched me with unblinking, angry eyes.

I sucked it up as best I could and explained that I had returned to speak to the Colonel. I stated that I had encountered the Captain near the Colonel's quarters in lingerie, and she had turned a gun on me and then fled.

The Colonel had me carried away for medical care and ordered everyone out of his private quarters in search of the rogue Captain. He stared at me as two soldiers crossed arms under my ass, and I hung onto their shoulders so they could carry me out.

I was given a local anesthetic in the field hospital and the bullet was pulled from my leg. I passed out anyway.

When I woke up, I was in the brig with two lumps under my pillow and three ghosts standing at the foot of my bed. I sat up and took a moment to gather my thoughts.

They looked paler and more translucent than before. Sanchez and Kahele were in bloody, blasted uniforms. Injuries showed from bullets and explosions. Kahele's tattoo was missing and white bone showed where it used to sit. He glowered at me. Sinead, wearing an undamaged uniform, glared at him.

I scrambled back to the head of the bed, pulling Gnorman and a standard issue military green canteen from under my pillow.

"I know you're angry," I started, "but you know me. I keep my word. If I've got this right there's a new genie in here that's going to be able to grant me three requests. I'm going to do my best to make this right, but I still need your help."

I put the little figure on the table and looked at him. "Gnorman, I've been thinking about what went wrong with the Captain. Am I correct in thinking that she was punished for gaming the system?"

He raised a thumb and looked over at Sinead. I turned my back on him and she spoke, "Can you explain?"

Gorman's bass rumbled, "Indeed she was. Genies are generally petty and spiteful and respond poorly to disrespect. I'd be bitter, too, if I were held captive and invisible and treated like a cosmic vending machine for wishes, but it's deeper than that. When The Rules are broken Magic acts on its own. It has a will and it is vindictive."

I could hear him capitalizing words as if they were proper nouns and knew I had a lot more questions for him when we had the time.

"There are legends in Faerie of those that sought to circumvent The Rules that would make your toenails fall off just to hear. There is a reason stories about genies are usually cautionary tales, even amongst you humans.

The chaos of the universe isn't as chaotic as it seems. Imbalances must be made right and there are Agents of Destiny who are put to the task."

Sanchez took it in and nodded. His eyes softened and his image wavered, shifting back into the Stetson and jeans. "Sergeant, I'd suggest being clear, concise, and accurate."

I relaxed as Kahele relaxed and shifted to his "comfortable" ghost look.

I made the old joke, "Dammit Sanchez, I'm a medic, not an editor." I steeled myself and nodded, "But I'll do my best."

I unscrewed the cap on the canteen and watched in curiosity as a dark cotton-candy cloud billowed forth silently, spinning out and coalescing into a platform upon which stood the silken-robed, long-legged, raven-haired form of Captain Evelyn Descharme. She looked capital P, pissed. Her eyes were full black behind her long lashes, with motes of silver dancing in their depths, and her teeth were all pointed. She spoke in an even, clipped, and precise tone that held more anger than her screams and gunshots of the previous night.

"Greetings, mortal. Know that I, the genie of the..." she took a deep, seething breath, "canteen, am here to grant your request. Speak it in my presence and, though it be great or small, it shall be granted. You are eligible for up to three requests."

I took a breath and spoke in a clear, calm voice. I swear, it wasn't shaky at all.

"Genie, I will speak my requests at once, I would have you fulfill them all in the order spoken when I am finished." I took a breath to continue and was frustrated to hear, "Request granted. What is your next request?"

I bit back my response and looked up, thinking furiously and welding words together in my head. I wobbled up to my feet and glared at her, afraid to say all the things that were going through my head, afraid to ask the questions I wanted, and angry that I couldn't make my final wish happen. I couldn't get O'Leary back or dig myself out of the mess I was in, but at least I could let Sinead, Sanchez, Kahele and all the other dead soldiers rest in peace.

"I request that all spirits within 100 miles of this camp be released from whatever bonds hold them so that they may move on as they see fit. I request that this canteen be thrown into the bottom of a volcano on the other side of the world."

I'd never know all of what had happened out here, but maybe this could put it to an end. My eye watered up as I stared into the angry, hateful eyes of the trapped Captain. I could feel my own hatred boiling up and gave as good as I got.

"At least you've got all your parts. I'm done." I saluted the genie and tossed the canteen at her.

There was a pulse of power that rippled out of the room and into the night as she said, "Requests granted." Lights flickered briefly before backup generators kicked in and I could hear an alarm in the distance.

Captain Descharme, the genie, pirouetted up into the air as her cotton-candy platform broke off from the canteen. It bounced once on the ground then flew into her hand. She snapped her fingers and disappeared.

I heard a soft, "Thanks, Little Buddy," and looked over to see Sanchez fading from view, relief clear on his face.

Kahele flexed, one arm over his head, the other pointing to the horizon. "I think the Great Beyond is that way!" He dropped the pose and smiled. "I don't want you to join us anytime soon, but, when the time comes, don't be a stranger, Danger." He turned in a single muscled column and faded as he stepped away.

I shifted my gaze to the last of my comrades, and she was already barely an outline. Tears immediately started flowing and my chest felt like I was being crushed under the hood of an exploded DAGOR. I couldn't breathe. I moved toward her and tried to envelop her in my arms one last time.

She whispered, "About that destiny..." and faded away with snorting laughter.

I fell onto my bed and I wept. Fully. Openly. Thoroughly. Until sleep welcomed me into a blissfully dark and empty silence.

17

I had a private interview with the Colonel that morning. The hookah was gone from the shelf in his office, apparently it had fallen and broken in the night.

I was informed that I was going to be returning home with two purple hearts, one for the convoy attack and one for being injured "saving his life," and the promise of a silver star for things I honestly don't remember doing. He, very carefully, never mentioned the Captain's full name and I was smart enough to not say anything but "Yes, sir. Thank you, sir," the entire time.

In a stunning coincidence, a military flight out of the camp to a civilian center and "home" from there was available the next day.

18

First class on an international flight is a little slice of heaven in the middle of a giant pain in the ass. There was a no-show for the civilian leg of the journey and the "injured hero" got bumped up. I had just buckled my safety belt, closed my window, and taken the first sip of a truly despicable, but potent, whiskey when the pilot's voice sounded over the intercom.

"Welcome aboard everyone and thank you for choosing our airline. I am Captain Francoeur, my co-pilot today is Lieutenant Ervin. I'm sorry to announce there will be a slight delay in taking off. Visibility has just dropped due to a sandstorm. I'm informed that it's going to pass in about thirty minutes, so we'll just taxi into place and wait our turn in the queue."

I nodded and reclined my chair. It actually reclined, like, more than three degrees. The whiskey and meds mixed in my belly taking all my pain and worry away, just like the plane was going to take me away. Back home to America.

I sat Gnorman on the edge of the fold down train and raised my glass. I stared at it with my one good eye trying to think of a toast. The plane jostled and I sloshed some of the whiskey onto myself.

"Typical," I said to the gnome. I drained the glass and swallowed back the bitterness that threatened to overwhelm me. They couldn't make me come back here.

I closed my eye and tried to bring up an image of O'Leary. I missed her. I missed the way she smelled of gun oil and flowers. I missed the milky curve of her neck and the freckles that dusted her shoulders. I missed the little happy sounds she would make when we managed to steal a moment alone in all the dirt and danger.

The shaking of the plane got worse. I could hear the wind outside howling and the engines revving up.

"This is your Captain speaking. It looks like the storm is ramping up outside. There are some small whirlwinds on the runway. We're going to have to reconnect with the skywalk and get you to de-plane until this passes."

I rubbed the shamrock tattoo in the webbing between the thumb and first finger of my left hand nervously. Thoughts of Cheryl jumped into my head. What could I tell her? What would she believe?

The plane jostled some more, and I idly flipped the window up to look at the coming storm.

Blazing black eyes with motes of silver dancing in their depths stared at me through the plastic. "Found you!"

I slammed the window back down and started screaming.

ABOUT US

AMY GEREIN

WRITER & ARTIST

Amy Gerein grew up with her nose stuck in a book and has always dreamed of both writing novels and illustrating picture books, so it wasn't much of a task to convince her to join the Debut anthology project. Despite growing up with her head in the clouds, Amy eventually wound up with an animal bioscience degree and can guarantee that she has spent way too much time contemplating the anatomy and physiology of mythical creatures.

While personally challenging at times, the Debut project was a great opportunity for Amy to grow in her work as a writer and an illustrator and a springboard for more to come. While she hopes she will have the opportunity to share future published work, she will continue to reside in the land of her imagination with an assortment of cryptids, mermaids, werecats, and dragons who just might make it to a story near you.

You can follow Amy's work at:

Facebook @amyofarg
Instagram @amyofarg

Irish Williams

Writer & Artist & Cover Artist

Irish Williams, a member of the Spud Pub team, may make a living as a background artist in Vancouver's animation industry but lives to create worlds through art and writing. Fascinated by how folktales and mythology give us glimpses into the topics and fears that concerned our predecessors enough to create them, Irish aims to continue this tradition in the modern age.

"I enjoy creating stories that focus on societies and culture, particularly how things change (or sometimes don't) over long periods of time. It boils down to that but how art and story gets expressed can vary widely; I mean, I have degrees in Visual Communication and Commercial

Animation. Art history was a requirement for both disciplines. When you take that class you either get a teacher who will just make you memorize who created what piece; or you'll get a professor who will force you to study the full history of the era in which the piece was created so you understand the context. You start looking differently at the world, even modern art and advertising. Stories are everywhere."

You can follow Irish's work at:
Instagram @firedanceratrea

ROMY POISSON

ARTIST

Romy is a self-taught artist currently living in Saskatoon, SK. Starting with the good old pencil and paper, she has taken the dive into digital art and finds her inspiration primarily in Fantasy character designs and illustrations. Currently she is working on the many illustrations of her various D&D groups as well as working on expanding her portfolio to commission as well as creating fun art pieces to be available on Redbubble.

You can follow Romy's work at:

Instagram @Styxxsardonyxart
Redbubble @Styxxsardonyx
Ko-Fi @Styxxsardonyx

Rachel Sikorski

Writer

Rachel Sikorski writes epic fantasy that takes place in a persistent universe called Saebetia. She loves to pen stories about morally grey heroes, sympathetic villains, and fickle gods. Throw in a few forbidden or doomed romances and voila! Currently she's working on finishing her debut novel to be titled 'Knowledge & Necromancy'. It follows a cocky mage with forbidden powers, an anxious historian with something to prove, and a sheltered diplomat with a world-changing secret as they navigate a war they were unwillingly thrown into.

While Rachel's writing or plotting, you can generally find her listening to power metal for inspiration at her favourite local coffee shop. She finds that bands like Sonata Arctica and Nightwish provide some of the most impactful songs that have led to the creation of some of her favourite stories and best plot points.

On the topic of inspiration, she also has a deep love of Tolkien and Tolkien-inspired works. She is on the board for the international Tales After Tolkien society which studies post-Tolkien media. When not typing her own works, Rachel sets up author interviews or other blog posts for the Society's blog and works on papers for the Medieval Congress in Kalamazoo. Previous topics she's written papers on include the lore of Diablo, how Tamora Pierce helped to kick-off the trend of Post-Tolkien media directed at young girls, and how worship of the Great Mother Goddess is used in everyday life within Pierce's works.

You can follow Rachel's work at:

Facebook @writerrachelsikorski
TikTok @writer_rachel_sirkorski
Youtube @rachelsikorski9858
Instagram @rachel_sikorski_writer
Twitter @rsikorskiwrites
Website @ authorrachelsikorski.com

Jenny Kong

Artist & Founder

Jenny is a fulltime 3D animator, part time artist, and three-quarter time indie publisher. She has worked on a variety of television shows, animated movies, live action movies, and AAA video games. She decided that being one of the owners of Spud Publishing Inc. is a thing she wanted to do.

Aside from the above mentioned, Jenny is also a mom to a cat in a dog's body, an avid gamer, and a reader of fantasy. She is allergic to the outside world. She loves indoor plants. Once in a blue moon she enjoys a hike or two, and spending time with friends and family in person.

Jenny aspires to be a professional couch burrito squalor goblin when she grows up.

You can follow Jenny's work at:

tumblr @jenny-kong
LinkedIn @jennykong
Instagram @jhengiskong
Tiktok @po_the_aussie_shepherd

CHENISE PUCHAILO

WRITER & FOUNDER

When not at her day job, former journalist Chen Puchailo in a professional aspirer! She is an aspiring social group co-ordinator, author, and publisher. Making up one half of Spud Publishing she is excited to not only produce Debut but be a part of it as well!

Chenise grew up in small town Dauphin, Manitoba, and currently lives in Saskatoon, Saskatchewan with her partner, and her beloved Mutt, Scotch. She has been writing since before she knew her letters, and reading as soon as she understood them. Literature in all its forms has always been a passion, alongside horses, and the outdoors. She hopes to bring forward many projects, both her own as a writer, and others as a publisher, after Debut.

You can follow Chenise's work at:

Instagram @eloraczyr
Twitter @NotARealPokemon

DON GAITENS

WRITER

Don is a neurospicy queer guy that strives toward the Renaissance-man ideal, without the actual Renaissance period misogyny or lack of personal hygiene. He has an abiding respect for the power of words to shape reality, a hatred of the Oxford comma and a deep belief in the responsibility of each person to think critically about the reality they are choosing to shape with their words. Following this path has led Don to become a major Lit-Geek with minors in martial arts, ballroom dance, outdoorsy stuff, LARP, TTRPGs and queer activism. He has wielded words as an actor, teacher, improvisor, playwright, slam-poet, sex-educator and now, novelist. He currently makes a living as a professional instructional designer and corporate trainer.

You can follow Don's work at:

Instagram @Dongeoneer
Twitter @Dongeoneer

Shaan Ali Khan

Senior Artist

Shaan is an animation storyboard artist and illustrator, having worked on projects such as Marvel's 'Avengers', HBO's 'Scavengers Reign', AMC's 'Pantheon', Netflix's 'Masters of the Universe: Revolution', and more. Since he was a kid, film and genre media were already heavily rewiring his brain in ways he wouldn't consciously recognize for decades. But when he remembers being 7 years old, watching George Lucas interviewed about creating the original Star Wars Trilogy and describing the process of technical hurdles, developing concepts, breaking down act structure etc., and it clicking right there: "Oh... PEOPLE make this stuff?! Like... they can just do that?!"

Storytelling has always been a dominant fixation for him, whether engaged as a viewer, an amateur writer, an artist, or studying theatre both on and off-stage. But it all came back to informing his work when drawing. After being introduced to storyboarding, it really became a culmination of everything he'd learned and loved to do as a creative.

Getting to collaborate on this project with friends old and new has been an incredible and inspiring venture. Shaan wants to thank and dedicate his contributions to those that inspired and supported him. An endless list of amazing teachers and mentors who understood and gave the guidance a scattershot kid with ADHD always needed. His brother Yousuf for showing him just how cool it was to see what an artist can do when they pick up a pencil. His incredible sisters, Sabeen and Sophie for their limitless love and support. His father Shaukat for ensuring his family was always taken care of, but also reading to and sharing stories for his young son every night. His late mother Shehnaz, who sacrificed so much for the betterment of her children. From her own experience as an artist when she was a young girl in Pakistan, she always pushed and celebrated her children's creative spirit, and her endless love and spirit touched everyone around her.

Lastly, Shaan wants to thank his beloved partner, Samantha. For her support through the hardest days, her laughter on the best days, and every moment in-between.

You can follow Shaan's work at:

Instagram @shaankhanart
Twitter @Khanimus

Diane Fickeria

Editor

An avid adventurer and person of many trades, Diane often finds herself dabbling in a myriad of projects, endeavors, and travel. A voracious reader, former middle school teacher, current teacher of adults, photographer, editor, writer, gamer, cosplayer, and outdoorswoman, she finds inspiration wherever she plops herself. Although she has edited, unofficially, on the side for many years, this will be her first published editing experience alongside the many contributors of this anthology. She currently resides in Orange County, New York, most likely petting her dog. Esto Benignus.

You can follow Diane's work at:

Facebook @FicktionPhotography